Praise for *Poor As I Am*

AND OTHER STORIES AT CHRISTMAS

"Utterly charming . . . clever and kind."
—2025 Utah Book Awards

"A collection of Christmas stories with wonderfully dry humor and heart. . . . a patchwork of relationships, emotions, and devotions. Some made me laugh, some made me cry."

—Reader C.

"Like sitting by a fire with a warm mug: nostalgic, sincere, and quietly moving . . . moments of unexpected depth . . . really captured the spirit of the season without falling into cliche."

—Reader G.

"Richard Paul Evans has some competition."

—Reader J.

Also by David Rodeback

The Dad Who Stayed and other stories
Hearts Together (a novel)

Poor As I Am

and other stories at Christmas

David Rodeback

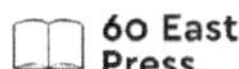

60 EAST PRESS — AMERICAN FORK, UTAH

60 East Press
867 N 60 E
American Fork, UT 84003
60eastpress.com

"The Case of the Missing Hair" first appeared in *Utah's Best Poetry and Prose 2023*, published in 2023 by LUW Press.

LCCN: 2023938269
Trade Paperback ISBN: 979-8-9883510-0-9
eBook ISBN: 979-8-9883510-1-6

Printed in the United States of America

No part of this book's text was written by or with the direct assistance of artificial intelligence (AI).

Book cover by BookCoverZone

Contents

For Kay

Poor As I Am

A MODERN NOVELLA OF CHRISTMAS EVES

1

The Girl on the Bus

OUR FIRST DECEMBER

IT DIDN'T START WHEN Anya chewed me out in the lab on Christmas Eve. Maybe it started when my parents decided they wanted a child, who turned out to be me. Or when I stumbled across a high school teacher who nurtured what he diagnosed as my gift for chemistry.

Later, when I wasn't nostalgic about a fine teacher or so discouraged that I blamed it on my very existence, I traced the beginning of my trouble to the Chemical Engineering Department's holiday party. It was the first Friday of December in my second year of graduate school. I traced much of my happiness to the same origin.

I needed a date for the party, so I asked the girl from the bus. It wasn't a random encounter. We'd been on the same bus most weekday mornings since late August, when the semester began. Sometimes she looked up and smiled a little, as I passed by on my way to the empty seats in the back. Some days that made her the only adult female who smiled at me anywhere outside the office or lab or some sort of customer service relationship.

It was October before we talked at all. One rare morning, the seat just behind her was empty, so I took it. I told her my name was Rick, and I learned that her name was Laurie. She was a first-year grad student in Bioinformatics. She wore no ring on the third finger of her left hand.

On a frozen, early December morning, someone got off and left the seat in front of her empty, so I switched seats. She smiled when I asked her to the party. She said yes. It was in a building on campus, and we agreed to meet there.

I waited for her that evening on the broad front steps of a large, tan, almost yellow building that looked colonial but said it was built just after World War II. That's when it dawned on me: I had only ever seen her sitting on the bus. I could only guess at her height or build. She could be the woman I saw in the distance, hurrying along the well-lit walkway across the quad, in a dark winter coat that reached her knees.

In fact she was that woman. I first recognized her by her hair. It was straight, light blonde, and curved cutely around her face. It didn't quite reach her shoulders.

She was right on time. We checked our coats just inside the main doors. The party was in the lobby.

Laurie wasn't short or tall or fat or skinny. I thought she was pretty in a dark purple dress she could have worn to present a paper at a conference. Some other women at the party were dressed just as conservatively. Some weren't.

As the evening progressed, I observed that she was less intimidated by professors and department chairs than I was. In fact, she didn't seem intimidated by anyone at all. She was good at academic small talk with me and everyone else, the kind where you play the interested, intelligent non-specialist to get people talking about whatever they most like to talk about.

Eventually I realized two more things: With her I wasn't keeping to the fringes of the group, as I usually did. And I was okay with that.

We planned to stay for an hour and a half, or less if we didn't like it. I thought we might ride the late bus home together, but I ended up walking her to the graduate library for her study group and taking the bus home alone.

"Thanks. It was fun," she said when we reached the library entrance. "See you on the bus."

On my way home on the bus that night, I imagined seeing her as I usually saw her, concentrating on a textbook. When she read, she puckered her lips slightly and was oblivious to everything and everyone around her—including me, as I watched her sometimes, from a few rows back.

A week later, I asked her to a free movie on campus and a late dollar-menu dinner at Wendy's. I expected a fellow bus-riding grad student to understand when I said all I could afford for us was the dollar menu. It was a reasonable expectation; there was a sense of "we're all in this together" among the grad students who walked or rode the city bus to the university every day. Bus passes were free to students, and free was exactly what a lot of us could afford.

There were other students on campus, mostly undergrads, who could afford sports cars, parking passes, and, for all I knew, their own private jets. They dressed differently, and they seemed to shop and eat out a lot more. The two groups didn't mix much socially, and academically we only paid attention to each other when we were teaching them. The perfect symbol of our separateness was that the graduate and undergraduate libraries were in separate buildings, hundreds of yards apart. We had privileges in theirs but didn't use them. They weren't allowed past the front desk in ours.

Laurie was, in fact, a kindred spirit. She understood my budget. She smiled and said, "Sounds fun. It's a date."

A FTER THE FILM WE both had Wendy's chili, fries, and a cup of water. She asked for an empty salad bowl and turned her late dinner into chili cheese fries. The cheese on the chili was optional, but no extra charge. I ate my fries and chili separately, with extra crackers because she gave me hers.

We were almost finished eating when her phone rang. Even poor grad students had cell phones.

"Do you mind?" she asked with apologetic eyes. "It's my mom."

I smiled. "Of course I don't mind. It's your mom."

I tried not to listen, but she was sitting right there. There wasn't much to hear. Her mom did most of the talking. Eventually Laurie said, "Sure, Mom," and reached into her purse. She pulled out a black American Express card, looked warily around us, then softly read the number into the phone, including the extra four-digit code.

"Sorry about that," she said after ending the call. "She wants to buy something online, and she left her card downstairs, so she's using mine."

As I cleared away our trash and began to walk her home, I thought about her AmEx card. The basic ones were green, and I'd seen silver and gold ones that I knew were a bigger deal. How big a deal did she have to be to have a black one?

"You must be tired," she said. "Or you've run out of things to say to me." Her friendly tone had a nervous edge.

"I've never seen a black AmEx card," I said cautiously.

"I don't see it much either. I almost never use it. But Mom and Dad insist that I have it."

"For emergencies?"

"That's what I think."

That's what I'd have thought too, but for me it was purely hypothetical. "Do they think otherwise?" I asked.

"They're all about status. An ordinary green one would be plenty for emergencies."

"What's the black one?"

"It's the Centurion. Sounds impressive, right? It's titanium, not plastic. The annual fee for just my card would pay four or five months of my rent."

Before that moment I didn't know I could be made to feel so small so quickly.

We had dined at Wendy's from the dollar menu.

On a date.

While she carried God's own AmEx card in her purse.

"How rich are you?" I felt more defensive than curious.

She looked at me soberly. I expected her to say it was none of my business.

"Rich enough that I find it obscene. Not rich enough that my parents do. Or my sister. The black card is for people on the 'if you have to ask the price you can't afford it' rung of the economic ladder."

"Wow," I said. "Tall ladder."

"No kidding. I probably sound spoiled or something. My parents say I'm ungrateful. I'm not saying money's a bad thing, all else being equal. I just don't like a lot of what comes with having way too much of it."

We walked in silence for another minute or two, while I writhed inside. I liked Laurie. I liked spending time with her. She seemed to like me. Then this.

I couldn't tell her.

I couldn't *not* tell her.

"I'm sorry," I said, with my eyes glued to the sidewalk.

"For what?"

"I'm sorry I couldn't afford a nicer dinner for our date."

"Rick, this is the first time my card's been out since I bought my plane ticket to come here. I flew coach. You're the first person here to know I have it, and possibly the last. I don't have a trust fund or a big, fat offshore bank account. Or a big, fat onshore bank account. It drives my parents wild that I won't spend their money—which I might, some of it, if it were just about the money. But it's a power thing. They want me living on money they control."

"What do you live on?"

"My fellowship. Plus I work part-time in a lab. They hate that too. For some reason it's wrong that their daughter should work to eat. Choosing to do that is so ungrateful of me."

"I don't understand. If you have money, why not use it? People do it all around us every day."

"I think I already answered that," she said.

"I guess you did," I said.

We stopped at a corner, waiting for a car to turn in front of us. We had crossed the street before she spoke again.

"Also, that's not the crowd I want to fit into."

"You want to fit in with starving students?"

"I want to fit in with people who care about something more than money and power. People who care enough to be committed to something else. By the way, it's an academic fellowship, just like yours."

I struggled to find the right words for a question—for myself, not her. It wasn't something I could ask out loud. *What about all the times when not having enough money is the main obstacle to the things you care about more than money?*

That wasn't quite the right question. More like, *What about times when you can't help the people you care about, when they really need help, or they can't help you, because no one has ten dollars more than they need to survive?*

I managed to look at her. All I said was, "I guess I still don't get it."

She glanced up at me, then back at the sidewalk, and we walked a little further.

Her voice was soft and serious. "Why did you ask me to your department party?"

"I needed a date, and you seemed nice. And smart."

"Thank you," she said. "Why did you ask me out tonight?"

"Because you are. Nice, I mean. And smart. I wanted to see you again."

"Because of my parents' money?"

"I didn't know about the money."

"Exactly. I want people to see me, not money or a black piece of metal. And speaking of things that aren't plastic, to compete for the guys they think I should date, I'd have to be into plastic surgery. Even more of it at regular intervals, if I caught one of them and wanted to keep him. Or wanted to throw him back and catch another one. A lobotomy would help too. Most of the rich guys I know—most of the guys I know period, even at school—have to be the only smart ones in their relationships. Which is pretty stupid, you know?"

Maybe I should have thought twice before commenting, but I didn't think once. "That's crazy," I said. "You don't need plastic surgery."

She positively glowed at me. If I hadn't been humiliated, my rational, dispassionate engineer's heart might have melted.

"See? I'd rather date guys who think that." She took my arm as we walked. "Guys who think I might enjoy a free movie and a late dinner from the dollar menu."

"You didn't mind that?"

"It was fun. Besides, I mostly eat at home, because that's what I can afford. Going out at all is a treat."

I wanted to ask if she was just saying that to make me feel better, or if she meant it. But I was starting to suspect she was serious.

"I don't know if I could do that," I said.

"Do what?"

"Have money and not use it."

"It's not that big a deal. Easy to say, I guess. I mean, sure, too little of it gets in the way of a lot of things, but so does too much of it. Too much money doesn't change people, I think. It just makes it more obvious who they are. I don't know whether that's true of people with too little money, but I wouldn't be surprised."

"Well, thanks for letting me pay, even if your card could buy the whole restaurant." I still felt very small, but she was being nice about it, and I thought I managed not to sound bitter.

We had reached her very plain, very ordinary apartment building. "Thanks for paying," she said. "And a really nice evening."

That's when she kissed me—on the cheek, not the lips, but still.

She disappeared inside, leaving me no opportunity—and clearly not expecting me—to kiss her back.

THE NEXT DAY WAS the first reading day before finals. Nobody's schedule was normal. Reading days came and went, and finals too, without Laurie and me riding the same bus a single time. Part of me missed her. Part of me was relieved.

I knew from our conversations that she planned to fly home for a few days between finals and Christmas, then fly back to school before Christmas, while her parents went on a long holiday cruise.

She had declined to join them. She said she preferred Christmas alone in her apartment.

A hundred times, in the days before she left, I thought of calling her. A few times I started to dial but didn't finish.

I liked her. I missed her. And she seemed to enjoy my company, which was unusual for college women in my experience.

Finally I did it. I punched in her entire number, pressed the green button—and got her voice mail.

"This is Laurie. If you're not selling something or fund-raising, thanks for calling and please leave a message."

"Laurie," I said, "this is Rick. Maybe you're in San Diego already. When you get back, I'd like to take you out again, if you want. Call me when you're not out of area. Merry Christmas."

Not that out-of-area calls were likely to be an issue for her, I thought after I ended the call. She probably had God's own cell phone plan too.

And she probably wouldn't call. In January, when I saw her on the bus again, she'd probably be both kind and honest. "Rick, I'm sorry," she'd say. "I enjoyed our dates, and you're a nice guy, but <insert excuse here>."

She wasn't looking for a relationship. She was too busy with school. Or I wasn't her type—which I already knew. If her black card meant anything, it surely meant that.

I told myself that her money and my lack of it didn't make me unworthy of her, but my heart knew better. Or maybe it was my mind. Things were getting confused. For a while I fought myself to a stalemate, but when she didn't call in the first day or two after she was due back from San Diego, I conceded the point.

Mostly conceded the point.

2

Okay If I Sit Here?

OUR FIRST CHRISTMAS EVE

I HAD THE LAB to myself just before Christmas. That was always productive, but I gave myself Christmas Eve off anyway. I stayed home and finally started reading *Les Misérables*, which I'd meant to do all year. Now and then my concentration failed.

Laurie should have been back already. She'd planned specifically to avoid being home in San Diego for Christmas. I wouldn't be home for Christmas either. Neither I nor my mother could afford the fare. The difference was, I wanted to be home.

My poverty was mild, not like the people I was reading about. It was also temporary. Eventually I'd finish school and get a job. Chemical engineering paid well enough if you were good.

I had always tried not to care about money. Until I met Laurie's AmEx card, I didn't know I cared so much. I tried to focus on other things, but by 10 p.m. on Christmas Eve I had cared myself into a dark place, literally and figuratively, and I didn't want to stay there. I needed light and Christmas music.

The only remedy I could devise was to dress up a little and walk several blocks to the cathedral downtown, where I knew there would be Midnight Mass. I wasn't Catholic—I wasn't anything, really—but I had seen information about the Mass on the cathedral's little sign when I walked past, and I knew there would be music and light.

I walked in at 11 p.m., an hour early, but it wasn't like a concert, where they locked the doors until half an hour before starting time. I took a seat near the back, at the end of a pew, near the side of the cathedral. I didn't want to take a better seat away from a real Catholic. I skimmed the evening's program, then opened a hymnal and thumbed through it until I found the Christmas hymns. I read them while the musicians warmed up. I could already tell I had found the proper antidote to my evening.

The choir was polishing a difficult passage. I closed my eyes and listened. I didn't notice someone sitting beside me in the gradually filling cathedral until a voice spoke softly.

"Pardon me. Is it okay if I sit here? Are you saving a seat for someone?"

I opened my eyes and half-glanced toward the intruder. I caught a glimpse of a navy blue skirt and leggings, with a winter coat folded on a navy blue lap.

I felt like it should be obvious, even to random strangers, that I was alone. I wanted to be annoyed at the interruption, but a conundrum distracted me. How should I reply? Her two questions required opposite answers. Yes, it was okay. No, I wasn't saving seats.

The coat looked familiar, I realized. The voice was familiar too. Laurie.

I looked up at her. She was looking at me, radiant but quizzical. Quizzical but radiant.

"Hi, Rick."

"Hi," I said, scrambling for something more. "How was San Diego?" I looked down at her hands.

"Warm outside, chilly inside where the parents were. In other words, normal. Is it okay if I sit by you? I don't know anyone else here."

"I don't mind if you don't mind."

"Thank you. I got your message. I owe you a call. Or an explanation."

"Not necessarily," I said. Not if you don't want to go out again, I thought.

"The thing is, until my degree's done, I don't do third dates."

I turned to her. "That seems arbitrary."

"It's not." She took a deep breath. "It's not arbitrary because, in my experience, the third date, or the fourth at the latest, is when guys start to expect . . . things."

I looked at her silently.

"Physical things," she said.

"I knew what you meant."

"I don't need the distraction right now or the drama. Especially the drama when they don't get what they want, but they think they can persuade me eventually. So no third dates. That's why I didn't call you back. Thanks for calling and asking though."

I shrugged.

"All I get is a shrug?"

"As opposed to what?"

"I thought you might protest that you're not that kind of guy." She cocked her head. "Are you that kind of guy?"

"No. Although my last third date was a long time ago, so technically it's all hypothetical."

A family sat directly in front of us, threatening our private moment. They consulted each other in whispers, then moved toward the front—but not before Laurie leaned closer and whispered in my ear. Her warm breath did strange, magical things to my pulse.

"The first two dates were fun. Thanks for asking again, despite the outcome."

"I almost didn't."

She was silent for a moment. Then she whispered, "Is this about my money?"

I shrugged.

"Another shrug." She sounded hurt. "At least we could talk before."

I summoned my courage and tried to explain. "I had a good time with you. But I took a girl with a black titanium Amex card—seriously, does God have one of those?—I took you to Wendy's for the dollar menu, because that's what I can afford. I'm sorry, but it was humiliating. And every time I wanted to call you, I relived the humiliation."

"You did call me."

I shrugged again, but I thought I'd better talk too. "Yes, I did."

"I had a good time too," she said. "Both times. Which is saying something. I'm not into parties, mostly."

Something seemed to be starting, and we turned toward the sound. It was just an announcement that seating was still available up front.

Laurie spoke softly. "I blew off one of Mom's luncheons and went to Wendy's for chili and fries, and I thought of you." She hesitated. "No, to be honest, I was thinking of you, so I went to Wendy's. Turns out I like the chili better when it's cold outside." She bit her bottom lip for a moment. "And I like it better with you."

Her eyes were shining, unless it was the lights hitting her just right. Beautiful, shining Laurie. She belonged in a cathedral.

I felt myself blushing. "I'm really not worth thinking about."

She smiled sweetly. "Wrong." She tapped her own cheek with a finger. "Plus it's written on your face that you like me too."

I just looked at her.

"Sorry if all of this sounds like junior high," she said. "You do like me, don't you? Between acute attacks of economic humiliation?"

I nodded. "During them too."

She looked toward the front and blew out a breath. "At first I wondered if you thought I was judging you for being poor, which I'm not. And I wouldn't. Then I thought you were judging me for being rich. But it's not me, is it? You're judging yourself for being poor."

I started to whisper something, then something else. Finally I just said, "I guess so."

She didn't reply. She didn't move, either. She watched the musicians up front.

The cathedral was almost full by 11:25 p.m., which surprised me until I saw in the program that there would be half an hour of music before the Mass.

At 11:26 she asked, "Is it still okay if I sit by you? I don't know anyone else here."

I nodded.

"Thank you," she said.

At 11:29 she asked, "Are you Catholic?"

"No."

"Are you religious?"

"Not really."

"Then why are you here?"

"Live Christmas music."

"Me too," she said. "But I guess I'm a little bit religious, at least enough to like the religious carols better than the other ones."

We listened to the music without speaking again, until it ended and the service itself was about to begin. In the brief interval she whispered, "Did you bring any money?"

"Five dollars."

"What are your plans for it?"

"Collection plate."

"I have a five," she said. "If I put it in the plate for both of us, will you spend some of your five on me tomorrow?"

"On Christmas?"

Her voice brightened. "Yes, I do believe tomorrow is Christmas."

"You don't do third dates," I said.

"We'll skip to the fourth date, if that's okay."

Something warmed inside me, but I was pretty tired. My words came out a little cold. "It's okay. How and where?"

"Your enthusiasm overwhelms me. You don't have to."

"Sorry, long day. My enthusiasm will catch up in a minute. Lunch at Wendy's again? If they're open?"

"You read my mind. I don't see myself needing fries, but I was hoping for a bowl of Christmas chili. Two bowls, actually. One for each of us. If you want."

"Sounds good," I said more warmly. "Why?"

"Why am I suspending my rule, sort of? I want to spend part of Christmas with you. Plus you and I need to have a serious chat, and during Mass it would just be rude."

My enthusiasm arrived just then, with a physical thrill that bypassed my rational mind entirely. She wanted us to spend part of Christmas together. While the rest of me wanted to put my arm around her and gaze with rapture into her eyes, my mind required an explanation.

"With me, as opposed to . . . ?"

"As opposed to alone in my apartment," she said equally seriously.

I had the presence of mind to act as if impossible things might be possible. "Okay," I said. "How about 2:00?"

"Perfect. Thank you."

"You're welcome," I said, because I couldn't think of anything else. Then I thought of something. "Thanks for making an exception for me."

I mostly watched the Mass after that. The solemnity and novelty of it, and maybe the joy and reverence of it too, intermittently pulled me away from my confused thoughts and feelings about the woman sitting next to me. I was better with books, computers, equations, data, theories. I had very little experience with women who were interested in me.

I stole a few glances. Some of the Christmas music brought tears to her eyes. She caught my eye a couple of times and smiled.

As I walked her home, she babbled enthusiastically about the music—all of it, piece by piece. What moved her most was the choir singing "O Come, O Come Emmanuel" a cappella and the whole congregation standing and singing "O Come, All Ye Faithful" with the orchestra playing at the front and the huge organ roaring behind us. I thought it was impressive too, but it didn't move me the same way. I didn't sing with her abandon, and my cheeks didn't show the tracks of tears when it was done.

"I'm more of a believer at Christmas," she said. "For some reason, when I sing 'O come, let us adore him' with a big organ, trumpets, and a thousand other people, that's what I want to do, come and adore him." She shrugged. "But I'm a bad believer, I guess, because then it pretty much wears off until next Christmas."

"I like the music," I said, "but I don't think it's a religious experience for me. Tonight was my first Mass, so it was partly just a curiosity."

We reached the front steps of her building and stopped. "Are you glad you went?" she asked.

"Yes," I said.

"Are you glad I went?"

I probably should have smiled. I just looked into her eyes and said, "Yes."

She smiled enough for both of us. "Thanks for walking me home from our impromptu non-third-date."

"You're welcome," I said.

"Pick me up here in eleven and a half hours?"

"Okay."

"It'll be fun."

I nodded and finally smiled.

She looked up at me a little shyly, I thought, and said, "If I turn my cheek toward you like this, will you know what to do with it?"

"Isn't that, you know, physical?"

"A kiss on the cheek isn't even close to what they want. Answer my question, please."

"Yes."

"Prove it."

I kissed her awkwardly on the cheek. She beamed.

"Your turn," she said.

I turned my head slightly and leaned down a bit. Her kiss was somehow both firm and gentle, and I wished I had shaved before Mass. "Merry Christmas, Rick."

"Merry Christmas, Laurie."

"Good night," she said, then giggled. "I mean, good morning!" She disappeared into her building before I could reply.

3

A Scarf and Gloves

OUR FIRST CHRISTMAS

I FLOATED HOME IN a happy, exhausted haze. Laurie was the only date who had ever kissed me, even on the cheek, and now she had done it on two occasions. Also, I had never kissed a date before. And it seemed likely that both those things would happen again later today.

Merry Christmas indeed.

When I got home, I was too tired to think for long about the girl who liked me enough to be hurt that I was put off by her money—and liked me enough to do something about it. And kiss me. And let me kiss her. I was also too tired to wonder for very long whether my response to her wealth was anything more than foolish pride. I set my alarm for noon, just in case, then fell asleep.

When it woke me, I opened the gifts Mom and my sister had sent, so I'd know what they were before our scheduled call at 12:30.

I had no Christmas tree; the gifts had been stacked next to my bookshelf for more than a week. If I could have afforded a tree, I wouldn't have had room for it. Calling my place a studio apartment was an injustice to studio apartments. My closet was as small as the wardrobe I kept in it, the bathroom was functional but not much larger, and the corner which passed for a kitchen was just enough for me, which wasn't saying much. The main area barely accommodated a bed, a desk, and a small bookcase.

But the rent was right, the location was good, the landlady kept an eye on things, the Internet connection was reliable, and the other tenants in the building were quiet enough that I could study at home. I had a decent chair for working at my desk, plus a secondhand folding chair I kept folded except for visitors, whom I never had. My little place was everything I needed and very little that I didn't need.

Mom's gifts were predictable but welcome: a used book of some interest, a scarf she had crocheted herself, a framed photo of her and my sister, a generous batch of snickerdoodles which had mostly survived their days with the Postal Service, and a Christmas card.

My sister's gifts were a pound of European chocolate bars, which must have set her back a few hours' babysitting wages, and a chatty letter about her life as a ninth grader. Dori—short for Theodora, a family name she didn't hate as much as everyone thought she should—began her letter with her usual candor.

> Dear Dufus,
> Life was more fun when you were an undergrad living at home. I miss you, especially at Christmas. I'd say you totally suck for running away from your little sister to go to grad school, except it wouldn't be true, because you don't <u>totally</u> suck. So anyway . . .

I would read and reread the entire letter, but first I skipped to the end, at the bottom of page five, to see how she signed it. "Love, Dorki," it said. I had called her that for about half her lifetime, though not lately. I knew she liked her friends to call her that, partly so others wouldn't think it was clever to call her a dork.

I set the letter aside to read over lunch and looked at the picture. It was recent. Mom looked a little older than I remembered, and Dori looked more grown up. They were the whole family, except me. Dad had been gone since Dori was a toddler, and the last time I'd been home for a family picture was the day I left for grad school, almost a year and a half ago. Mom had sent me that picture the previous Christmas.

I propped the framed photo on the bookshelf, in front of some books, next to last year's photo, and considered the changes in Dori. Last year she was cute. This year she was pretty, even if she didn't put much effort into it. I wondered if the guys at school noticed anything more than her intelligence and her sarcastic wit. I wondered if any of them liked those things in her and could see past her perfect GPA, her refusal to use makeup, and her utilitarian haircut, to see the beauty I saw.

She had Mom's looks. I had Dad's. The opposite would have been tragic, at least for her.

For lunch I had my usual breakfast, a bowl of plain oatmeal, and too many snickerdoodles for dessert. It was a big batch, so even after my binge I could ration and enjoy a cookie or two every day for a couple of weeks.

I called Mom and Dori, and we talked for most of an hour. They'd said that's all the gift they wanted this year, but I'd also sent them a small gift certificate, so they could go out for ice cream, and two stickers with my school's logo.

At 1:45 p.m. I left my apartment, then immediately went back in to get the scarf. I didn't wear scarves, but it was cold, and I needed to be able to tell Mom I'd worn it. For now I stuffed it into my coat pocket. My other pocket held dessert for our dollar menu lunch: four snickerdoodles in a plastic bag.

At 2:00 p.m. sharp I rang Laurie's bell. I heard someone on the stairs inside. Then the door opened and she bounced out. "Hi! Merry Christmas!" she exulted.

"Merry Christmas," I said, smiling but not bouncing.

"What did you do today already?" she asked, so I told her. She was disappointed that I hadn't brought the picture of Mom and Dori with me. "I could have called my family," she said. "Mom and Dad have sat phones. But I thought I'd wait and see if they call me. They probably won't."

"Did you open any presents?" I asked.

"Four. One from myself, a book I've been wanting to read. Three from my roommates: some chocolate, a video, and enough microwave popcorn to get me through the video."

"That's nice. Nothing from your parents?"

"Not today. I opened a few things early in San Diego, but I left them there. I can't really use them. What I could have used was a scarf to replace the one I lost last week. I may have to break down and buy one on sale tomorrow. Good thing it's sunny today."

That was when I decided Fate was a romantic, even if my ego wasn't. Laurie caught me smiling.

"What? You think it's funny that a rich girl doesn't have a scarf?" Her tone was gentler than her words, but I assumed she wasn't just teasing me.

"It's not that."

"What, then?"

We stopped at a corner. "Mom made a gift for me, which I will never use, unless I wear it once so I can say I did. That's why I brought it. Now I want to give it to you." I pulled out the scarf. "Compliments of my mother and her son. If you like it, you should keep it."

She held it almost reverently. It was blue and green, and something in the yarn made it shimmer in the sunlight. "Your mom made this? It's beautiful!"

"Thank you. She's a beautiful person."

"You won't get in trouble for giving it away?"

"Nope."

"Are you sure?"

"I could send her a picture of me wearing it. But if I tell her I was on a date with a girl who lost her scarf, and I gave it to her, and she loved it, so I told her to keep it, she'll be even happier. Besides, it'll look a lot better on you."

She put it around her neck and glowed like it was Christmas—which, of course, it was.

"Do you have anything else up your sleeve?" she asked.

"They sent me a batch of snickerdoodles. I brought four of them for our dessert."

"Perfect! Anything else?"

"Nope."

"Then here's what I brought for you. I noticed you needed gloves. They're work gloves, technically, even though they're just cloth, but they'll be warmer than nothing, and they don't take up much space in a pocket or a laptop case. I didn't wrap them."

She handed me a pair of brown fabric gloves with the cardboard still on them, but she didn't let go when I took them. I looked up to see concern in her eyes.

"They're not nearly as wonderful as a handmade scarf. They were only $1.99. I even left the price tag on, in case you want to return them."

"Thank you," I said seriously. "I can definitely use these."

She smiled shyly and let go. Then her fingers were stroking the scarf. "This is so beautiful. Warm too. Are you going to put them on?"

My hands weren't cold at the moment, but I pulled off the cardboard and the little plastic connector thing and pulled on both gloves. They looked small but stretched a lot, so the fit was perfect.

I held up both hands to show her, and we both smiled. "They're just right. I'm taking them off now, but not forever. It's too warm for gloves at the moment."

She was still smiling. "Okay."

We crossed the street while I slipped them into my pocket.

"Are you sure you like them?" she asked. "They're the best I could do at the convenience store this morning—within my budget, at least."

I grinned. "Do you always tell people how much you paid for their gifts?"

Her expression was an adorable mix of chagrin and amusement. "I can't believe I did that. No, never. Until today."

"If you promise not to tell my mom, I'll tell you something."

"What are we? Five years old?" She chuckled. "I promise."

"I wouldn't have used the scarf, but I'll actually use the gloves. I like them. Thank you!"

Over lunch we talked about our parents, who weren't very much alike, and our sisters, who were alike in some ways. She wanted to hear some of Dori's letter, if I didn't mind. I read her the whole thing. She listened with a gentle, introspective smile, mostly, but I caught her brushing away a tear or two.

I didn't ask what she was thinking. If she'd wanted to tell me, she wouldn't have focused so intently on her chili when I finished reading.

Finally she looked up. Now her smile seemed sad. All she said was, "Thanks for reading that. Dori must be an amazing sister."

"I like her," I said.

We ate slowly, but it wasn't as if anyone was waiting for our table. Wendy's was mostly empty. I broke out the first two cookies, and we nibbled those slowly too.

It wasn't long before she asked, "Didn't you say four cookies? What would a girl have to do to get you to produce the other two?"

"I'm glad you like them."

"I do like them. But you didn't answer my question."

"I don't know. Ask, maybe. No, wait. You said we need a serious talk?"

"I guess I did."

"So how about we do that, then more cookies?"

"That's fair." Her face and tone turned earnest. "I like you. You know that, right? I mean, I don't want to be forward, but I've tried not to leave too much room for doubt. I don't go past the second date for anyone, but here we are."

I ignored my heart and tried to be calm and rational. "You've been pretty clear. In what ways do you like me?"

"You're kind and gentle and smart. You study hard. The geek in me enjoys your dry, geeky sense of humor. I like talking with you. And here's a new one from today: I like the way you talk about your mom and your sister. I can't imagine my sister talking about me that way, but I wish she would. It's like they really matter to you, but you don't have to keep saying it. It's just obvious when you talk about them."

I nodded, and she continued. "I like them too. I guess you noticed Dori's letter made me cry. I'm jealous of you for having a family like that."

I should have felt and said something sympathetic, but I was more selfish than that. I just smiled and hoped she'd keep listing things she liked about me.

"I've already told you I like how you seem interested in me, not my money."

My smile probably faded a little just then. That was still a painful subject.

"You're welcome to talk too," she said.

I could smile at that. "Why would I interrupt a girl who's listing what she likes about me? I'm not stupid."

"Suppose I tell you that was the whole list?" Her eyes twinkled.

"Is it?"

"It's all you're getting now."

I nodded. "Therefore, what?"

"Therefore what what?"

"You like me. I like you," I said. "Therefore, what?"

She looked at me with big, beautiful, serious eyes and took a deep breath.

"Therefore I need to know if this money thing is going to be a for us."

"A problem in what way?" I asked, stupidly feigning ignorance.

She gave me the impatient look I deserved. "Are you willing and able to get over your pride or whatever and believe I'm content to live on a shoestring, and I don't fall back on my parents' money as soon as I want a new pair of shoes? And I'm not just slumming with you or making some sort of political point?"

She probably didn't deserve the hurt look I gave her, but it was genuine. "So I may be a slummee or whatever, but there's more to me than that?"

"I'm sorry. I said that wrong. I'm not slumming at all."

I softened. "You kind of are, now that I think about it."

"I'm not. I just want a different life from my parents. I want to be happy, and I can't do that living their life. I've tried. I was miserable. Right now, I want to study hard, earn my degree, and go on dinner dates to places with a dollar menu. After that I want a normal life with normal problems, surrounded by normal people."

She giggled, and her eyes sparkled. "Or people like you. Normal isn't everything." Then she was serious again. "So what do you think? Can we get past the piles of money?"

I'd smiled briefly at her teasing, but now I said soberly, "I think I've made some progress since yesterday. I'm willing to try. I really like you."

"You're willing to try?" She didn't sound pleased.

"Yes."

"Not good enough. I need you to succeed. I want you to succeed."

Could I fight for her? Fight myself for her? I could. "When I said I'll try, I meant I may not be perfect right away. But I'll keep trying until I succeed."

"And if you're tempted to relapse?"

"*When* I'm tempted, I'll try harder. You're worth it."

"Whatever it takes?"

"Yes. For as long it takes. Even if you have to chew me out again," I said soberly.

"Because I'm worth it?"

"You're worth a lot more than that," I said as seriously as I had ever said anything.

Her gaze softened, but she still looked concerned.

"What's your next worry?" I asked.

"That I'm acting like a spoiled rich girl and badgering you until I get my way. I don't want that. I don't want to be the dominant one in our relationship. If we're going to have a relationship."

"You want me to be dominant?"

"No," she said. "Does one of us have to be?"

"I don't see why," I said. "Equal partners?"

"Perfect."

I tried to look puzzled, so I wouldn't have to feel brave. "Does this mean we're dating?"

She was deliberately obtuse too, and it was adorable. "We're on a date. It's not our first," she said, as if thinking things through with great care. "We're setting the stage for more. We might be dating."

Brave would be better after all, I thought. "Does this mean we're dating seriously?"

Her eyes held mine for a long moment. "I am willing to be as serious as you want to be, as long as we don't go too fast, and we can both be serious about our studies at the same time."

"Be patient and get to know each other?" I asked. "Take it slow?"

"I'm open to the possibilities," she said.

My mind was still catching up, but my heart was fine on its own for a while.

"So am I," I said.

We looked at each other, and I hoped my eyes held as much fondness as hers. Then I had a thought.

"What?" she asked.

"What what?"

"I saw a thought. Something you could tell me?"

I smiled and nodded. "Yeah, it was this: wow, that happened fast."

She beamed. "I don't know. Seems like I've been here a long time without meeting a nice guy like you."

"Yeah," I said. "Even longer for me. And not a guy, exactly. Is that all the serious conversation you wanted to have today?"

She nodded.

"Okay. Give me your hand." Things had changed for us in the last few minutes, if I could ask confidently for her hand.

Now she seemed shy. She held out her hand, and I put a cookie in it.

"Thank you," she said.

"You're welcome. Now your other hand, please."

I gave her the other cookie.

"Isn't one of these for you?" she asked.

"They're both for you. I ate about dozen for lunch."

"I'm not sitting here and eating two cookies in front of you, while you eat none."

"I guess I could eat another one. For you."

She returned one and lifted the other. "Thanks for bringing dessert."

When the cookies were gone, I cleared the table and helped her with her coat. Before we went out into the cold, I tried to arrange her scarf the way she had before, and she actually let me. Then I pulled out my new gloves.

"Give me your hand again," I said.

"I'm not wearing your new gloves while your hands freeze."

"If we're going to be dating, we need to trust each other."

She held out her right hand, and I put a glove on it. The other glove went on my left hand.

"Now give me your other hand." I took it with my bare hand, and interlaced my fingers with hers. "Is that better?"

She beamed. "I feel like I should share my scarf somehow."

"Sounds dangerous."

"I guess it might be. You'll just have to think warm thoughts."

"That won't be a problem," I said.

I held her hand all the way to her place, enjoying what felt to me like an important conversation about utterly unimportant things.

At her front steps I mustered my courage again. "I don't see any mistletoe, but if we're officially dating, we don't need it, right?"

"Hold that thought." She climbed onto the first step, so we were eye to eye.

She took the glove off her hand and put it in my coat pocket—a small intimacy which thrilled me. Then she took the glove off my hand too, which thrilled me even more. She took my face in her hands and said, "Thank you."

"I haven't kissed you yet. Sure you'll want to thank me?"

She smiled gently. "Thank you for the best Christmas I've had in years."

"You're welcome. It's a pretty good Christmas for me too."

"You miss your family more than I miss mine."

"I got some nice gloves."

"And a girlfriend," she said. "Am I better than a pair of gloves, at least?"

"Maybe less practical," I teased.

"I can be practical. I can also be warmer than a pair of gloves."

"I take it back."

"I was pretty forward," she said tentatively.

"Some guys need forward, I think." Some guys could get lost in her big, earnest eyes.

"I was afraid you'd push me away," she said.

"I think I'm done doing that," I said. "I'm going to kiss you now."

Her eyes twinkled. "Thanks for the warning."

4

What Do You Want to Do?

OUR FIRST DAY AFTER CHRISTMAS

O N OUR FIFTH CHEAP date, on the day after Christmas, over hot chocolate at one of the few shops that was open on campus, she asked me, "What do you want to do with your degree?"

"Industry, maybe some teaching eventually."

"Husband and father too?"

My pulsed quickened. "I thought we were going slowly." I didn't mind our direction of travel.

"We're just getting acquainted."

"Okay. And yes to marriage and family."

"Maybe I'm old-fashioned," she said, "but I think you need a woman for that. And speaking for my gender as a whole, we're not exactly falling at your feet. You should probably get to work. You're not getting any younger."

I loved her impish grin.

"I'm not from Saudi Arabia or Southern Utah," I said. "I only need one. What do you want to do?"

"I want enough of a career that I can work from home while I raise some children, if I'm fortunate enough to have any, then go back to work full-time. I don't have to be CEO or anything. And I refuse to be a single mom, so I guess I'll need a husband. As you say, I only need one. And maybe I'll like being a mom so much that I won't want to work if I don't have to. If I have to, that's okay too."

"Not like your own mom."

"True, but a lot like Nanny Marie."

"Wow. My girlfriend had a nanny." I smiled in wonder. "First you have to finish your degree."

"Because things don't always go as planned," she said. "Plus I love it. And I'm good at it."

"Not the life of a wealthy heiress?"

"No. It's like my family and I are from two different planets. They think I should live on theirs, and they're not above crass manipulation to get me there, or punishing me if that doesn't work. For my own good, of course, even if I can barely breathe in their atmosphere."

"I'm sure they're not all bad," I said.

"No. We're just different. Irreconcilably incompatible. They expect me to do my duty to the family and be their little rich girl, and the only part of that I like is girl."

"I like that you're a girl."

She smiled. "In case you missed my subtext," she said, "I'm happier, here and now, than I could ever be in their world."

"I still don't completely understand that. Or very much at all."

"It used to be mostly rebellion, I think, when I was, like, twelve. But it's not that anymore. I never liked who I was in that world, and there was never anything there that I wanted to be. I hope you don't think I'm narcissistic, but I love this me. And here I can see the path from who I am to who I want to be. I can't do that in their world."

"You think maybe they accidentally switched babies in the maternity ward?"

"I actually used to think that. I told Nanny once, but she said it wasn't that. She said I—" She blushed slightly and shook her head. "Never mind. I can't say it."

"Yes, you can."

She looked at me silently.

"You don't have to tell me if you don't want to," I said.

"I think I want to. But only you." She put her head on my shoulder. "Nanny's devoutly religious. She has some interesting ideas. Maybe strange ideas. I don't know.

"She says every two or three generations, God sends a misfit into a bad family, someone different and good, who can save the family, if they want to be saved, or at least escape its gravity. Actually, someone who can help God save the family. God does the saving, she says."

Her cheeks flushed. "In my family she thinks that's me. That's why she stayed with me even after she could have retired."

"May I tell you something?" I asked seriously. It was something light and warm and new.

"My self-image is completely out of control? You can tell me. I deserve it."

"You know I'm not religious. But I think she might be right about you." I took her hand and held it tightly. "I haven't met your family, but I think I believe her."

She didn't move, not even to breathe, almost. I saw her start to blush again, but then it mostly went away. "Do you know you who are?" she asked.

"That's debatable," I said. "Who am I?"

"The sweetest man I ever met. You're much too good for me. And you're about to be kissed."

She was right about that last part, at least.

5

Candor in the Library

OUR SECOND DECEMBER

THE FOLLOWING YEAR, IN mid-December, Laurie and I were having one of our countless library dates. It was still an hour until closing time, and as far as we could see, we had the fifth floor to ourselves.

She yawned discretely. "If I read one more sentence, my eyes may roll back into my head and stick there forever," she said.

"I've been staring at the same page for ten minutes," I replied. "Shall I walk you home?"

"We could do that, or . . ." Her eyes twinkled.

"Or what?"

"We could sit on that couch over there and talk for a while."

"Talk in the library?" I asked. "Or is that a euphemism?" On library dates we sat on different sides of a table, so we could study something besides each other.

"Making out in the library would be fun, but let's just sit and talk. I'm sure we won't bother anyone."

When we were comfortably situated on the not-very-comfortable sofa, I asked, "So what do you want to talk about?"

"Whatever," she said. "As long as we can cuddle while we talk. Think they'll wake us up at closing time, if we fall asleep?"

"If not sooner," I said. Dozing off was a real possibility. We both spent nearly every available hour working and studying, and most of the evenings got pretty late. "Though we haven't seen any anti-romance patrols tonight."

"Not that much to patrol between finals and January, I guess, except at our table." She sighed contentedly. "We probably looked like we were studying."

"We were studying," I said.

"Yes, but there was romance in our hearts. And we look a little more suspicious now."

"We could try for a lot more suspicious," I said.

"I like you," she said with feeling.

A few minutes later, she leaned back on the sofa, closed her eyes, and said, "As a library patron, I feel deliciously naughty. But there are things we could actually talk about."

"You talk. I'll listen."

"Okay. You know how we both say 'I love you' when we say goodbye, among other times?"

"Yeah."

"It's true, isn't it?"

"Yeah."

"Next time I say that," she said, "I want you to remember something."

"Okay. What?"

She looked at me. "I want you to remember that this year with you has been the happiest year of my life. Thank you."

I just looked at her for a moment. I was still amazed sometimes that we'd been together for so long, and I was the one she wanted.

"I should be thanking you," I said quietly.

She shook her head. "I'm serious."

"So am I."

Now she glared.

"Okay," I said. "You're welcome. But it's a happy year for me too, thanks to you."

"I'm glad," she said. "Do you mind if we talk about the future for minute?"

"Not at all, " I said. I didn't feel ready for that, but I couldn't say it.

"I have two years left to finish my degree. You have two years left to finish yours."

"Maybe three," I said.

"Or maybe three. Where do you see us after that?"

I dodged the question. "Where do you see us?"

"You want the whole truth?"

I hesitated. "Do I?"

"Let's find out. How can I put this? I see us having better places to snuggle than the library. I see us not having to stop and go home at an arbitrary hour, when we're together, because we're already home. I see a simple ring on my finger, with one small but pretty stone, and an even simpler ring on yours. And since neither of us would cheat on a spouse, it follows, if we're going to be snuggling, etc., especially et cetera, we'll have given each other those rings."

We had talked before about having a future together, so there were no surprises in what she was saying, and hearing her describe it helped my joy drown out my terror. But I was still a coward, so I chose the most trivial part of what she'd said and replied to that.

"You don't want a big, elaborate ring? Isn't that what girls dream about?"

"I did want that, briefly. I was about nine. Is this about my money?"

"More about my lack of money, I guess."

She didn't chew me out, even if I deserved it, and she didn't look hurt. That was good. She just said, "*Our* lack of money."

"Okay," I said. It was time to be less of a coward. "Are you proposing that we officially merge our possessive pronouns?" I intended the question to sound less serious than it was. Or more serious. I wasn't sure.

She hesitated. She was probably wondering about my question too. "My proposing would be sort of backwards, wouldn't it?"

"I guess so."

She snuggled closer. "What I'm saying is, there's no great rush, and we both have degrees to finish, but when we feel like we're ready, I'm open to the possibilities." She smiled—mischievously, but there was something more. "Well, I'm saying that and some other things. I dream of changing my last name to yours, setting up housekeeping together in some cozy little cottage, and raising our babies there. If you want that too. And I'm still not proposing. I'm just telling you my thoughts and dreams."

"When you said candid, you weren't kidding," I said appreciatively. I was feeling better and better about the future. "You could keep your last name. People do that."

"I don't love my last name, inasmuch as I got it from my parents."

"Makes sense. Any more candor for me?"

"How about this? Before we can raise our babies, we have to make our babies." She giggled. "You're blushing."

"You're not."

"I feel like I might blush soon, if that counts for anything."

I chuckled. "Not really."

"Rick, I don't mean to hog all the candor, if you have some for me."

She made me want to be brave and candid too.

"Okay," I said. "I dream about that too. I won't always be poor. I'll have a good job. That's sort of the point of the degree. But I'll probably never be rich. And sometimes it still eats at me that for now I can't afford to take you to a decent restaurant."

She sat up suddenly and took my face in her hands—not violently, but not tenderly either. "Stop it! We've been together for a year. I need you to get it through your thick, macho skull, and anything else you try to think with, that I don't care about my family's money. I don't want it. I don't have it. I love that I don't have it.

"I don't care that you're a starving student, or that I am. Those dollar-menu dates we can barely afford are amazing. So are these library dates, which are free if you don't count tuition, which our fellowships pay anyway. And if I have to live on a shoestring for the rest of my life, that's wonderful too, if it's with you."

There was a fire in her eyes that I hadn't seen for a while.

She took a deep breath. "My parents started on a shoestring. I know I've said this before. Then they got some money, and I mostly lost my parents. They're not criminals, as far as I know, but they're useless. Worse than useless. They're parasites. As parents go, they're petty, manipulative, and only selectively interested. They didn't used to be like that. If you and I ever have money, we will *not* be like them."

"When you do candor, you really do candor."

She visibly relaxed. "I've been wanting to say all that again. I just have to try not to say most of it to them. The larger point is, I love you. I love that you love me. We can't let money change that—the money we have or the money we don't."

"Okay," I said.

"Just 'okay'?"

"Not just okay. But I feel like I'm smaller than you deserve. Socially, economically, you know."

"And I feel like the luckiest girl in the world. But the idea that money still comes between us? That's in your head, not mine, and it may just break my heart."

"I'm sorry."

"Don't be sorry," she said. "Just promise me it won't break my heart."

I looked into her eyes again, which was good medicine for just about anything that might ail me. "I promise. My relapses are getting less frequent and less severe."

"Thank you," she said. Then she kissed me. Eagerly, urgently, at length. I happily did my part.

"I love you," she said, when we stopped to breathe.

"I love you too," I said. "And I have a confession."

She eyed me suspiciously. "A happy one, I hope."

"I think we have to consider it happy, in view of our discussion. I've been saving money for an engagement ring, but it's going to be a while."

Her smile was dazzling, unrestrained. "I can wait. How much have you saved?"

"Not enough," I said. "However much that is. I'm sure it's more than $573. There's the engagement ring and the wedding band too."

"Don't forget your ring. I'm saving for that, because great minds think alike. So far, about $340. That's my confession. But I don't know how much is enough either." She grinned. "I see a ring-shopping date in our future, if only for research."

"Soon?"

"How about when I get home from San Diego? Christmas Eve, maybe? What a fun thing to do at Christmas!"

"Shop for things we can't afford?" I smiled broadly, so she wouldn't think I was relapsing again.

"Shop for things we can eventually afford. Besides, it will give me something to look forward to while I'm home. I can use that."

"Okay. Dollar-menu date?"

"Maybe. Let's shop first, then decide. Maybe we'll want to give the ring funds a tiny little boost instead."

It was closing time, so I walked her home. The weight of my relative poverty was noticeably less crushing than before.

6

Surprise

OUR SECOND DECEMBER,
CONTINUED

TWO DAYS LATER, OVER the phone, Laurie announced, "I have a surprise for you. I'm not sure it's a happy one, but it's definitely a surprise. Want to meet my parents tomorrow?"

I was silent for a heartbeat. "Sure, I guess."

"But what? I thought I heard a 'but.'"

"I sort of thought you were hiding me from them."

"You really need to know me better," she said. "I've been hiding them from you."

"I think I understand."

"You'll understand a lot better after spending some time with them. Here's how it works. They come to town, stay in the nicest hotel they can find, invite me to brunch the next morning, complain about the hotel, invite themselves to my apartment, forget about the hotel when they see my little studio flat, tell me I should be living somewhere bigger and nicer because they can afford it, take me shopping for things I don't want or need, then—here's where you come in—take us out to dinner someplace really nice, where there's not enough food but it's really fancy. And expensive. That's the crucial part."

"Sounds like fun," I lied.

She sighed. "No, but it's necessary. And whatever they buy me that I don't need, I'll return, if I can, and donate it to our ring funds. That way they feel good about the gesture, and I get something I actually want."

"Then I hope they buy you something expensive," I said. "I doubt they'll like me."

"They won't. Before dinner they'll already have walked me through a short list of their rich friends' sons, the guys I should be dating. And I'll have told them that I am dating someone. That's why they'll invite you to dinner. Before they meet you, Dad will say, 'I hope you're being careful.' Mom will ask if it's serious, and at some point she'll wonder aloud if we're sleeping together.

"Maybe I'll say, 'No, Mom, we're not fooling around. We're fairly serious about school and life.' She'll wonder if that's snarky daughter code for 'No, Mom, I'm trying not to be like you.' She'll be right, but we won't argue. That comes later."

Laurie had started talking about her parents' visit in a matter-of-fact tone, but now she sounded morose. I didn't want her to feel even worse, if she continued, but I knew she wasn't finished.

"Will you argue at dinner?" I asked. "That would be sad."

"I hope not. It would also be rude. The next morning, before they leave, Dad will say, 'We were watching you two at dinner. You're obviously fond of each other.' I'll interrupt and say we're way beyond that. He'll say, 'There are more important considerations than love. You need to end this.'"

A cold chill gripped my heart. I tried to ignore it and kept listening.

"Mom will give me a speech about won't I be happier marrying someone more like me? I'll say no, I'm not a lesbian, I'm not marrying a rich girl. She will very patiently explain that she meant someone of my own class.

"I'll be much happier that way, Dad will say.

"I'll say they'll be happier. I'll be miserable. I'll tell them you make me happy, and you have plenty of class for me. Which is true. I'll try not to say you have more class than they do, which is also true."

She fell silent for a moment, and I didn't know what to say. Now I was morose too.

When she continued, her voice shook. "About then the yelling will start. I might do some of it. They'll do more. Mom, mostly. Then Dad will want to make peace before they leave. So we'll stop arguing and say a few kind words about looking forward to my visit next week, and I'll wish them a safe trip, and we'll be done." She sniffed, and I might have heard a tiny sob. "Lucky you, you only have to be there for dinner."

My rational engineer's heart was breaking for her. "Hard to imagine you yelling," I said. "Even when I deserve it, you're not loud about it."

"I've never heard you yell either," she said. "It's a welcome contrast."

"I never want to yell at you," I said.

"Even when I deserve it?"

"When would that be, exactly?"

"Seriously?" she asked.

"Yeah. Seriously."

"You really need to get me off the pedestal. It's not real."

I tried to understand, but I didn't. "What do I think about you that's not real?"

"Sometimes you call me angelic." Her voice still trembled. "I'm no angel."

"You are to me."

"Like I said, get me off the pedestal."

"Tell me," I said. "Who's a better authority than I am on what you are to me?"

She was quiet for a long moment. "Sooner or later, probably sooner, I'll fall off my pedestal, and someone will get hurt. Probably you. Probably me too. Good chance it will be this weekend."

"I'm pretty sure the you I love is the real one," I said. "I've never thought you were perfect, but I can still think you're my angel."

This silence was longer than the last, and I had no idea what to expect when she finally spoke.

"I wish I could kiss you right now," she said.

"So do I." I had a thought. "Ever notice that I have to reach down a little to kiss you? So no pedestal. Unless I'm on one too."

Another silence.

"That's actually possible," she said, "now that I think about it."

"What if we're both just on a higher plane?" I asked.

Her quick laugh was a relief. "Let's go with that. You're a lot like your mother."

"That is a higher plane." I said. "What do you mean?"

"Kind, gentle, understated, soft-spoken, smart, good. She's so sweet to me. I can't wait to meet her in person."

"She adores you," I said. "And you're a lot like her too."

"Thank you. What do you mean?"

"Stubbornly practical, but not unpleasant about it. You take care of the small stuff, but you don't worry too much about trivia. You're kind, loving, unselfish, smart. Strong when you need to be, when something matters to you. Or someone."

The next silence ended when she said, "I love you. After tomorrow you can tell me if I'm like my mother. You have to tell me the truth."

I HAD A FULL twenty-four hours to imagine what her parents would be like. I hadn't even seen a picture. I figured they couldn't be as bad as she said and still produce such a daughter, with or without an excellent nanny. I resolved to see the good in them, especially any resemblance to Laurie I could detect. That would make it easy.

I was plenty nervous when they picked me up in their rented Lexus SUV. It didn't help that Laurie and her mom sat in the back, leaving me in the front with her dad. But it was a short ride to the restaurant, and soon we were seated at a square table, on adjacent sides, where at least we could hold hands. I was across from her dad, and she was across from her mom.

Laurie reached for my hand below the table and gave it a long squeeze. I met her eyes, where I saw concern and only a hint of a smile. She probably saw the same in mine. She let go of my hand and turned to look at her parents. I followed her lead.

Her dad had sharp, narrow features, not at all like Laurie's. He was balding, and what hair he had was cut short and gradually turning from brown to silver. His dark eyes, narrow nose, and thin lips gave him a look of intensity. When he smiled, he seemed more aggressive than friendly or relaxed. At least that was my initial impression.

Her mom looked like a very slightly older version of Laurie. She had no more wrinkles at the corners of her eyes and mouth than Laurie did, and her hair was the same light blonde. There was something different about her eyes, but it wasn't the color. I couldn't decide whether it was just age or something else. I was tempted to think she looked more calculating and less intelligent than Laurie, but that sounded too much like my own bias.

To my relief they seemed friendly and genuinely interested, as we began to get acquainted. They were no more concerned or reserved than parents should be, when meeting a man with designs on their daughter. They asked me about my family, my studies, and my professional interests and aspirations.

I quickly ran out of things to say about myself, so I was glad when they began to reminisce about their own college years and beyond. They talked about building their financial consulting business from the ground up, and how their standard of living shot up almost overnight, when they began to get some traction, and how things just kept getting better. A bigger house in a better neighborhood. An even bigger house in an exclusive neighborhood. A nanny for Laurie and her younger sister, Vicky, short for Victoria. Important friends becoming clients and vice versa. I wasn't all that interested in the business or the social climbing, but I tried to be a good listener.

It was easy to be interested when they started telling me about Laurie as a little girl. Some of it was things she had never mentioned, like equestrian training. Vicky had been desperate to start at age seven, her mom said, when Laurie was nine, but Laurie was terrified of horses, so they waited another year, because Vicky didn't want to do it alone.

"Even then," her mom said, "Laurie refused to get on a horse for about the first month. She'd just sit there watching Vicky ride. Vicky was a natural. She rode competitively for a while, until she got distracted by tennis in high school."

"And boys," her dad interjected.

"And boys," her mom echoed. "She played a lot of mixed doubles."

I turned to Laurie. "You eventually got on a horse, right?"

She hesitated, then nodded.

"Laurie ended up liking long horseback rides through the countryside," said her mom. "She never wanted to compete."

"I went on a couple of horseback trips in Scouts," I said, "but that was all. I liked it, but I haven't done it since."

"It's an expensive avocation," her dad said. "Especially if you actually own a horse or two. I think we were up to four or five for a while."

Her mom smiled. "It was Nanny Marie who finally coaxed Laurie onto the horse. That woman was a treasure. She was our third nanny, and she stayed the longest by far. We kept her on as housekeeper, once Vicky didn't need a nanny anymore, because the girls loved her so much."

"Third time's the charm," said her dad. "The others didn't work out so well."

"She was our fourth nanny," Laurie said. "You always forget Juliette. She only stayed that one summer, but she was nice."

Her mom's face darkened and her dad looked pensive. His cheeks might have flushed, but it was hard to tell with his tan.

After a fraught moment I thought I might have understood, her mom turned to me. "We should tell you about her awkward teenager phase. It lasted from age ten to about her junior year in college."

Laurie pursed her lips and blushed slightly but said nothing. Who wouldn't be embarrassed, I thought, by parental stories about their teenage years? I warned myself not to enjoy them too much, but I had to smile a little. Her parents were opening up to me, telling me things you tell a welcome guest.

They told me about thirteen-year-old Laurie having a huge crush on Braden, a high school boy in the neighborhood. "He pulled into the driveway in his new Porsche convertible one afternoon," her dad said, "and the silly girl ran out and jumped into the passenger seat and buckled in. But he wasn't there for her. She just thought he was. She mistook daydream for reality, I think."

Her mom chuckled. "He was picking up my sister's daughter, Tiffany. She was staying with us then. She was sixteen or seventeen. Braden laughed pretty hard at Laurie—but then so did we. Tiffany didn't think it was all that funny, as I recall. She said something about Laurie being awfully pretentious for a plain, frumpy little girl. That was just mean."

Laurie stared silently at her plate as they talked.

Her dad picked up the narrative. "Laurie wouldn't come out of her bedroom suite for about two days. When she finally did emerge, the only person she would talk to or even acknowledge was Nanny Marie. That lasted maybe a week."

I turned to Laurie with a hesitant smile—which disappeared immediately. Her face was redder than before; her lips were thin, pale lines; and her eyes flashed. She was glaring at her parents.

They were enjoying themselves a little too much, I thought, but they were just being parents. I jumped in to rescue her.

"I'm sure it wasn't long before handsome boys in expensive convertibles came to the house for Laurie," I said.

"Well, yes," said her mom. "Sort of. They would bring her flowers and invite her out on some kind of nice date or other, but I don't remember her actually going out with them."

"I went on plenty of dates in high school," Laurie said quietly and almost flatly, as if she were restraining herself.

"Of course you did," said her mom. "I was thinking of dates who actually picked you up." She turned to me. "Once she had her own car, starting the day after her sixteenth birthday, she would agree to meet a boy somewhere for a date, but she wouldn't let him pick her up."

Her dad smiled, but the effect was grim. "One boy came by to pick her up anyway, for the Homecoming dance, I think it was, even after she told him not to. She refused to go to the dance at all—and he'd borrowed his dad's Lamborghini. We were mortified, of course. Doubly so, since it was Congressman Howard's son."

"He's Senator Howard now," her mom said. "The dad, I mean. She missed a real opportunity with that one. The son really liked her. I heard he found someone else to take to the dance at the last minute, so at least he wasn't publicly humiliated, and the damage to our standing was less than it could have been."

Laurie stared daggers at her mom, but her voice was still flat and controlled. "What you don't remember, somehow, is that what I missed that night was an opportunity to be roofied and date-raped. Kelsee Bethers had that honor in my place."

"Laurie!" Her mom sounded scandalized.

"Mother?"

"I never believed those rumors, and you shouldn't either. Really, people will say just about anything about you these days, if you're prominent enough."

"They weren't just rumors," Laurie said quietly to me, with evident sadness. "His family was important, and hers wasn't. They paid her off, and she withdrew the charges and moved away."

Her mom didn't let it go. "Honey, really, dredging up those old stories after all these years! The Howards are our friends."

"They're not my friends. Kelsee was my friend." She turned back to me. "She was a few steps lower on the social ladder—nobody important, the way some people calculate those things—but she was kind of effortlessly beautiful, so she attracted boys anyway. She was quiet and sweet. Smart too. A lot quieter after Homecoming."

What struck me most was not the sorrow in Laurie's eyes. It was the trust in her face when she looked at me, but not when she looked at her parents.

"I will say this for Laurie," her dad said. "She was a first-rate student, and she was almost always well behaved in public. She only came home drunk once that I know of. She drove home that way, which wasn't smart, but fortunately she didn't get caught or hit anyone. Missed the driveway on her way in, but the damage was minor. Could have been a lot worse. She was so plastered, I don't think she even realized she'd vomited all over the dashboard and the console."

Laurie's voice had some acid in it. "That was Vicky, Dad."

"Really? Are you sure?" asked her mom.

She huffed. "Hard to forget combing partially digested Buffalo wings out of her hair."

Her dad looked bemused. "I could have sworn that was you."

"Me too," added her Mom.

"It was Vicky," Laurie said. She was more animated now, but still not loud. "You know, the dark-haired, younger daughter who went to rehab for a while? As opposed to the blonde, older daughter who never once missed the driveway, because she never came home drunk or high?"

Her mom shrugged. "I guess you must be right. That's just not how I remember it."

"I'm not surprised. You two were away somewhere. It was just Nanny and me home with Vicky that weekend."

"And the dessert menus have arrived," her dad said. "Perfect timing."

I decided I didn't need dessert. Not for $14 of these people's money. I said I was pretty full from dinner, which wasn't quite true.

But her dad was right. The timing was good. I wasn't enjoying the stories anymore, and I was having to work to keep my cool. I wanted a good way to tell Laurie's parents what I thought about their using her for sport and forgetting which daughter did the bad stuff. This was far beneath normal parent behavior.

I wanted something short of direct confrontation, so I wouldn't just make things worse. Refusing dessert wasn't much, but it was something.

"Please, Rick," said her dad. "For one night, forget your thrifty upbringing. Order whatever looks tempting."

I opened my mouth to decline again, or maybe to defend my thrifty upbringing—or Laurie after all—but Laurie squeezed my hand and looked into my eyes. She was trying to smile, but it wasn't working. "Would you help me eat my dessert, please?"

Maybe I imagined it, but something in her eyes told me she could see my struggle, and she appreciated both my wanting to protest and my determination not to.

"Sure," I said. "If you want me to." I took a couple of seconds to enjoy her eyes. Then I added, "Thank you."

At that she really did smile a little. She looked up at the waiter, when he reappeared. "We'll share the grilled pears à la mode. Two spoons, please. Thank you."

She turned to me. "They're really good."

Her parents said that was a great idea and ordered two more of the same. I wondered if they were trying to placate their daughter, but she ignored them. She spoke to me as if we were alone at the table.

"Nanny would take slices of fresh, ripe Bartlett pears and drizzle them with this buttery, sugary sauce straight from heaven. She put some vanilla in it too. Then she'd grill them just right and top them with vanilla ice cream at the table, so the pears would still be hot when we ate them. It was my favorite dessert."

I smiled at her little burst of happiness, and she smiled a little more brightly in response. Then she bit her bottom lip adorably.

"It's . . . possible . . . that I love those grilled pears as much as I love you, and I've loved them a lot longer. Sorry."

The look we shared then was as intimate as a kiss.

When I thought to glance at her parents again, they were watching us and frowning. I could think of only one way to reach out to them.

"Thanks for dinner," I said. "This is the fanciest dinner I've ever eaten." I wasn't exaggerating.

Her dad nodded slightly. "You're welcome. It's not a new experience for Laurie. We've tried to surround her with the finer things, when she'll let us. Life shouldn't be lived from the dollar menu."

Something twisted in my gut. Laurie's eyes went hard and cold, and they were riveted on her dad.

Her mom turned to him. "Do you remember that little place we found on Lanai, when we stayed at the Four Seasons for, what was it, three weeks? That chef was some kind of wizard."

Laurie turned the same cold eyes to her mom, who met her gaze and looked completely unfazed.

Dessert arrived. Laurie reached for a dessert spoon, filled it with equal portions of grilled pear and ice cream, and fixed me with her gaze. She subtly moistened her lips with the tip of her tongue. While I wondered if she did that consciously, and if her parents had seen it, she fed me the first bite.

It really might have come from heaven. She beamed when she saw that on my face. The look in her eyes might have made a spoonful of sawdust taste pretty great too.

I also wondered if she wanted us to feed each other. We'd done that before, but it would provoke her parents. She handed me the spoon, still smiling, and we fed ourselves.

No one spoke.

When a single bite remained, I pushed the plate toward her slightly.

I didn't hear her words, but I read them on her lips. "For you." Her eyes sparkled, and she pushed the plate back toward me.

"Thank you," I mouthed, and enjoyed the last bite almost as much as the first.

On the way back to my apartment, we sat in the same seats as before. Nobody said much. When we reached my place, I thanked them for dinner again, and for the ride, and started to get out.

"I'm getting out too," Laurie announced, opening her door. "Thanks for dinner."

I couldn't see her mom's expression, but I heard disapproval. "I didn't realize you'd be staying here."

Laurie glanced at me, then back at her mom. "I'm not. It's a lovely evening. Rick can walk me home. Breakfast in the morning?" There was a catch in her voice.

"Seven forty-five," said her dad.

Doors closed, and the rented Lexus pulled away. I put my arm around her.

"The element of surprise," she said as we watched them leave. "Sometimes it works."

7

After Dinner

OUR SECOND DECEMBER, CONTINUED (AGAIN)

LAURIE'S PARENTS ZOOMED A little too fast toward the stop sign at the end of the block, then rolled through it and turned the corner. When they were out of sight, she bowed her head and slumped her shoulders.

"Long day for you," I said.

She didn't look up. "I need a really big hug."

"Want to come in?"

"I need it sooner than that." Her face crumpled. I pulled her to my chest and wrapped both arms around her.

"I'm so sorry," she said after a minute. Her voice was high pitched and unsteady. "They were awful to you, from the very first minute, and then I made it worse. I tried to be patient. I really did. But I lost my temper anyway, and I had to push back. I'm sorry."

I was bewildered. "I guess I missed something. I thought it went okay for a while. They were rough on you later, and kind of cold at the end."

"They're angry now," she said. "They were going to unload on me after we dropped you off. Tell me what a bad, ungrateful daughter I am. How wrong you are for me. Maybe how wrong I am for you. How I'm betraying the family."

I was torn between thinking she was imagining things, or at least badly overreacting, and a new sense of despair that I simply had not seen what she saw at dinner. Or I had seen it, but not for what it was.

I didn't know what to say. Again. I just held her and waited. I thought she might explain, but she surprised me again. "Are you okay?" she asked. "Do you hate them? Do you hate me?"

"I could never hate you," I said. "I'm okay. I guess I don't hate them, exactly, but it seems like there's some ugly stuff I didn't understand. I really thought most of tonight went okay. Well, some of it. The first part."

She pushed away enough that she could look up at me. "How could you think any of that was okay?"

"They were sort of friendly for a while, I thought. They opened up to me, like I was a welcome guest. At least not completely unwelcome. I didn't like them going overboard with the teenager stories, but parents do that. It's not necessarily malicious. The date rape thing was creepy, but before that?" I shrugged. "I guess I thought it mostly went okay for a while."

"You keep saying that. Are you blind?"

I was still trying to find a response that wasn't defensive when she spoke again. She was almost yelling, and I saw tears on her cheeks.

"You were right there! You saw their looks. You heard every condescending word. How could you not . . . ?" She shook her head. "How can you think . . . ?"

She looked away, still shaking her head. I had never seen such a frown on her face. Knowing I caused it—or helped cause it—was a gut punch. As if seeing her tears weren't bad enough.

"I'm sorry, okay?" I felt guilty and, yes, defensive, and—without wanting to—maybe I sounded harsh. "I guess I'm just an idiot. I'll shut up and let you explain."

"Don't be a martyr," she said. "You're better than that."

I took a deep breath and didn't say the first two or three things that came to mind.

"Please explain," I said quietly, after a long moment. "I want to understand everything. I just don't yet."

I watched her try to calm down, and I tried to do the same. Finally she looked up with eyes that weren't angry anymore, just distressed. "We both know you're not an idiot. You're a smart, kind, decent man, and I love you." She hung her head. "My parents would be happier right now, if they knew they'd managed to come between us for even a minute or two."

"I love you too," I said. "I just don't understand everything yet." I pulled her into another hug. "What can we do to make you happier and make them . . . less happy? With us."

"This is a good start," she murmured. "If you feel trapped between me and my parents, I'm sorry."

"I guess I do, a little. Not where I want to be."

She looked up. "Where do want to be?"

"Firmly on your side, wherever that is."

"Wherever . . . what?"

"I want to understand. I just don't yet. But I'm on your side."

She nodded, and I felt her relax a little, but it was a minute or more before she spoke again. "Could we walk? Please? Not too fast. There's no hurry. But you should know there's maybe a one-in-three chance they'll be waiting for us at my apartment. That could be ugly."

"Want to go somewhere else? Or stay here?"

"I already told them I'm not staying the night, so I can't sleep on your couch. Also, you don't have a couch." She sniffed. "There's nowhere else to go. By the way, Mom was socially, not morally, offended when she thought I was staying."

We turned and plodded down the sidewalk, hand in hand.

"We could hang out at a bar or maybe a coffee shop for a while, or just keep walking," I said.

"I've angered them enough for one night. Things will be better if I'm brave."

Her voice faltered, and my heart ached for her. But I still didn't see what she saw.

I let go of her hand, put my arm around her waist, and squeezed. I didn't know if it was possible to transfer courage to someone that way, or if I had any of my own to give. But at least I could reinforce the idea that she wasn't alone. I was on her side. Wherever that was. Wherever she was.

Especially if her parents were waiting for us at her apartment.

She took a few deep breaths, and then her voice was steadier. "Let's just keep walking me home, and I'll try to explain. I will explain. Everything. Maybe even calmly. Sort of."

We walked another thirty yards or so before she began.

"The first thing they did to you intentionally tonight—to us, I guess—was not let us sit together on the way to the restaurant. You looked uncomfortable up there with Dad, and that's exactly what they wanted."

"Are they really that petty?" I asked.

"Hold that thought," she said. She sounded almost calm. "Did you notice how they set up the contrast between you wanting a good engineering career and them wanting to conquer the whole stupid world?"

"No," I answered honestly. "I guess I see it now. But I already knew that about them. I just figured they were being who they are. I did notice the name dropping."

"They were definitely being who they are. They're arrogant and condescending. As far as they're concerned, a chemical engineer, even a fine one, soon enough a PhD, is far beneath them and their daughter."

"Okay."

She glanced up at me for an instant, and I thought she was going to complain that I sounded unconvinced, which I was. I still thought she was exaggerating.

She didn't complain, but her voice was less calm. "Did you ever hear me talk about anything equestrian in my life? Anything at all?"

"No."

"That's because horses were a very small part of my life. I liked riding, but I didn't do a lot. You know I did a lot of reading, and some local theater—but you don't have to be rich to read books, and I didn't get lead roles, so none of that even registers with them. Rich people do horses, so that's what they remember. If crocheting scarves with yarn spun from actual gold were a thing, they'd have had us doing that, and believe me, you'd have heard about it tonight."

"You should do some theater again someday, if you still like it," I said.

"Maybe we should do some together. But what I loved most about it was being someone else for a while. I don't need that anymore. I like who am, most days.

"It was Vicky who was terrified of horses. She insisted on just watching my lessons for the first month, but later she did great. She competed for a couple of years, and she was good. For me a horse was just a nice companion for escaping everything for a while."

She gave me a squeeze. "Like I said, I don't need to escape all that much anymore. But I hate it when they rearrange their memories so Vicky did all the good stuff, and I did all the bad, embarrassing stuff. That's why I lost my temper and mentioned Nanny Juliette. Mom caught Dad having a little summer fling with her."

"Yeah, I got that one. Saw it in their faces."

"I shouldn't have mentioned her at dinner," she said. "It was a cheap shot. Anyway, did you notice that every boy who ever wanted to date me arrived in an outrageously expensive car?"

"Yes and no."

We were passing under a street light, so I could see her clearly. She turned to me and pursed her lips.

The arm that had been around her fell to my side.

"Tell me about the no," she said.

"I noticed, but why would I think twice about it? That was the socioeconomic circle you lived in. Why did you insist on meeting your dates somewhere else, instead of letting them pick you up?"

She sounded peeved. "You're smart," she said. "You tell me."

"Are you angry with me?" I asked. "You seem a little angry. With me."

She hesitated. "No. A little frustrated. I'm sorry, but how could you not see what they were doing?"

"I'm trying very hard to see."

"Can you see why wouldn't I ride with any of those rich boys?"

"So you could get home on your own, without them?"

"Definitely. And?"

"To avoid . . . awkward car scenes? And going places you didn't want to go?"

"Yes. Literally and metaphorically. And the boys I dated who weren't rich, well, I didn't want them to be intimidated if they came to pick me up. And I didn't want to listen to my parents mocking the older, cheaper cars they drove. Or the clothes they wore or their haircuts or whatever."

She took my hand and we kept walking,

"I wanted a used Honda, when I was sixteen. They wanted to buy me something outrageously expensive. We compromised on a new Acura, which is more expensive, but still basically a Honda. I'm surprised they didn't tell you that story too, including how we went to two luxury dealerships first, and I refused to get out of the car.

"I sold the Acura after I drove it to school for freshman year, once I made sure I could get around without it. The title was in my name by then, so I could do that."

She stopped walking and pulled me gently around to face her. "You at least noticed that they can't believe a senator's son would date-rape my friend, right? Or they don't care?" Now she looked hurt. Deeply hurt.

I nodded. "That was pretty bad."

"Do you believe me when I tell you he actually did it?"

"Yeah."

"They don't even care that it could have been me. Almost was."

"I'm sorry about your friend," I said. "But I'm glad it wasn't you."

She looked me in the eye. "I wonder what they would have done. I've wondered that a lot."

I reached for her, and she came to me. "I'm glad you never had to find out. But you're their daughter. They'd have to take your side for that one."

"I hope so. But I really don't know."

It was minute or two before we resumed walking, silently at first. Finally I squeezed her hand and spoke. "When we shared dessert, was that you trying to upset them even more?"

"No. I can see why you might wonder, but that was about me loving you and wanting to show you. And needing to escape. We were in our own beautiful world for a few minutes, where Mom and Dad didn't exist."

She shrugged. "Which was probably rude, and they weren't pleased, but after their performance I can't bring myself to care. You patched over it a little anyway."

"I tried. Not sure it worked."

"It didn't. That's why they made a big deal about being on Lanai."

"Where's Lanai?"

"One of the Hawaiian Islands. Kind of small. Basically, rich people go there and stay at the Four Seasons—for three extravagant weeks, in our case. That was Mom and Dad reaffirming for themselves and for me, at least, that we're money and you're not."

"I guess that one was lost on me."

"They were okay with that. It confirmed for them that you're inferior, which I know isn't true. Oh, and speaking of inferiority, that time when I jumped into my crush's Porsche?"

"I wanted to laugh," I confessed.

"That's okay. But it wasn't Tiffany who said I was awfully pretentious for such a plain, frumpy girl." Her chin trembled again. "It was Dad. I shrieked at him, asked him how he could say such a thing. So Mom said she thought frumpy and plain were the right words. She said I apparently wanted to be that way. Tiffany smirked and said something about me being the ugly duckling, so it's not like she was the nice one in this picture. There wasn't a nice one."

"Except you."

"I wasn't very nice that day either."

"Thanks for explaining all that," I said. "I understand better now."

"Do you believe me? That they were being deliberately offensive from the beginning?"

"Yeah. At first I thought you were overreacting, but now I believe you."

She searched my face. "You look angry now. I hope it's not with me."

"They hurt you, I get angry. At them."

"Thank you. But they're out of here tomorrow. We have bigger fish to fry. This girl you love is staying, and she's a real piece of work. Are you sure you want to be part of this sad, cruel, dysfunctional . . . whatever this is?"

"I think the key thing is, this piece of work is the girl I love."

"Even if she has major issues with her parents, and vice versa?"

"Everybody has issues."

"I don't suppose your mom would adopt me."

I laughed. "Absolutely not. Then you'd be my sister. I don't want you to be my sister. Not what she has in mind for you either."

She smiled for the first time in a while. "I'm going to learn to make that dessert for you. I'll get Nanny to teach me."

As we approached her apartment, she squeezed my hand more tightly. We scanned the parked vehicles along the street, looking for her parents' rental. It wasn't there. When we didn't see it in her building's small parking lot either, I felt her relax.

She pulled us to a stop under a light near the corner of her building, and I watched her scan the lot again. "We seem to have this moment to ourselves," she said. "Let's enjoy the parent-free view."

My eyes were on her. I saw the tracks of a few tears, but also a tired smile. "I'm enjoying the view," I murmured.

She glanced up and smiled more brightly.

"Are you okay now?" I asked.

Her smile faded. She took in a deep breath and blew it out. It was just cold enough that we could see our breath. "You know, except for my parents, my life is as perfect as tonight's dessert."

"I wish tonight had gone better," I said earnestly. "I wish I'd realized what they were doing. Maybe I could have helped somehow."

"You helped by being there. You helped by listening. You're helping now."

"It's still hard for me to believe they could be all bad, when I consider the daughter they made."

She gave me a wry look. "I guess they're not the devil, but look how they treated the man their daughter loves. He's a good man, and they don't care. He makes their daughter happy. Chronically happy. They. Don't. Care. I wish I weren't wired to care what they think."

"What can I do to help?"

"Want to come to breakfast with them? I won't be so tired, so my part should go better."

"I don't think I'm invited."

"I just invited you. So come if you want to. It'll give them a chance to flex their good manners muscles. Or not. You never know how cold things will get when they don't get their way."

"I'll come in a heartbeat, if you think it will help you. If it won't just provoke them."

"Let me try to think rationally about that for a minute, while you take your sweet time escorting me to my door. Then I'll think about it some more while you kiss me."

"I must not be much of a kisser," I said.

She smiled a little, but mostly she looked puzzled. "It was a long day and I'm exhausted. I have to ask you to explain."

"Simple. I'd like my kisses to make rational thought impossible, like yours do for me. Multitasking of any kind should be impossible."

Now there was mischief in her smile. "We'll see how it goes."

At her door she kissed me harder than I expected, and I reciprocated. Rational thought didn't seem to be involved.

She rested her head on my shoulder. "Best part of my day," she murmured. "I was not thinking about breakfast with my parents."

"What were you thinking about?"

"Taking you upstairs and just falling asleep in your arms tonight. And waking up there in the morning. Probably not a good idea."

"Probably not. Sounds amazing, though."

"I feel safe with you—in all sorts of ways. Even that one."

"Not sure about that one right now."

"I know, right? Do you feel safe with me? I mean, you'd be smart to wonder about that. But does your heart at least feel safe? I'd understand some doubts, after an evening with my parents."

"My doubts are about them, not you."

I felt her nod. "I ought to feel as safe with my parents as I do with you. Even safer. But I don't. I feel really lucky to have you."

"Then we're both very lucky."

She breathed deeply. "I should go to breakfast without you. That's what I think. But I'll be okay. Could we do lunch later?"

"Lunch is good. Are you sure?"

"I've had the same parents all my life. Well, the same biological parents. Nanny Marie mostly raised me. Anyway, Mom and Dad and I have had arguments like this since long before you were in the picture. I cry a little afterward, and I rage a little too, but then I'm okay. Distance helps a lot, and there will be plenty of that after about 9:30 a.m. tomorrow. I can look forward to that and to lunch with you. Could we make it an early lunch? Please?"

Her breath was warm on my neck. I reached up to stroke her cheek, and she purred.

"Just call me when you're done. I wish I knew . . . ," I started over. "I wish I could put myself between you and all your troubles, instead of making some of them worse."

She hesitated. "You don't really think you're making them worse, do you? You're the antidote to my troubles. You're the man who makes me happy, remember? Whether they like it or not?"

"I just wish they wouldn't hurt you because of me."

"They think they're helping me. I'm officially the difficult daughter. Good thing I got tough somewhere along the way."

"I love that."

"I thought you loved my gentle side and tried to avoid my tough side," she said with a hint of a smile.

"The tough side's pretty important. I'm afraid you'll need it with me."

So much for the smile. "Tell me we're not talking about money again," she said.

"Just real life. That's tough enough."

"I can deal with real life," she said, instantly happier. Then I was instantly happier too, because her gentle side and I were kissing again.

We finally came up for air. I was almost desperate to stay with her, which meant it was time to go. "Good luck with breakfast," I said.

"When it starts, I can already be thinking how it's almost over."

"You'll see them again in a few days, when you go home."

"I have that figured out too. On the way back I'm stopping in Vegas to see Nanny Marie for a couple of days. I can look forward to that. It's been a year, and I miss her a lot more than I miss my parents."

"I wish I could go with you," I said. "At least to visit her."

"I wish you could too. But don't worry. I promise to think about you a lot, and Nanny will insist on hearing all about you and us, and I will love telling her."

8

While You Were Away

STILL OUR SECOND DECEMBER

WHILE LAURIE WAS IN Las Vegas, I arrived home from my day on campus to find a note on my door.

"Richard, this is Andrew Martin, Laurie's father. I'm back in town briefly and need to speak with you. Please call. Let's meet for dinner tonight whenever is convenient. Don't tell Laurie, please."

At first I worried that something had happened to Laurie, but he wouldn't have come to town to tell me that, if he told me at all. Still, it didn't take a genius or even an engineer to guess that Laurie and I would be the main topic of conversation. For an instant I hoped he might want to apologize in person, but that didn't seem likely.

I wondered what he would do if I didn't call. For all he knew, I could have stayed late at the lab. Unless he was somewhere watching me.

If I didn't call, he'd probably just knock on my door before the evening was over. So I called. He offered no clues, and I didn't ask.

I dressed up a little and walked to his hotel. We met at the restaurant off the lobby at 6:30 p.m. The food was good, and he made small talk about business and the town. He didn't seem hostile, and if I hadn't known it was all just a prelude, I might have enjoyed it a little. As we finished our entrees, he finally got to the point.

"Richard, let us speak as men. You are fond of my daughter, and she is fond of you. That much is obvious. If you care for her future at all, surely you can see that she should marry someone who is more nearly her social and economic equal. She can't do that as long as she's seeing you, because she won't date anyone more suitable with you in the picture." He spoke calmly and firmly, as a man accustomed to getting his way without argument.

He stopped to sip his wine. Then he fixed his eyes on me and continued. "If you really care for her long-term welfare and happiness, you'll move on, so she can move on."

When I didn't reply immediately, he continued. "Has she told you about the job I have for her?"

"No, sir. She hasn't."

"My partners and I are acquiring a small biotech firm with poor management and even less marketing vision, but very promising technology. I want her to help me run it for a while. She has the scientific mind I lack, and a firm mind for business, I think. She'd start as VP of Technology, earning six figures plus equity. I've even offered to wait until she finishes her degree here. She really hasn't told you about this?"

"No, sir. As I said."

"I'm not surprised. She would say it's not relevant, since she refuses to consider it."

"You think that's my fault?" I asked. "I wouldn't stand in her way, if that's what she wanted."

"No, no, no. In this sense, at least, you're more of a symptom than the problem itself. And I'm not asking you to persuade her. Not even you could do that, I'm fairly certain. She wants, how shall I say, a flatter career arc, something she can scale back for a while to raise children, and then reenter when she's ready. She's wanted that longer than she's known you."

"You're right," I said. "I couldn't persuade her."

He shook his head. "Nanny Marie is her hero—a nanny, of all people! She—Laurie—repeatedly served us notice of our parental inadequacies, along with Nanny Marie's many virtues, all through her teenage years."

"She's told me quite a lot about Nanny Marie."

"Small wonder. But here's the thing. My daughter has a gift for her field of study, and I have the financial means. It would be a tragedy to see all of that wasted in the interest of raising children—which she'll have to do herself. It's not just that she'll refuse to hire someone, because she wants to do it herself. She refuses to be wealthy enough to hire someone."

I spoke carefully. "If you don't blame all of that on me, and you don't think I'm standing in the way of her career, then what? I should just dump her? For her own good?"

"What I hope is that losing you, which needs to happen anyway, will jar her back to a proper sense of who she is, who she can and should be, and she'll ultimately decide to take her place in the family."

He stopped and stared at me. I stared back and didn't speak. My own concerns about her money and my lack of it had seemed just and honorable to me, but his concerns about the same thing seemed hopelessly shallow and small. Maybe that's how mine looked to her. That would explain a lot.

He finally spoke. "It could be good for you too. I've checked into you and your family," he said. "You were never wealthy, of course, but since your late father passed, your mother has struggled mightily to make ends meet at all. You yourself live on a shoestring here—not because you choose to, like my daughter does in her current, interminable rebellious phase. You do it because you have to. I'm sure it's all very admirable. But even when you finish your degree and take a job, you will never be well off. You don't have the drive I had, the will to succeed at all costs, beyond all limits and expectations. I believe Laurie has that, if she'll stop repressing it. My daughter deserves to marry someone who has it too, for her own happiness and for the long-term good of the family."

He looked at me expectantly, and I finally spoke. "Sir, if I thought that way, your daughter would have broken up with me before there was anything to break."

Now his eyes flashed, and he replied more sharply. "Surely you don't believe she can be happy in the lifestyle your middle class income will support."

There should have been a lot to say to him, but there wasn't. I couldn't change who he was or what he thought of me or Laurie. There was no point in my thinking or speaking of anyone but her.

"Where Laurie's happiness is concerned," I said, "I've learned to listen to her instead of making assumptions. Or proclamations."

I thought my words might provoke him, but his businesslike expression returned. He regarded me for a moment, then pulled something from an inner pocket of his suit jacket. He reached across the table and placed it in front of me. It was a cashier's check.

"The payoff amount for your mother's mortgage is a hair under $35,000. You'll forgive me for looking that up. Another $20,000 will buy her a decent new car. Your sister's college fund could use $20,000 as well, I'm sure. And $75,000 for you will put far more money in your own bank account than you've ever seen in one place, I suspect. So stop seeing my daughter, help your family, and get something for yourself in the bargain."

I probably should have been upset that he looked into my family's finances, or that he was using them to pry me away from his daughter, but his thoughts had stopped mattering to me. Maybe

I'd be offended later, but for now I was too busy thinking this could have been a bad movie. He was actually bribing me to break up with his daughter!

Unless he was testing me.

I picked up the check. It was made out to me for $150,000. I put it back on the table, face down. It really could have been a movie scene, because somehow I knew my lines.

"I don't know if you're testing me, sir, but I'm going to assume that you're not. Some things are not for sale," I said calmly. "I'd like to think that, as a father, you'd want your daughter to be one of those."

"I will write you a personal check for an additional $100,000 right now," he said with equal calm.

"I agree that you lowballed your opening bid. But there's nothing up for auction here, sir."

"I'll tell you what," he said, clearly trying to be personable and firm at the same time. "I need to make a call for a few minutes—not about you or my daughter—so I'll excuse myself briefly. While I'm gone, order yourself a drink or dessert, or both, and think about how much good you can do for your family today, if you get this right. You could make it a Christmas to remember."

He put a credit card—not a black AmEx—in the folder for the server to pick up, then left and went outside. I dropped my grocery money for the week—$30—on the table to pay for my half of the meal and part of a tip. Then I took out a pen and wrote "VOID" in large letters across the front of the check. I left it face down on his side of the table, grabbed my coat, and left the restaurant by a side door.

My walk home took over an hour. I fumed at Mr. Martin's offers and shook my head at each new layer of irony I uncovered, as I thought about Laurie and me and her parents. I laughed a few times too, but caustically, because things had become so bizarre. Nothing about this was genuinely funny.

I was pleased with myself for defending his daughter's immeasurable worth, when he tried to put a price on her, and proud that I hadn't even considered accepting his money. Mom and Dori wouldn't want or accept help on those terms anyway. As for me, my only regret was leaving my $30 on the table. The ring fund might have to buy my groceries this week.

When I reached my apartment, there was still almost an hour before Laurie's scheduled call. I spent it sitting motionless on my bed, wondering if I should tell her, and how and when. I couldn't *not* tell her, I realized after failing to persuade myself otherwise. But should I tell her in person or on the phone? What words should I use? Would she cry, laugh, rage?

Maybe all of those.

My phone rang, and I thumbed the green button. "Joe's Exotic Bathhouse and Beer Hall. Joe speaking," I said gruffly.

The game would go on, with each of us saying progressively more outrageous things, until one of us broke character and burst out laughing—which I did as soon as she giggled and said, "Joe, I was calling for my boyfriend, but you sound sexier. Are you available?"

It felt good to laugh.

"It's good to hear your fake voice," she said. "And your real laugh."

She told me how much she'd missed me and caught me up on what she and Nanny Marie had been doing—mostly talking about me, apparently. Then I heard her sigh. "I had long, bad talk with Mom on the phone today. I guess the daily arguments in person weren't enough."

Some of those had been ugly. I'd heard all about them in our daily calls.

"So I wanted to ask," she said, "do you know how to cut titanium?"

"Your card? I think a hacksaw will work. There's a laser at the lab that would be more fun. Why?"

"My phone's dying. I'll call you back from Nanny's house phone in a minute, okay?"

Half a minute later, she picked up where we'd left off. "I left my AmEx card with Mom and Dad. Told them I wouldn't be using it anymore. She says they're sending it back to me. I want to send it back to them in pieces, and I'd love for you to help me. Laser date when I get back?"

"Sure. The lab's pretty empty this week. We won't be in anyone's way."

"Thank you. I won't be visiting them anymore, and that's all I was willing to use it for anyway."

This was big. And sad. "I'm sorry."

"So am I. Ready for my next thing?"

If she had to ask, maybe I wasn't. "Sure," I said.

"Something Mom said, or maybe the way she said it, makes me think you'll be hearing from Dad soon. They're determined to break us up. Big surprise, right? For my own happiness, of course."

"What do you think they'll do?" I asked. And how will I tell you what they did? I thought. I still hadn't figured that out.

"I guess they could threaten to hurt you or your family somehow, but that's not their style. Maybe try to persuade you it's for your own good, which you'll have to decide, or mine, which it's absolutely not. If you still won't dump me, maybe they'll offer you money. As far as they know, money can buy practically everything. They'd be overjoyed if it could finally buy me as well."

"That's sick," I said, and meant it. "How much do you think you're worth to them?"

"Low six figures, if I'm lucky." She was trying to sound light-hearted, but her voice was strained.

"You think they'd really do that?" I asked, wondering if it was wrong of me to pretend, even briefly, that they hadn't already done it.

"I've been asking myself the same question. I think they really would."

I gathered my courage. "I wish you were wrong about that. A girl should be able to respect her parents."

"I know, right?" She was silent for a moment. "Wait. Did you just . . . He already did it, didn't he?"

"He's in town. At least he was. We had dinner tonight."

"Rick, I am so, so sorry."

I told her all about it. After I mentioned the cashier's check, I heard her crying softly, and I wondered if she wanted to ask me what I'd decided. She had the right to doubt me, after all my worries about money.

I told her what I had done before she could ask. She just kept crying, and my heart wasn't doing too well either.

Finally she said softly, "You're my hero." I heard a deep breath. "You showed Dad a real man. I wish Mom and Vicky had seen it too."

"I don't. Meeting Vicky would be interesting, but I don't like being outnumbered by hostile forces."

"My hero could have handled it."

"Yeah, maybe. If I really am your hero, that's the best thing I've ever been."

"You've been that for a long time. Where did you get the $30?" she asked.

"My grocery money for the week."

"Will you starve? I can share."

"I'll be okay."

"I'll still make you dinner at least twice this week, with plenty of leftovers. You'll also get your favorite dessert, kisses from me, right?"

"Zero calories," I said. "Over 100% of the USDA's recommended daily affection."

"The government recommendations are way too pessimistic."

Just the thought of kissing stripped away some of the evening's distress. I hoped it did the same for her.

"On that note, I have to go," she said. "Nanny and I are baking cookies for someone. Sorry it's not you. And don't get the idea that I know how to bake. See you soon."

"Not soon enough," I said earnestly.

"Mind reader. Warm up that laser, okay? I love you."

THREE DAYS BEFORE CHRISTMAS, she came home and introduced me to Nanny Marie, who'd come with her at the last minute. We met for a late lunch at Wendy's, then went to Laurie's small apartment and talked into the night. Mostly, I listened to a different set of tales from Laurie's childhood, but they also coaxed plenty of my own memories out of me.

I found a way to talk with Nanny alone for ten minutes before we said good night. There was something I wanted from her for later. She offered it before I could ask.

Two days before Christmas, Laurie and I went to the lab and cut her titanium AmEx card into precisely uniform ribbons. At the campus post office we dropped the pieces into an envelope and mailed them to her parents.

"I hope there's a penalty for destroying the card," she said. "I hope it's a big one. Sorry if that's childish, but I'm their child. Somehow."

We had the lobby to ourselves. As soon as the envelope disappeared into the mail slot, she turned to me, threw her arms around me, and kissed me for a whole minute.

"I was going to ask how you're feeling," I said, "but I have my own data now. You feel really good. So do I."

"You feel wonderful," she said. "I feel liberated. Exhilarated. A little bit scared, because I basically just disowned my parents. That's how they'll take it. But they've earned it."

"Good thing you still have Nanny," I said. "You'd be an orphan." I instantly feared that I'd said a bad thing, but she took it with a smile.

"You would still love me as an orphan," she said.

She was right.

9

A Beautiful Setting

OUR SECOND CHRISTMAS EVE

ON THE DAY BEFORE Christmas, we met for an afternoon of pricing rings. I looked forward to the company, but it was difficult not to be discouraged, thinking about jewelry I couldn't afford for a while.

Laurie didn't seem bothered, and I didn't tell her I was.

"First, we find the right ring," she said as we approached the first store. She was businesslike and cheerful. "Something simple. Then the stone. I don't want a diamond."

"You have to let me buy you a real diamond, not a fake, even if it's small."

"We're too real for fakes," she said. "But I want an emerald."

"Don't people use diamonds for this?" I asked.

"Mostly. So what?"

"So why an emerald?"

"I've wanted one for a long time," she said. "But I have a new reason too. You have beautiful emerald eyes. When you're not around for me to look at, I can look at my finger and see a piece of you."

I had to smile. "Are you making this up as we go along?"

She gave me a mischievous look. "I really have wanted an emerald for a long time. The other thing's new."

Maybe I could catch the spirit of this after all. "You wouldn't rather have a red ruby, for my bloodshot grad student eyes?"

"Very funny. Not a ruby."

We spent two hours visiting four different shops. The fifth one didn't look like much. It occupied a small stone building across from the town square. A brass marker declared the building historic.

We almost skipped it. We'd learned what we needed to know. But the shop was cute and inviting, so we stopped. We stayed half an hour, then longer, because that's where we found our rings. Even the sizes were already right.

With a small emerald, the price would be $1,210 for the engagement ring, the stone, and her matching wedding band. They'd solder her two rings together for free after the wedding.

That was more money than I had, but I'd expected an even higher price. It was an attainable goal. And there was no rush. We were just there for research. I told Laurie I was encouraged.

Even if the rings were gone by the time we could afford them, Laurie said, now we knew what we wanted, and we'd know the first place to look. She was encouraged too.

Before long, I was more than encouraged. I was eager and nervous, because I knew three things she didn't know.

They were having a 40 percent off sale for Christmas. I hadn't noticed that at first, and she hadn't noticed it at all.

Mom's letter that morning said she'd put $230 in my bank account from selling my two old bicycles.

And I had brought my checkbook, on the unlikely chance that we wanted to put down a deposit or something.

When Laurie excused herself to use the restroom, it was time for me to be bold.

The jeweler looked old enough to be my grandfather. He was lanky and tall, so that when he leaned over the counter, our eyes were at the same level. "If I buy these right now," I asked him, "how long would it take you to mount the emerald? I know it's Christmas Eve, but I just decided to propose tonight. With or without the ring, but with it would be better."

A smile lit his face. "As you see, I'm not busy this afternoon." He checked his watch. "Come back in two hours, just before closing. If she's with you, tell her you need the restroom. I'll meet you in the back, and I'll have everything ready. You can come back later for your band, and I'll give her the same discount." He hesitated. "Maybe I shouldn't say this, but I see a lot of couples, a lot of future brides. This one is special."

Laurie returned before I could agree or ask him to explain.

We decided to walk through downtown, enjoying the decorations, then finish at the town square, where the paved walks wound among snow-covered trees and past the occasional statue. I tried not to sound nervous with anticipation, as we chatted. And I made sure our route to the square went past the jewelry shop.

This was going to work. Fate was clearly a romantic.

"Oh, look!" she said. "There's the shop with our rings."

"Just in time too," I said. "Now I need a restroom. I hope they're still open."

"Looks like it."

Not ten minutes later, we crossed the street to the square. Darkness had fallen, and it was beautifully lit.

"Did you look at rings again?" I asked.

"A little. I didn't see mine, but I'm not sure it was in a display case before."

"If that's the one you want, I'll give it to you someday."

She beamed. "That's the one I want. When we can we afford it."

"So someday, when I propose to you, am I supposed to have your dad's permission first?"

"That is so last-century," she said. "I'm a person, not his chattel. In a perfect world, I guess you should ask both my parents for their blessing. You won't get it, but you could ask. You should do it in a letter, not a visit, so it's less convenient for them to kill you."

"Okay. Am I supposed to kneel?"

"When you talk to my parents? No."

"When I ask you."

"Oh. Well, you could, but not if we're in public somewhere. You don't have to kneel."

"Good," I said without thinking. "The snow's a little sloppy."

"What?"

I figured I had two seconds, tops, to distract her before she figured it out, or ten seconds if I kissed her. So I kissed her.

Then I said, "Every really significant thing happens in the winter for us, and we might be outdoors. I expect snow."

"I guess you're right."

I stopped us amid the trees, when no one else was near, and pulled her into a hug. "For example, it's winter now, and the trees and the snow are beautiful, and you are even more beautiful, and I'd really like to kiss you again. That seems significant."

"You know what we need?" she asked.

"What?"

"Fewer speeches about kissing. More kissing."

A blissful minute or two later, she said, "Now, will there be anything else?"

"Like what?"

"I don't know. I guess if you want to make a romantic little speech now, it would be okay, but only until we catch our breath. Then you should kiss me again. If we're still alone."

"What would you like me to say?"

"Whatever comes to mind." She grinned too innocently. "You could list some of the many things you love about me."

"Okay, I guess I have one idea."

"I'll be honest," she said. "I was hoping for more than one. But hurry up and say it. I've almost caught my breath."

"May I take your glove off? I have a romantic thought about your hand."

"Weirdo. One hand or both?"

"One's enough, I guess."

She held up her hands. "Your choice."

I pretended to deliberate. "This one, I think." I took her left hand and removed her glove. After I kissed her hand, I pressed it between mine.

"This is nice," she said, "but does your little speech come with words?"

"Yeah, it does. I love your hands. I don't exactly know what makes a hand pretty, but yours are pretty. And holding your hand, and you holding mine, is almost enough to make me believe in heaven."

"That's a good speech."

"I'm not finished yet."

"Okay."

"Will you marry me? Because I have this ring in my pocket that would look a lot better on your finger." I pulled out the box and opened it.

Her jaw dropped and her eyes went wide. "What? How did you . . . ? Did you steal it?"

"No. But first things first. Marry me? Please?"

"Yes! Of course!"

I'd been confident of her answer, but my relief was overwhelming. We just stood there and smiled at each other for a minute. She was radiant, and she wasn't just Laurie now. She was *my* Laurie.

"Give me your hand," I said softly.

Her eyes twinkled, and she held up her right hand. I squeezed it.

"I meant your other hand."

"I know." She held it out.

The ring still fit perfectly. She looked down at it, then up at me.

"Come with me," she said, taking my hand. A few yards further down the path, there was a stone border along one side, several inches higher than the path itself. She stepped up onto it, so we were eye to eye. Then we were kissing—as long and ardently as we dared in a public place.

When she pulled away, it was only a quarter-inch or so.

"I've never had a fiancé to kiss before," she said. "This is nice. Thanks for picking a time when there's no one else in the park."

Her breath brushed my lips as she spoke, and it was all I could do to reply in words before I kissed her again.

"Lucky accident," I said. Then time stood still—until we heard voices approaching.

"To be continued," I murmured. "Thank you for saying yes."

"Thank you for asking," she said. "And still wanting me, now that you've met the gene pool."

We set off slowly down the path, hand in hand. She overflowed with questions.

I told her about the sale she hadn't noticed at the jewelry store, but she was too good at math to think that was enough. So I explained the money Mom gave me from selling my bikes, and how the jeweler worked extra quickly to mount the stone. And how he'd said he could tell she was special. I mentioned that last part to distract her from thinking I should have told her of the change in our future-related finances before doing anything drastic like proposing.

I didn't have to worry.

"I love Christmas Eve!" she exulted. "Almost as much as I love you."

"I don't have your parents' blessing, and I never will," I said soberly. "But I will write them a letter."

"That's more than enough," she said.

"It's less than enough. That's why I asked Nanny Marie for her blessing when she was here." I glanced at her, wanting to see her face.

Her eyes were dancing. "And?"

"We have her very enthusiastic blessing."

"No wonder she was all aglow. And so tearful. I thought it was just saying goodbye. When shall we get married?"

"Yesterday?" I asked.

"Sorry. We're too poor for a time machine. But you seem eager to get your hands on me. For the record, I approve. Next suggestion?"

We said things like that to each other sometimes, but early in our relationship we'd discovered that we both wanted to save some physical intimacies for marriage. The funny thing was, we had different reasons. Mom had raised me a certain way, and I wanted to be able to look her in the eye. Laurie had watched friends and neighbors who had no such scruples, and she'd grown up seeing the wreckage, not to mention fending off unwelcome advances. Some things were too consequential to play with, she said.

"I think we should discuss the possibilities," I said, "including what kind of wedding you want. Then we can decide."

"Tonight?"

"We can't get a license that fast," I said. "But I like the thought."

"I mean, do you want to discuss it tonight?"

"Not really. We should wait 'til the euphoria wears off."

She smiled. "What if it doesn't?"

"A little of it might. We'll make better decisions that way. Right now, I'm content to enjoy your answer."

"Were you nervous?" she asked.

"Very."

"Even though you pretty much knew what I would say?"

"I was still nervous."

"I love how you did it. Total surprise, beautiful setting. It'll be a wonderful memory. It already is. What kind of wedding do you want?"

"One with you in it," I said. "What about you?"

"Small, simple, nice. Doesn't have to be in a church. Something we can afford, because my parents won't be helping. They probably won't even be there."

"I'm sorry."

"Me too. But it's their choice. Besides, Mom and Dad would both want a royal wedding, for slightly different reasons. Soon or later, do you think?"

"I'm open to the possibilities," I said. "Are we talking about this now?"

"No, this is just the pre-meeting. What are the possibilities?"

"After graduation. Next Christmas Eve. Fall. Summer. Spring. Groundhog Day. Whatever works. I can wait a while, if we decide that's best. Any thoughts?"

"Well, yesterday's already off the table," she said. "After graduation sounds sensible in some ways, almost unbearable in others. Next Christmas Eve would be fun, but it might be hard for the people who'd want to come. And we have to make it possible for my parents to attend, even if they won't. Lots of equations with lots of variables."

"We'll solve them together," I said.

"And have fun doing it." She reached for my waist and gave me a squeeze through my coat. "Let's err on the side of sooner."

WE WENT TO MIDNIGHT Mass and hardly said a word. We just held each other, watched, listened, and sang the congregational hymns—and caught each other looking at her ring.

I had her home by 2:30 a.m., and I was home by 2:45. But for a good breeze and the wind chill, we might have been out later. We could have walked and talked—or just walked—until dawn.

I told Mom and Dori the joyous news in our Christmas call that morning, and I promised them Laurie and I would call together that afternoon, after our now-traditional early Christmas dinner at Wendy's.

We couldn't wait to see each other until mid-afternoon, so early dinner turned into lunch. We knew from experience that we'd feel terribly sorry for the people there who had to work on Christmas Day, so we took them small gifts. They said no one had ever done that before. When the manager overheard us talking about wedding dates and realized we were newly engaged, she treated us to large Frosties, an unimaginable luxury.

We called Mom and Dori from my apartment. They'd talked with Laurie before, but this time they talked with her a lot more than with me. Dori was happy and bouncy. Mom was happy and tearful. Laurie was gracious and smiled a lot. Then we called Nanny Marie, and she and Laurie both cried.

B Y THE TIME WE'D been engaged for 48 hours, we'd decided that Presidents Day weekend was our first choice for the wedding, so we could enjoy the long weekend together without school. Any honeymoon we could afford would be short and close to home. Our second choice was the first weekend in March. Laurie had checked her parents' calendars online, to make sure we picked dates when they could come if they chose to.

We were still deciding whether I should send that letter to her parents before or after she told them she was engaged. Maybe both letters in the same envelope, she said, and her parents wouldn't like either of them.

10

What Can I Give Her?

OUR THIRD CHRISTMAS EVE

A YEAR LATER, ON December 23, we were at the hospital. Laurie was scared. I was practically frantic and trying desperately not to show it.

She'd worked through the summer to finish her degree ahead of schedule, because, as she put it, morning sickness had set in a year or two earlier than we planned. She took that surprise like she took every challenge in our life together: more cheerfully than I did. I did my best to mimic her good spirits, and I helped her as much as I could.

Her defense was right at the end of her second trimester. She felt great, and it went well—and with that her degree was finished.

Then the doctor found a problem which meant that a normal labor would be extremely dangerous. There was a good chance neither Laurie nor our little girl would survive it.

"Not to worry," said the obstetrician. "We'll keep an eye on things, and unless there are indications sooner, we'll schedule a C-section at 37 weeks. We'll be fine."

"What if there isn't much warning, and labor starts earlier than that?" I asked.

"We'll suppress the labor if we can and do the C-section right away," she said. "But it's not likely."

Surgery was scheduled for December 28. If all went well, mom and baby would be home to start the New Year.

Laurie went into labor on the afternoon of December 23. By evening it clearly wasn't false labor, and the drugs that usually suppressed it weren't working. There would be no calm, conveniently scheduled C-section. There would be an emergency, late-evening C-section, starting within minutes and involving a mom who was already exhausted and a baby who, according to the monitors, was beginning to be distressed.

When the doctors and nurses talked to Laurie, they spoke only of the baby's welfare. When they talked to me, they seemed more worried about Laurie. I didn't know what to believe. I was scared for both of them—and myself, when I considered the possibility of losing one of them and having to tell the other what had happened. Or losing them both.

The orderlies came to wheel Laurie to the OR, but the nurse put them off for two minutes. She told us, "They won't be ready in the OR for a few minutes anyway. It won't hurt anybody if you take two minutes for yourselves. Then we have to go."

Laurie nodded soberly and turned to me. The first part of the anesthesia was starting to take effect, making her voice too calm for her words. "Honey, I'm scared. I know this fuss isn't just about Baby. What if I don't make it?"

"Then you will be in heaven," I said, "and I will be the loneliest man on earth." Later that evening, when I had time to think, I would wonder if the part about me was a terribly selfish thing to think and say at that moment.

One tear rolled sideways down her cheek and onto her pillow. "That too," she said. "What if . . . ?"

"Don't." I squeezed her hand and tried to be the strong, optimistic one—because she needed that from me, not because I felt it. "I don't know the answers to all the what-ifs. But I'm going to envision my beautiful wife with my beautiful newborn daughter, because that's what I'll see in an hour or two."

"How can you be sure?"

"I have to be."

"Will you be okay while we're in there?" she asked.

"I'll pray."

"You don't pray."

"I do tonight."

She sighed, nodded, and seemed to relax. I figured it was the anesthesia.

"I love you," she said, so faintly that I could barely hear it.

"I love you. I'll see you soon. Both of you."

I kissed her, put one hand on her belly and the other on her cheek, then finally stepped back, and they wheeled her away.

The next hour and a half were an agonized blur. They told me they would call the waiting room from the OR with an update, and I thought they said it would be within half an hour. An hour passed, and still there was nothing.

Midnight came and went, and I had the surgical waiting room to myself. My awkward, quiet prayers grew more frequent and more desperate.

A worker pushing a cart down the hall looked in, saw me, and said, "Hey, it's Christmas Eve. Have a Christmas cookie while you wait."

I took the cookie, which was in a little paper bag, thanked him, and watched him go. I just held the bag for a while, then slipped it into my coat pocket.

I stopped watching the clock.

Finally the surgeon came. "Don't get up," she said.

She stood in front of me, looking exhausted. I couldn't read her expression. I was glad I was sitting. I felt too weak to stand.

"Sorry that took so long," she said. "I can only imagine what you've been going through out here. Your wife and your daughter will be fine. I won't kid you; it was complicated, even dicey for a little while. Truth is, for a minute or two I wondered if we might lose them both."

She explained things to a level of detail I would ordinarily have appreciated, and I tried to focus. But I scarcely even heard her explanation, and I didn't understand it. The next thing that actually registered in my head was a repetition of the good news she brought.

"They're both safe, and they're both out of the OR. Your wife lost a lot of blood, as I said, but she's in recovery, and your daughter's in the NICU. That's just precautionary. We'll probably move her to the regular nursery in few minutes, as soon as the on-call pediatrician signs off. She's very healthy."

She put a steady hand on my shoulder. "As long as you're okay, I think the whole family will be just fine."

"Thank you, Doctor," I said. It was all I could say. "Thank you."

She offered a tired smile and nodded. "Give them a little while to get settled—might be half an hour or more—and then you can see both of them. Can't say which will be first, but a nurse will come and get you as soon as one of them is ready."

"Thank you."

"You're more than welcome, Dad. Congratulations. You have a beautiful daughter and a beautiful wife. Merry Christmas."

She disappeared.

"Thank you too, God," I whispered.

I felt a little stronger. I stood and wandered the empty waiting room, stopping now and then at the windows but looking inward all the same. Every few minutes, I found myself saying softly, "Thank you, God."

The initial tsunami of relief subsided, leaving me drained and drowsy. To stay awake I picked up a book but kept standing. It was a children's picture book. Maybe I could actually read at that level, I thought with a tired smile. Earlier I hadn't been able to read anything at all.

I flipped through a few pages, admiring the beautiful illustrations without paying much attention to the words, except to notice they were from a Christmas carol. Finally my eyes settled on one line from the song: "What can I give him, poor as I am?"

I didn't get past that line. In my head it became, "What can I give *her*?" Then, "What can I give *them*?" What could I give my girls, poor as we were?

Poor as I was.

I thought as hard I could, but every possibility felt too small, and I didn't want mere tokens—or a cop-out.

What if the baby was ready first? I had no idea what to call her. We'd bounced from one name to another for months, never settling on any of them for more than a few days. And did I even remember how to talk to a baby? Dori was the only baby I had ever known up close, and that was a decade and a half ago.

Before my eyes appeared a middle-aged nurse with an ample figure, a Santa hat on her head, and a jolly twinkle in her eye. "You must be Rick. I'm Susannah, your spirit guide. We're going to see your daughter, then your wife. The baby's out of the NICU. She's looking great for 36 weeks. Already seems quite opinionated too. Does it run in the family?"

I could only nod.

"Congratulations, by the way. Follow me."

Five minutes later, properly scrubbed, I was sitting in a chair, holding my tiny daughter in my arms. "Hi," I said. "I'm Dad. You came early."

She peered through half-open eyelids. I couldn't think of anything else to say.

"Give her your little finger," Susannah said. "If you can do it without dropping her." She chuckled at her own wit.

The baby took my finger and held it. I was surprised at her strength.

"I'll be back in a few minutes," said my spirit guide.

For the longest time I just watched the swaddled bundle in my arms. Then one tiny arm wriggled free. It seemed to move randomly. Her eyes stayed mostly closed.

Finally I said, "Little one, the only thing I can think to give you for Christmas is a promise: I'll remember that your mom is an angel, and I'll treat her accordingly. And since you must be an angel too, the same goes for you."

My spirit guide returned. "Ready to take her to her mom?" she asked. "I'll show you the way." She took my daughter and laid her in a tiny cart, which looked a lot safer than my carrying her in my condition.

"Have they met?" I asked, as I wheeled our baby down the hall. "On the outside, I mean."

"Your wife was pretty groggy, but, yeah, sort of."

I saw a restroom and winced. "Truth is, I need a restroom. Would you take her the rest of the way? I'll meet you there."

"I'd love to. Don't forget to gel after you scrub."

She told me where to find my family and rolled away. I felt like a coward, but I really did need a restroom. I also wanted to pray—awkwardly, uncharacteristically, and redundantly, yes, but

I wanted to. I wondered if praying in the restroom was blasphemous or sinful or maybe just weird.

A few minutes later, I stood in the doorway of Laurie's room. She didn't see me at first. I just watched her, wondering how someone so exhausted could be so radiant. She talked softly to the baby in her arms. I started to weep.

I didn't realize she was looking at me until she said weakly, "Why don't you come cry with your family, instead of doing it alone in the doorway?" I saw tears on her face too.

I stood near her bed.

"Have you two met?" she asked.

"We had a good chat."

"Then I won't introduce you. I'll just go straight to, 'Look what you gave me for Christmas!'"

And vice versa, I thought, but all I could do was smile and nod.

"They said things were rough for a while, but we're both going to be okay." She blew out a breath. "Kind of feels like it wasn't easy, even if it wasn't labor. Apparently I lost a lot of blood."

"That's what they told me."

"Meanwhile, you look like death." Her grin was half-exhausted, half-impish. "Sorry, bad joke. Come and sit. I don't suppose you brought any food."

I remembered the cookie in my pocket. It was still in its bag when I handed it to her. "Somebody gave me this in the waiting room."

She looked inside, then looked up with an exaggerated pout.

"Unfortunately, I'm pretty sure I have to share this. Do you really want your half?"

"It's all yours if you want it."

"That's really not an option. It's a snickerdoodle. But I'll take the big half."

I STAYED AT THE hospital all day and into the evening. At 11:00 p.m. the nurse helped Laurie get the baby settled for a two-hour nap until her next feeding, then stepped out.

"I have to go soon," I told Laurie.

"Visiting hours don't apply to new dads," she said.

"It's not that. And you need to sleep."

"I can sleep with you here." She giggled. "You know what I mean. Where are you going?"

"You know what day this is, right?"

Her face brightened. "I forgot it's Christmas Eve! We have a Christmas Eve baby! Are you going to Midnight Mass?"

I nodded.

Her chin trembled and her eyes were wet. "Not just for the music?"

I shook my head.

A tear rolled down each of her cheeks. She reached for me, and I bent over her so she could hug me.

Her voice was higher-pitched than before. "Tell God I said thanks too. For everything. But especially for you and our beautiful little girl."

11

I Guess You Never Know

OUR FOURTH CHRISTMAS EVE

ONE CHRISTMAS EVE LATER, I left our apartment for campus at the usual time. My doctoral research was going well overall, but I was struggling to make sense of some recent data. And the truth was, I couldn't stay home all day.

The baby had been ill—seriously ill, to the point that she was hospitalized and we began to fear we might lose her. Another infection could have been disastrous, so they sent her home before we thought she was ready. They taught us how to change her antibiotic IV, which scared me, and had us wearing masks at home and taking other precautions. Laurie cared for her night and day. She was beyond exhausted.

All this had begun just after Thanksgiving, not more than a month after Laurie had finally emerged from a postpartum depression that ran long and deep. I'd helped as much as I could, as much as she would let me, but it was never enough. I began to wonder if I should defy her wishes and contact her family. Maybe her mom or sister could come and help somehow. Before it was over, Nanny Marie made three trips, staying two or three weeks at a time. Now she was stuck at home in Las Vegas, recovering from a hip replacement she'd postponed for our sake.

Halfway through Laurie's week of sleeping at the hospital every night with the baby, I complained to her that she couldn't catch a break. As soon as she was well, the baby got sick.

"You're wrong about that," she said. "I caught a big break. I'm better now, so I can take extra care of our little girl."

Laurie really was an angel. I, not so much.

Part of me wanted to stay home again today and take care of them both, but part of me was relieved when Laurie insisted I go to work. The work needed doing, we both knew. And maybe she knew I needed to escape for a while.

She was asleep when I left. That became a welcome excuse not to tell her immediately about the note from the landlord that was taped to the front door.

He was running out of patience, and we were running out of time. He expected the second half of the month's rent by December 26. I couldn't blame him. By then it would be ten days overdue.

We didn't have the money, or we'd have paid it already. We'd spent it on some expensive prescriptions that weren't fully covered by insurance. We wouldn't have money again until early January, when the last semester of my fellowship funded. I crumpled the note, put it in my coat pocket, and spent the next several hours trying to escape it too.

I had to try to do something useful.

In early afternoon, another PhD candidate, Anya, pulled up a chair and sat down near my desk in the lab. "What's wrong?" she asked. "Still not finding it?"

"No, but that's okay. I'll figure it out." I was very good with data.

"How's the baby?"

"Better, thank you."

"And Laurie?"

"Exhausted but okay."

"So if one's better and one's okay, why do you look like some-body died?" she asked earnestly. "It's Christmas Eve. Be happy!"

"That's easy for you to say," I complained. I knew it was the wrong thing to say. But sometimes fear and self-pity overpowered good sense. Lately, for me, they overpowered a lot of things.

"What do you mean?" she asked.

"You're by yourself. You don't have to worry about a spouse or a child. You don't have to balance school and family. You can just study and work."

She looked as if she wanted to incinerate me by willpower alone.

"What?" I asked crossly.

"What do you mean what? You're one of the good guys. The really good guys. But you're being a total jerk."

I just looked at her.

"You moron! Don't you get it? Another way of saying I'm by myself is, I'm alone. You have everything. When you get home from school, you have a wife and daughter to adore. Do you have any idea how much I want what you have? I love what I do, but I'd give it up for a while, if I had to, to have a family like yours."

I wanted to protest . . . to say . . . something . . . but I didn't know what, and she didn't give me a chance anyway.

"So you're having trouble making the rent for a month or two. You'll get your degree and your job, and that won't be a problem anymore. You'll still have your family—unless you stay stupid."

She swiped at a tear and stood up. "I'm sorry. I'm sure I won't always be alone. And you won't always be an ass. Merry Christ-mas, Rick. Laurie and the baby too. See you next week."

After she left, I couldn't even pretend to work. I gave up and left. But I didn't go home. I just walked.

I walked until I found myself at an import shop on Main Street, looking at a pretty scarf I'd have given Laurie for Christmas, if I could have given her a scarf for Christmas. I started calculating whether I could steal it successfully, and I thought I probably could. On a normal day, I'd no more have thought seriously about that than I'd have cheated on her.

I didn't steal it.

I stopped in front of a pawn shop and thought about pawning my wedding ring. Maybe it would pay half a month's rent. But how would I tell Laurie? I'd keep the pawnshop as a last resort. I checked its hours. It would be open the day after tomorrow.

I walked past a few banks, wondering if anyone had successfully robbed an American bank in the last 20 years. Not that I could or would.

I walked by the train station and remembered Anna Karenina, who stepped in front of a train. That was cowardly and selfish, I'd always thought. Or maybe it was the only thing left that she could do.

I stood on the platform for a while, staring at the tracks.

Maybe if I just got on a train and left forever, Laurie's parents would take her and the baby in, and they'd never have to worry about rent or the next meal.

Pawning my ring would at least buy me a train ticket. But that was too dramatic, and I didn't think I could live that way, not having them with me, knowing I had left them, even if they were okay. Maybe I was selfish, but I couldn't hurt myself that way. I couldn't hurt Laurie that way either, and I didn't know anymore what was selfish and what wasn't. But I knew how things had been for Mom and Dori and me, without Dad.

Maybe I was a coward like Anna Karenina. Or just a pathetic failure at a man's most basic duties.

I found myself outside St. Peter's. It was hours too early for Midnight Mass, but I went in and sat in our usual place, at the far end of third pew from the rear. I put my arms on the back of the pew in front of me, put my head down on my arms, and . . .

Didn't pray.

Didn't cry either.

Didn't fall asleep.

I managed not to think, mostly. It was sort of like resting, and I probably needed that. Once I seemed to hear Laurie's voice in my head, saying something she'd said a few times lately.

"You're exhausted too. It's not just me."

I sat that way for a long time. When I finally looked up, there was a priest sitting near me, with maybe two feet of pew between us. He was at least ten years older than me. He stared straight ahead, as if deep in thought.

"Father?" I said.

He started.

"Sorry. Is that what I should call you?" I asked.

"Oh, yes, of course. That works. Father Mike, if you wish."

"I'm Rick."

"Son," he said, "I don't want to intrude. If you want to sit here and pray, I'll leave you alone."

"I wasn't praying. I don't . . . pray." I felt guilty confessing that to a priest.

"If you just want to sit, that's okay too."

"I'm not Catholic."

"I guess you didn't see the 'Catholics Only' sign at the door," he said seriously.

"No, I'm sorry, I'll—" I started to stand up, but he put a hand on my shoulder.

"There isn't a sign. There never has been. There never will be. You're more than welcome here."

"Thank you."

"If you're not Catholic, what are you?"

"Nothing, really. My mom's a lapsed Mormon. I guess my dad was an extremely lapsed Baptist. My wife's family was Presbyterian, before they began to worship money. Laurie and I come to Midnight Mass here every year."

"For the Mass or the music?"

"The music. Sorry."

"I love the music," he said. "That's why I'd come, if I didn't have to anyway. Are you coming tonight?"

"I doubt it."

"Why not?"

I shrugged.

"Am I just bothering you?" he asked.

"No, it's okay."

"Good, because I have some chores to do, and talking is a good way to procrastinate them. What shall we talk about?"

"Father, you don't know me. When you look at me, what do you see?"

"I see darkness and light."

"Aren't they incompatible?" I asked.

"That's why they're fighting," he said.

"You're pretty good."

"Don't give me too much credit. That's what I see in almost everyone. Occupational hazard. Plus they're both actually there, and they always fight."

"Do you ever see just darkness?"

"It's theoretically possible, but no. Why do I think you mean yourself?"

"Do you ever see just light?"

"In small children. Once in a while in older people, often very old. Do you?"

"I look at my daughter, and I see only light. I look at my wife and see no darkness, only light."

"You are a fortunate man indeed. Not just to have such a wife and child, but to see them that way."

"I wish they were so fortunate."

He regarded me silently for a moment. I thought he was about to ask what was wrong with me, but he asked about them. "Are they well?"

"The baby's been pretty sick. She was in the hospital for a while, but she's doing better. Today's her first birthday. Laurie's completely exhausted from taking care of her, and I can only help so much."

"Do you have medical insurance?" he asked. He seemed very practical for a priest.

"Yes. Just not rent money, and not that much for food. Enough, but Christmas dinner might be peanut butter sandwiches."

He nodded. "You a student?"

"Chemical engineering. PhD in May, if all goes well."

"So your poverty is temporary."

"I guess so. But why does it feel so dark? Never mind, I know. There's a good chance we'll see an eviction notice on our door within a few days. How am I going to tell her?"

"She knows money is tight, does she not?"

"Of course. She knows we're paying half our rent every two weeks, by special arrangement with the landlord, and she knows we haven't paid the second half for December yet. She doesn't know what the landlord said in his note this morning. He's out of patience. We can pay him in January, when my fellowship comes in, but I don't think we have until January."

"What will you do?"

"I don't know. I could quit school and get a job, but it wouldn't pay in time. And it wouldn't be very smart in the long run."

We talked for a while after that, and it was probably supposed to help, but the darkness started to close in again. Finally I said, "Her parents have more money than they know what to do with. If I were out of the picture, they'd take her back. Then everyone would be fine."

"Sure they would," he said, "if money is everything. If there's literally nothing else we need to live."

"Right now, it's almost everything."

"Christmas isn't supposed to be like that," he said.

"I'm not much of a Christian."

"Okay, but you know the Christmas story, right?"

"Sure."

"Do you see any similarities between yourself and anyone in that story?"

"Someone called me an ass today."

Father Mike laughed heartily. "Not the character I meant. Try again."

"I suppose you're about to tell me that Christmas is about a baby, a mother, and a husband, or something like that."

"Mostly a baby, but yes. Do you think Joseph knew who that baby was?"

"Sure. An angel explained it to him, right?"

"Correct. Do you think they could have found a room in the Bethlehem Four Seasons if they'd had the money?"

"Of course."

"Do you think Joseph wanted his beloved—speaking of light—to give birth to the Son of God in a barn? Well, probably a cave."

"No."

"How do you suppose he felt about being unable to provide something splendid—or even decent—for them?'

"I know how he felt," I said. "Humiliated. Frightened. Unworthy."

"He probably felt some of those things again when they had to flee to Egypt, to avoid Herod's Slaughter of the Innocents," said Father Mike.

"Probably."

"So what do you do, if you're Joseph, when you're humiliated, frightened, and feeling unworthy?"

"Father, you tell me, because right now I have absolutely no idea."

"Okay. Maybe it's easy to say, but you swallow your pride, rejoice at what you have, hold them as close as you can, keep them as safe as you can, and trust in God as much as you can. Someday, in your case probably soon, things will start to get better. They probably won't get better all at once. God usually works in small steps, not stunning miracles. But hard times don't make you a failure—as a person or a husband or a father or a man."

"And son . . ."

I looked up.

"If there's an eviction notice on your door in the next few days, come back and see me. Maybe we can help. In the meantime, I'll pray for you and your family." He smiled gently. "And your landlord."

"We're not Catholic."

Now he grinned. "What a coincidence! Neither were Mary and Joseph. May I give you a stern piece of counsel about your immediate future?"

"I probably deserve it."

"Don't come to Mass tonight. You're exhausted. Your wife's exhausted. There's a Mass on TV and the radio and even the Internet, with a rebroadcast or two later. The music will be fabulous. Stay home with your wife and daughter. Take care of them. Get some sleep. Then come back to us next year, here or wherever you land after graduation. If it's here, be sure to say hello."

I looked down. "That's good counsel."

"Yes, it is. So's this. If you need to pick up a few dollars, Target needs people to help with returns on the day after Christmas. Be there at 5:30 a.m. with photo ID and your Social Security card. For now, stay a little longer if you want, then go home to your family. They need you, not just your money."

I nodded. "Okay."

"Have a little faith, my son. God is good. And present."

He stood, said he had chores waiting, wished me and my little family a merry Christmas, and left me alone in the pew.

I left the church and wandered the streets until it was time for me to be home from school. Things still were not sweetness and light, but a tired sadness had mostly replaced my desperation.

I still didn't know how to tell Laurie about the landlord.

I QUIETLY LET MYSELF in the front door, but Laurie was awake, sitting in our tiny living room on our battered couch, feeding the baby with a bottle.

"You're awake," I said softly.

"Enough for a kiss."

I bent down and we shared a quick kiss. It was the best I'd felt all day, but it didn't last.

"How was your day?" she asked.

"Not good."

"The landlord came by this afternoon," she said.

My heart fell. "I'm sorry. He left a note this morning, but you were asleep."

"What did it say?" she asked.

Where I found the strength to report such news, I didn't know. "If he doesn't have the rest of the rent by the 26th, we're out at the end of the month."

"Well," she said, "wait until you hear what he told me."

"I'm so sorry," I said, as the knot in my stomach tightened.

"Don't be sorry," she said gently. "You haven't heard it yet."

"I can imagine."

"Apparently not. He said he'd be an idiot to turn out good tenants like us. If we can catch up by mid-January, he'll be fine."

Hope began to push its way through my fear and shame. "I'll have my fellowship on the 7th," I said. "Sometimes a day early."

"I know, right? We'll be okay. And since you're about to ask, we had a pretty good day here. She's noticeably stronger. Come sit by us."

I sat next to her and started to sob. She didn't have a free hand, but she leaned her head on my shoulder.

"Tears of relief?" she asked after a minute or two.

"Partly."

I felt her nod. "You had a serious relapse of 'look what a poor husband did to his wife who should be rich,' didn't you? While you were gone?"

"I'm sorry," I whispered.

"Tell me about your day."

I told her about Anya and Father Mike and wandering the streets. Her eyes filled with tears from the very beginning and stayed that way.

I didn't tell her about the things I'd thought of doing but hadn't done.

"So are peanut butter sandwiches what you want for Christmas dinner?" she asked.

"That would be okay," I said.

She smiled. "It really would, but I was thinking ham and potatoes and some nice rolls and an assortment of fresh fruits and vegetables. I'm pretty hammered, though. You'll have to help me with some cooking."

She stood and put the baby in her bassinet, which we always rolled to the living room during the day.

I gave her a wan smile. "A girl can dream. Maybe we can do that next year."

"That's the spirit," she said. "Come to the kitchen."

She pulled me up and steered me toward our tiny kitchen. "See? Not next year. Tomorrow."

On the table was a big box of groceries. I could see a ham, a bag of potatoes, and a bunch of other things we couldn't afford. A homemade card had four large words in bold, red permanent marker: "Merry Christmas from Santa!"

"There's a chocolate cake too," Laurie said, "but we're starting that tonight and calling it someone's birthday cake."

"Who?" I asked, wanting to cry again.

"Our daughter. It's her birthday."

"That's not what I meant." I gestured weakly toward the groceries. "Who did this?"

"No idea. Did you tell Father Mike where we live?"

"No."

"Must be a neighbor," she concluded. "Or neighbors. Maybe the landlord? I guess you never know."

12

Midnight Mass

ONE MORE CHRISTMAS EVE

YEARS LATER, A FAMILY from out of town arrived early for Midnight Mass and sat at the end of the third pew from the back. There was a lovely wife, who was aging more gracefully than her husband. He sat to her right, at the end of the pew, gently cradling a quiet bundle on his lap. To her left sat a towheaded boy, about nine, still wearing his parka, looking cranky and sleepy in equal measures. To the boy's left sat a dark-haired girl of about fourteen, looking existentially bored.

The boy turned to his parents and said for the third time in the last hour, "This is stupid. We should be sleeping in our hotel. But where we really should be is home, sleeping in our beds."

"It's not actually stupid," said his mom.

"Yes, it is. It's almost midnight, and it's Christmas Eve. Why couldn't we stay home for Christmas, like we always do?"

"We're not even Catholic," the girl said. "And shouldn't I have some say in where we go on my birthday?" She looked at the bundle in her father's arms. "At least The Thing gets to sleep through this."

Her dad smiled, ignored the provocation, and spoke softly. "I hope she sleeps through this, but she might not."

"Mass is long," the mom added, "and there's going to be some music tonight that's pretty hard to sleep through."

The girl shook her head. "I don't know what made you two think you needed another baby anyway. You almost died, Mom, like when you had me."

That was an exaggeration, her parents knew. The third time had been less scary than the first.

"Dying in childbirth is so not a good idea," added their first-born.

The boy asked eagerly, "Did you almost die when you had me?"

His sister glared. "We almost died when we saw you. All of us." She looked at her mom. "Why do that? Why take the risk? I mean, you know they invented birth control, right? Were you pretending to be Catholic or something?"

"Honey, maybe that's not the best way to talk, when we're at Catholic Mass." The mom looked and sounded amused, not angry, and it had the desired effect on her daughter.

"You're right. I'm sorry."

"To answer your questions, your dad and I—"

The glare was back. "On second thought, Mom, don't be gross. Please? Why is talking about that around me so much fun for you?"

"Actually, teasing you about it is what's fun for me, and that's not what I was about to do. I was going to tell you what we're doing tomorrow."

"Not opening presents," groused the boy. "We left those at home."

"Not all of them," said their mom. "We girls get scarves from Grandma. The boys get gloves. We all get Aunt Dori's snickerdoodles. There will be other gifts at home the day after tomorrow."

He was visibly unimpressed. "Do we at least get Christmas dinner?"

"Yes," she said.

He brightened. "At a restaurant? With ham? And mashed potatoes? And soda? And pie? Is it a buffet?"

His sister elbowed him. "All you think about is your stomach."

He bloomed with righteous indignation. "Wrong. I think about my taste buds too." He turned to his parents. "She hit me with her elbow! Really hard! I think she broke my ribs."

His parents ignored his injuries.

The mom explained, "First we're going for a walk in a little neighborhood not far from here, where we'll show you two old houses and an apartment building. I checked the weather. We'll be glad for the gloves and the scarves. Then we'll walk through the town square, and then we'll visit the university for a few minutes. I wish the buses were running on Christmas, so we could ride them there and back. We're also visiting an old priest, Father Mike."

"Hey, that's my name!" said the boy.

"Yes," she said. "Interesting coincidence, isn't it? He's not here tonight, but he will be tomorrow. We're going by the hospital for a little while, just to see it. And all day long Dad and I are going to tell you about things that happened when we lived here. Then we'll go to dinner, before it gets too late."

"At a restaurant?" asked the boy.

"Yes," said his dad, amused. "We're having Christmas dinner at a restaurant."

"Ham? Mashed potatoes?"

His sister looked exasperated. "You are the biggest of all possible losers."

"I don't think they don't serve ham there," said the dad, "and they have a different kind of potatoes."

The girl looked at him suspiciously. "What is this restaurant?"

He smiled broadly. "We're having Christmas dinner at Wendy's."

She searched both parents' faces for some sign that he was kidding.

"And because the people there have to work on Christmas, we're taking them little gifts."

"So my brother is a loser and my parents are weird," she said. "Move along. Nothing to see here."

"This is so cool," the boy exclaimed. "Can I have a *ham*burger?" He elbowed his sister, and she responded in kind.

He was opening his mouth to protest again, when his mom silenced him with a look.

"You may have two, if you're that hungry," said his dad. "You kids may order whatever you want, within reason, but Mom and I are eating from the value menu. It used to be the dollar menu, believe it or not."

The girl was unimpressed. "What does all this have to do with Christmas? Or with you two deciding we needed a little sister?"

Her parents exchanged a warm look, and her mom spoke. "If you listen tomorrow and hear what there is to hear and see what there is to see, and you still can't answer that question for yourself, we'll try to tell you."

"It's going to be something mushy about love, isn't it? Because this is where you fell in love? Can I just stay at the hotel all day? At least it has cable."

"No," said her mom. "You're an essential part of this family."

"Like I could forget," she said. "But tomorrow's Christmas, and none of this is about Christmas."

Her dad shrugged. "That's mostly true."

The girl looked suspicious. "Wait, you agree with me? Mostly?" She looked at her mom. "He agrees with me. What's wrong with this picture?"

"That's because you're right," said her mom. "Most of what we're doing tomorrow is not about Christmas."

"Then why are we doing it on Christmas?"

"Because, at least for us, Christmas is about it."

The girl was silent for a moment. Then she muttered, "Too deep for me, Mom."

Her mom spoke gently. "Rachel, maybe for a while tomorrow you can be deep enough for it. Let's get ready to listen now. The music's about to start."

The boy spoke up. "I already finished my book. Does anyone have a book I can borrow?"

His mom smiled. "I happen to have a new Christmas book."

"Will you read it to me?" he asked with eager confidence.

"Not during the music or the Mass. Read it to yourself. And you may want to notice that, according to the program, the choir's about to sing the same words you'll be reading. I know you don't care about that sort of thing, at least not yet, but they're from a poem by a woman named Christina Rossetti. We sing them at Christmas."

What her children didn't notice during some of the music, but her husband did, was that every so often a tear ran down her cheek. What she noticed, but her children didn't, was that he shed a few tears as the cathedral children's choir finished its first carol.

> What can I give Him,
> Poor as I am? —
> If I were a Shepherd
> I would bring a lamb;
> If I were a Wise Man
> I would do my part, —

Yet what I can I give Him, —
Give my heart.[1]

A few minutes later, between songs, when parental eyes happened to be dry, the girl leaned forward, looked down the pew, and whispered to her dad, "Can I at least hold Anya for a while, so I don't have to just sit here? I won't wake her up."

---

1. Christina Rossetti, "A Christmas Carol" (1872), often sung as "In the Bleak Midwinter."

Eight Short Stories

AT CHRISTMAS

The Case of the Missing Hair

OUR PARENTS ALMOST SHUT down our investigation, which parents can do, when you're eleven and they don't think it's important.

"Timmy, I know you love the books," said Dad one Sunday at dinner. It was after Thanksgiving but not super close to Christmas. "So do I. But you and Jason are not the Hardy Boys. You can't run around investigating anyone you want, whenever you think there's a mystery."

"They were a lot older," Mom said, "and they could drive. They also had a boat, as I recall." Which was true, I knew from my reading, but this investigation didn't need a car or a boat.

"Also," Dad said, "their father, Fenton Hardy, was a licensed detective, so he could help his sons and sort of keep an eye on them. More than that, though, you're sticking your noses into things that are none of your business, and eleven-year-olds don't have mature enough judgment to avoid hurting people unnecessarily."

I knew what was next.

"It's not your business why Pastor John is bald," Dad said. "It was rude and disrespectful of you to ask, especially in front of your Sunday school class."

I felt myself turning red. "Did he tell you?"

"No, that was your Sunday school teacher."

Mrs. Brott's superpower was making Sunday school even less fun than actual school, especially for boys. The girls didn't seem to mind so much.

"I'm curious," Mom said. "Why did you ask him that?"

"We wanted to know why he's bald when other people have hair." I said "duh" after that, which was a mistake.

Dad frowned. "Is Jason in this too?"

"We flipped a nickel to see who would ask Pastor John."

"I should have known," said Dad. "For your punishment you're not allowed to play with him after school this week or on Saturday. You may not use the Internet for anything but school assignments. And next Sunday we're visiting Pastor John so you can apologize."

I wasn't scared of Pastor John, but the rest of it was bad. I didn't complain, because they'd just say it wasn't the first time we'd embarrassed our moms and dads during an investigation.

"And you have to tell us you're sorry," Dad said.

I just stared at them.

"Well?" Dad asked.

"I'm sorry." I hoped he wouldn't ask what I was sorry for, because it wasn't for asking Pastor John why he was bald. To be a detective, even when you're a kid, you have to ask people questions without being sorry. I was sorry my parents didn't understand that. I was sorry I was in trouble.

If they'd known what we were really investigating, I'd have been in more trouble.

At church they have a men's restroom and a women's restroom, and if you're one you don't want to go into the other by acci-dent. There's also a handicapped restroom, and it's the same one whether you're a boy or a girl. It's in the same hall, but hardly anyone uses it. Unlike the others, you're supposed to lock it when you get inside.

One Sunday, between the service and Sunday school, when everybody wants to use the restrooms, we ducked into that one so we wouldn't have to wait. Also, who likes a crowd around when you're peeing?

We were all the way inside before we noticed the girl. Ginny was older, like maybe fourteen. She was super thin, except for her face. She wasn't using the toilet, thank heaven (as Mom says). She stood at the sink, looking in the mirror, and she was bald. It took us a second, but we realized the hairy thing in her hand was a wig.

I thought she would yell at us, but she just stared at us in the mirror. Her eyes were sad. Or tired, maybe.

It took another second to realize we should say we were sorry and leave, which we did.

We couldn't tell our parents, because we'd get in trouble for walking in on a girl in the bathroom. We also couldn't think of any reason a girl would be bald. We whispered about that all the way to Sunday school, but it was a mystery.

That day the pastor came to our class to teach us part of the lesson, and when he was done he asked, "Do you have any questions?" We thought a bald man would know why someone would be bald, so we asked.

Other kids laughed, but we were serious. Mrs. Brott didn't think it was funny either. It wasn't a huge surprise that she ratted me out to Mom and Dad.

ONE OF THE IMPORTANT things Jase and I learned from our dads' old Hardy Boys mysteries and the newer ones in our school library was this: you don't stop investigating just because something goes wrong and it gets harder.

Since I was grounded from the Internet, except for school assignments, we went to the library at recess. We started with the dictionary. We knew how to use it. We looked up *bald* and *baldness*. It told us what the words meant, which we already knew, but it didn't explain why some people are bald.

We looked on the science shelves for a book about baldness, or maybe hair, but there wasn't one. The librarian asked us what we were looking for. "Nothing," said Jase, and we left.

We kept trying to think of reasons why a girl would be bald, but everything we thought of sounded stupid.

"Maybe she likes how she looks with no hair," Jase said, "but her parents make her wear a wig at church."

"Maybe her head gets so hot that she can't sleep at night," I said, "but she doesn't like how she looks when she's bald."

Like I said. Stupid.

One of the sixth grade teachers was old and mostly bald, but he was also mean, so we didn't ask him. He might tell our parents, and that would be bad for our investigation.

After school we looked for books about hair and baldness at our houses, Jase at his and I at mine. We didn't find any.

Our next idea was to follow Ginny. Surveillance was fun—and Saturday morning was our church Christmas breakfast. She'd probably be there. Almost the whole congregation went, including people we didn't remember seeing at church on Sundays.

Breakfast was in the church gym. (Churches would be totally boring without gyms.) After I ate my pancakes and bacon, I sneaked away from Mom and Dad. They were busy talking with the Tillotsons across the table about boring stuff, as usual. Jase escaped his parents too. We planned it that way, because surveillance goes better if you're not alone, so the person you're following doesn't notice that it's always the same person following her.

We'd been watching Ginny already, as much as we could. She'd had three sips of her orange juice and a bite or two of her pancake. She whispered something to her mom, then got up and walked out of the gym.

We followed her. We stopped at the door from the gym to the foyer. It had swung closed behind her. We were talking about who should go first when the door opened and she almost bumped into us.

"Excuse me," she said, and went around us. She went back to where her family was sitting, picked up her phone from the table, and started back toward the door. We went to a different door, so we could sneak around to the foyer through the hall.

We were quiet. When we peeked around the corner, she was sitting in an armchair. No one else was around, and her eyes were closed. She wasn't smiling, and I thought her face looked thinner. She just sat there and didn't move.

We checked to see that her eyes were still closed and sneaked toward the place where people hang their coats, so we could watch and she wouldn't notice us.

She sat and sat and sat and still didn't move. We watched and watched and watched and almost didn't breathe.

The door from the gym burst open, which startled us so much that we almost made sounds. Three more girls came out and surrounded Ginny in her chair. The one who talked was Jo, which we knew she spelled without an "e."

"Here you are, G. Are you okay?"

Ginny nodded.

"Did you eat?"

She shrugged. "Some."

"We want to show you your Christmas present. But we have to do it on the stage, where no one will see. Five minutes?"

Ginny smiled a little. "Okay."

The other three girls went back to the gym. Ginny stayed in her chair, leaned back, and closed her eyes.

When you're best friends, sometimes you don't have to talk to say things. Jase and I looked at each other for a second. Then we both nodded.

We checked that Ginny's eyes were still closed and sneaked away, one at a time.

The stage faced out into the gym, so people could sit in the gym and see what was happening on the stage, if the curtains weren't closed. But this morning the curtains were closed.

We knew a hallway we could use to get to the stage from the back without going through the gym, but we had to hurry to get there before the girls did.

Partway down the hall, we bumped into a man we didn't know. "Slow down, boys," he said. "Where are you going in such a hurry?"

Jase and I looked at each other.

"Too much orange juice," Jase said. You have to think quickly to be a detective.

"We have to pee," I said.

Fortunately, that hallway was how you got to the restrooms too. The man frowned and stepped aside.

We tried to walk funny, like we needed to pee, in case he was watching us. We were almost to the boy's restroom when we ran into some more people—and it was Ginny's friends. I actually bumped into Zoe.

"Sorry," I said, and I really was, because I thought we were too late.

"In here for a minute," said Jo. I thought she meant Jase and me, but she didn't. The girls disappeared into their restroom.

We slipped through the backstage door and onto the stage. It had a high ceiling with lots of lights. Thin black curtains hung down from metal tracks so you could move them around. On one side, fastened to the wall, was a steel ladder painted brown. It started about six feet off the floor and went up to a ledge maybe twelve feet up. We didn't know what the ledge was for, but we were pretty sure the reason why the ladder didn't start down near the floor was because it would be too easy for boys to climb it, including detectives like us.

It wasn't a problem though. They kept folding chairs on the stage for when they used it as an extra classroom, and there was a locked wooden cabinet next to the ladder. We climbed from a chair to the top of the cabinet, then onto the bottom rung.

The ledge was always super dusty, so we had to be careful. When you do surveillance, you shouldn't sneeze.

We could lie on our stomachs and peek over the edge at whoever was on the stage. For a minute that was nobody. Then the backstage door opened. The first girl up the steps was Melanie, or Mel for short. Zoe was with her. Then Jo appeared, holding Ginny's hand and pulling her along.

When they were all up on the stage together, and we were watching and they didn't know, the other three smiled really big at Ginny. She only smiled a little.

"We thought about it a lot," said Mel.

"We talked about it too," added Zoe.

"Talked about what?" Ginny asked. Her voice was quiet and husky.

"What to give you for Christmas, silly." Jo said. "Are you ready?"

"Okay," said Ginny.

"Ready, girls?" Jo asked. "One, two, three."

What they did after three made us almost make a noise, which would have ruined our surveillance. And if we hadn't been lying down, we might have fallen down onto the stage too, which would have made more noise and also hurt a lot.

All the girls, except Ginny, reached up into their hair and pulled it off. They were bald too. Their hair was wigs.

I looked at Jase. His eyes were really big. Mine too, probably.

"Merry Christmas!" said the three of them together.

"Do you like it?" Jo asked.

Ginny was smiling now, but she was crying too, which was weird. "I love it," she said. "You're the best friends ever. It's perfect. Thank you."

There was hugging and more smiling, and we weren't sure, but all four girls might have cried.

"Could I get a picture?" Ginny asked. "Please?" She pulled off her own hair.

They pulled out their phones and took some selfies with all their heads bald. Then they helped each other put their wigs back on and took some more. Then the backstage door opened, and a bunch of little kids ran onto the stage, followed by an adult who was telling them where to go. That's when we noticed that the stage was set up for a Christmas manger scene.

We were stuck there, up on the ledge, until it was over, but even with the curtain opened, no one in the gym could see us if we were careful.

A FTER THE LITTLE KIDS' manger scene, which didn't look as lame as I expected, the kids left the stage, the curtain closed, and everybody started singing Christmas songs. We climbed down from the ledge. Someone had moved the folding chair, but we were detectives on a case, so we didn't mind dropping a few extra feet down to the stage.

When I took my seat during "Silent Night," Mom looked at me sideways, then turned toward me and frowned. She was looking at my shirt, so I looked at my shirt. It was covered with dust. So were my pants.

After the song ended and somebody said a prayer about Christmas, mostly, my family and Jase's family met in the foyer on the way out, pretty close to the chair where we watched Ginny. His parents stared at me and frowned. My parents stared at him and frowned.

"Where have you two been?" asked my mom.

"How did you get so dusty?" asked his mom.

We both started to brush off the dust, but our moms stopped us. His said, "Not here. You'll make a mess."

Mine said, "Do that outside."

"Where were you?" asked his mom.

Lying is wrong most of the time. But to be a good detective, you have to be able to lie sometimes. It works better when what you say is partly true.

"We were on the stage," I said.

"They needed help with the little kids," Jase said.

"It was dusty," I said.

"Yeah, dusty," Jase said. "We almost sneezed during the manger scene."

Our parents looked at us for a moment. Then Jase's dad said, "Good for you. Helping out for once."

It was a close call, but detectives have those all the time, if they have good cases like the Hardy Boys always do.

At church on Sunday, we realized there was a problem. It wasn't just Ginny anymore, and even if we split up, we couldn't do surveillance on four girls or even three, unless they stayed together.

During the sermon I saw Ginny get up and leave. Jase followed her after a minute. Then I saw Mel get up and follow Jase. I instantly faked a coughing fit and followed her.

When I got to the foyer, I didn't see Jase anywhere. Mel and Ginny were standing in a corner, hugging. I didn't think they were watching me. I walked past them, then stopped and pretended to look for a cough drop in my pants pocket.

"Bad day?" Mel asked Ginny.

"It's a good day," Ginny said. "I love my Christmas gift. Thanks again."

"Why are you crying?" Mel asked.

"For a while I didn't think I'd get another Christmas, but now I will."

They stopped talking after that, and I kept walking until I got to the drinking fountain. I faked a cough every three or four steps.

I didn't see Jase until I was back in the chapel. He was sitting with his family again.

Aftet church Dad said, "Timothy owes you an apology." We were talking to Pastor John in his office. We sat in three chairs in front of his desk. I was in the middle.

Pastor John was sort of smiling. "Really? Tim, what have you done that requires an apology?"

"I'm sorry I asked you why you're bald," I said.

Mom patted my knee.

Pastor John grinned. "Are you really?"

I shrugged.

"He is," Mom said.

"Thank you, Tim," said Pastor John. "I accept your apology. May I ask you a few questions?"

"Sure," I said.

"Why did you ask?"

"I wanted to know."

"That's the best reason. What if you and I make a deal?"

"Okay," I said hesitantly.

"Anytime that's the real reason—because you want to know—it's okay to ask me." He glanced at Mom and Dad, like he wanted it to be okay with them.

"I don't think Mrs. Brott will like that deal," I said.

"No problem," said Pastor John. "If you have questions she wouldn't like, don't ask them when I visit your class. Ask them here."

"Okay."

"Excellent. Do you still want to know why I'm bald?"

I was pretty sure my eyes got wide. I looked at Dad, then Mom, to see if it was okay. I couldn't tell.

"Yes," I said.

"It's part of aging, getting older. Some people do it sooner than others. In my family the men do it pretty early, most of us. It bothers some men that they don't have the great hair they used to have, but it's never bothered me that much, and my wife says it doesn't bother her. So I'm okay with it. Plus I save money on haircuts and shampoo."

I nodded. "Can I ask another question?"

"Please do," he said.

Ginny wasn't a man or a boy, so I asked, "Do the women in your family go bald too?"

"Tim." Mom sounded tired.

Pastor John's eyes twinkled. "No. Women's hair often gets thinner with age, but women usually don't go bald."

"Okay," I said. Mom elbowed me gently. "Thank you," I added.

"You're welcome. Is there anything else?"

I shook my head.

He stood, and we stood too. "Thanks for coming to see me," he said.

"**P**ASTOR JOHN IS NICE," I said in the car on the way home.

"Yes, he is," Mom said. "Nicer than you deserve, in this case."

For once I was smart and kept my mouth shut.

"I have a question," said Dad after a minute. "Why did you want to know why Pastor John is bald?"

"Why did you wonder about women going bald?" Mom asked. "Have you ever seen a bald woman?"

I had to think fast. It seemed like a bad time to lie, but I needed to tell the truth in a way that wouldn't get me in any more trouble. "Do you know Ginny Lambson?" I asked.

"The Lambsons' youngest daughter?" Mom asked. "We know who she is. She's about fourteen, I think."

"She wears a wig," I said. "She's bald."

"Did you see this?" Mom asked.

"Jase and me saw her putting it on once at church."

"Did you ask her why she's bald too?" Dad asked.

"Good heavens, I hope not," said Mom.

"No," I said. "It was a mystery, and we decided to solve it."

"So asking Pastor John was part of your investigation," Dad said.

"Yup."

"I think you mean 'yes,'" Mom said. She cared about that stuff.

"Yes," I said.

Mom and Dad shared a look, and I wondered how much more trouble I was in.

"Timmy," Mom said, "have you noticed, the last few months, that when Pastor John prays for the sick people in the congregation, he mentions someone named Virginia?"

"I don't listen to that part," I said. "And I don't know anyone named Virginia."

"Ginny is short for Virginia."

"Ginny is sick?" I asked.

"She's been very sick," Mom said. "With cancer."

I knew cancer was bad. "Does cancer make you bald?"

"I think it's the therapy that makes you bald," she said.

"Is that like medicine?"

"Yes. It does unpleasant things to your body, but it's meant to kill the cancer."

"Is she going to die?" We'd never had a case about somebody dying. It felt bad, but not bad enough that I wanted to stop being a detective or anything like that.

"We're all going to die, son," said Dad. That got him another look from Mom.

"I mean soon," I said sadly, and I wasn't faking it. "From cancer."

"From what I heard," Mom said, "she's doing well. The cancer is gone, at least for now. The treatment was successful."

That was good. "Will it grow back?"

"Sometimes it does. They'll watch for it, so they can catch it early, when it's easier to treat."

"I mean, will her hair grow back?"

"Probably. Remember how beautiful it was?" Mom asked.

"Not really."

"Well, in the meantime she wears a wig."

We pulled into the driveway, and that was the end of our talk.

I thought about Ginny and cancer and dying, and her hair and her wig. After Mom said grace at dinner, I asked, "Should I pray for Ginny, when I say my prayers at night?"

Mom used the smile that meant she was about to cry. "That would be a very good thing."

"Will it help?" I asked.

"Prayers help," Mom said, at the same time Dad said, "Yes."

"Okay," I said. "I'll do it."

A couple of tears really did roll down Mom's cheeks. Moms are girls, and girls are weird and cry a lot. Somebody should investigate that, but it probably shouldn't be Jase and me.

Then I thought about Ginny's friends. "Are there other girls at church who have cancer?"

Mom's eyes went wide. "Good heavens! I hope not. I don't know of any."

Maybe I did, but I didn't say it yet.

"It's not contagious," Dad said. "It's not like a cold or the flu or the measles. You don't get it from someone else. Some people just get it."

Dad might have been wrong about that, but it was time for dessert.

J ASE AND I COULDN'T talk about the investigation at school on Monday. Not even at recess, because we were playing basketball with other boys. When you're a detective there's a thing called confidentialness, which means you don't tell extra people anything they don't need to know. So we had to wait until I went to Jase's house after school.

First he wanted to know whether my visit to Pastor John's office was scary, which it wasn't. Then I told him Ginny had cancer, which was why she was bald, and her three friends probably had cancer too.

His face wrinkled some around his eyes, which meant he was thinking hard. After a minute he said, "You might be wrong about something. This doesn't make sense."

"Why not?"

"They all acted like the others being bald like Ginny was a happy thing. I don't think having cancer makes you happy."

He was right. It didn't make sense, and I should have noticed that. Jase was pretty smart. That's important for a detective.

We couldn't figure it out, so at dinner I gave up and asked Mom and Dad, "Is having cancer ever happy?"

"It's a sad, scary thing," Mom said.

"We thought so."

"You and Jason?"

"Yup. Yes."

Mom nodded. "Why do you ask?"

To find out what I wanted to know, if Mom and Dad even knew it, I had to tell them things that might get me in trouble again. So I had to be careful.

"Remember when we got all dusty on the stage?"

"Yes," Mom said.

"We didn't go up there to help, at first. We went to see what was there. That was before any of the little kids got there. That's where we saw Ginny, with Jo and Mel and Zoe."

"They're best friends," Mom said.

"Why are they bald too? Do they all have cancer?"

"What are you talking about?" Dad asked.

"Tell us exactly what you saw," Mom said.

So I told them how they all pulled their hair off—their wigs—to show Ginny that they were bald too, and it was her Christmas present, and they were all happy and took selfies.

Mom started to weep, which made sense, if they all had cancer.

"Cancer is very sad," I said.

Mom sniffed, and her voice was shaky. "Yes, but that's not why I'm crying."

I probably looked puzzled, because I was.

"First of all, Tim, can I tell you one of my favorite things about this Christmas? I've been thinking about this."

"Okay."

"Your dad and I have a son who cares about other people, not just himself."

"I do?" I really didn't understand. "That's about Christmas?"

"Remember when you asked about praying for Ginny? Have you been doing that?"

"Yes."

"She's not your friend. You barely know her. But you know she's sick, so you pray for her. That's a very good thing. Very kind of you."

"Okay." I knew it was good to be kind sometimes.

"Well, those other girls are Ginny's good friends. They care about her a lot. They're very fine friends."

"Because they all got cancer?"

"I'm pretty sure they don't have cancer."

"Then why are they bald?" I asked.

She was still crying a little. She looked at Dad and said, "You explain. I'll cry."

He nodded. "Tim, imagine how sad you'd be, especially if you were a girl, and all your beautiful hair fell out. How would you like to go to school and church and everywhere else that way?"

"That's why they wear wigs, right?"

"That's why Ginny wears a wig. Part of the reason, at least," Dad said. "It's hard when you're different in such an obvious way, especially for teenagers. But even if she wore a wig, she'd know she was different. She'd feel different, not just sick."

Which made sense, but it didn't answer my question, so I repeated it. "If they don't have cancer, why are the other girls bald?"

Mom sniffed, and I looked at her. Dad put a hand on her arm. She sniffed again, and her voice was still shaky. "Jo and the others don't have cancer. Their hair didn't fall out."

"Yes, it did," I protested.

"No, it didn't," Mom said. "They're such amazing friends that"—she sniffed again—"when Ginny's hair fell out . . ." She looked at Dad.

There were tears in Dad's eyes too, maybe, but he wasn't actually crying. Dads cry a lot less than moms.

"They shaved their heads and got wigs too," Dad said.

"Why would they do that?" I demanded.

"Why do you think?"

"It doesn't make sense," I said. "They wouldn't need wigs if they didn't cut off all their hair."

"I assume they didn't want Ginny to feel different and left out," Dad said, "especially at Christmas. So they shaved their heads and got wigs too, so she wouldn't feel alone. They're incredibly good friends."

"Do you understand?" Mom asked. "They did it because they're her friends. I heard you can donate your hair to be made into wigs for cancer patients, so they might have helped other people too."

"They're probably in trouble," I said. Some things are just obvious.

"Why do you think that?" Dad asked.

"If I cut all my hair off, you'd be pissed," I said.

"Timothy! Language!" Mom protested.

"You'd be mad," I said.

Mom's voice softened. "I think you mean angry. But no, if you did that to help a sick friend, we'd be very proud, not angry. But I'll bet they talked to their parents before they did it."

I knew what that meant. If I ever had ideas like that, I should tell Mom and Dad before I did them.

Our investigation was over. The mystery was solved. I needed to tell Jase as soon as I could. But first I had another question.

"So if Jase gets cancer and loses his hair, I should shave my head too? And if I get cancer and lose my hair, he should shave his?"

"I hope that doesn't happen, and it's very unlikely," Dad said. "So rare that you shouldn't worry about it. But I do think you should be that good a friend in other ways, when your friends need you."

I didn't know what he meant, but I nodded. "Can I use your phone?"

"Why?" Mom asked. "It's Christmas Eve."

"Jase and me do investigations together. I need to tell him we solved it."

"Jase and I. You may call him on one condition," Mom said. "After you tell him about Ginny's amazing friends, be sure to thank him for being your good friend. Wish him a merry Christmas too, of course."

It was kind of mushy, but I could do that. It wasn't like we didn't already know we were best friends.

I told him we were going to need a new investigation, and the other stuff. Just before we hung up, I said, "Jase, I probably wouldn't shave my head for you."

He laughed a little. "Yeah, you would."

Yeah, I probably would.

What I said last was, "Merry Christmas, Detective."

He said, "Merry Christmas, Detective," and we hung up.

<h1 style="text-align:center">Orange Juice</h1>

ON MY BREAK I strolled around the block, admiring the trees which lined the streets. They had burst into pinks and whites over the weekend, making downtown smell like spring. They must be especially stalwart trees, I thought, to bloom so abundantly amid the concrete, asphalt, and exhaust fumes. The very idea of them was intoxicating.

At the last possible instant I saw and dodged a blond, pant-suited, high-heeled woman as she hurried in the other direction. Her eyes were glued to her smart phone. I kept walking but turned my head, seeking any sign that she'd noticed the near miss her large coffee and possibly her phone screen had just survived. It was pointless to snarl; she was already several yards behind me and moving fast. At least I wasn't wearing her coffee.

Maybe she was watching premarket trades. I did, when I dressed like her for work. The markets would open in an hour. How many stockbrokers worked in these glass towers? How many lawyers and accountants?

The blow to the side of my head stopped me in my tracks. The temporary "ROAD WORK" sign hadn't been there earlier. My skull hit the metal with a dull thud, not a clang, but I felt like a clapper.

I gathered my shattered thoughts, brushed off concerned questions from solicitous passersby who weren't on their screens, and walked on. Five minutes later I was in the ladies' room at work, deciding the bump wasn't bleeding and wouldn't be visible under my hair. Five minutes after that, I was at Table Six, trying to be pleasant and wishing the ibuprofen would kick in already.

"Here you go, Frank," I said. "One large, fresh-squeezed orange juice and your check. Thanks for coming in."

He sat alone in his usual booth, the second from the end, looking too much like my grandpa. My memory of Grandpa, at least. It wasn't a good look: wrinkly, saggy, haphazardly shaven, unsmiling, eightyish, with protruding, bloodshot eyes. I caught a whiff of old age, maybe stale urine, amid the breakfast aromas. His blue-gray-green plaid flannel shirt could have been Grandpa's, if the cuffs had frayed. His limp gray slacks were Grandpa's. So were his lonely strands of silver hair.

I knew Frank wasn't Grandpa. Grandpa had been dead for years. I knew I was projecting my feelings about Grandpa onto Frank, but I did it anyway. I automatically braced myself for crankiness and disapproval.

He'd come well after the late breakfast rush, as usual, so we weren't slammed. I could linger, while he turned the check over and examined it, also as usual. We still did checks by hand, but I figured he'd have doubted a computer's calculations too.

"Did I get the math right?" I always did. Even with a headache, there weren't that many ways to go wrong, adding up $4.85 for the juice and $0.35 for sales tax.

There was one good thing about seeing Frank almost daily. His tip would be two dollars, which was crazy generous, percentage-wise.

Grandpa gave me two dollars once, when I was seventeen. Made me promise not to put it in my college fund, as I'd done with his larger gifts. Told me to find a boy and buy him an ice cream cone.

Said I was turning into one of those "feministic" girls who studied too much and didn't care enough about attracting a good man someday and settling down.

By then I'd long since abandoned hope for Grandpa's approval, and I was tired of his criticism. So I told him I liked guys well enough, but I wouldn't dumb down or sex up my personality for them.

He complained about my language.

I didn't stop resenting him when he died. Now I remembered him by resenting Frank, who'd never said a critical word to me. I knew it didn't make logical sense. But it made emotional sense.

Frank had been in almost every weekday for weeks. Lately he always sat in my area. He'd sip his juice for half an hour, then shuffle out. He never brought a newspaper or a book. I never saw Grandpa reading either, despite his floor-to-ceiling roomful of books.

They had the same blank stare.

I was only one-third of Frank's age, give or take, but if I was ever old enough for grandchildren, I wanted to make my exit before I lost the capacity to be cheerful and kind to them. In any case I wanted to go before my life shriveled into dreary use-lessness—which certain people thought had already happened. Mom, for example. She'd had such high hopes for me, visions of pant suits, heels, office buildings, corporate power—a life she never had—and now I waited tables in a diner. Worse, far worse, it was my choice.

"You always get the math right," Frank rumbled. "You should be an accountant."

"I am an accountant."

He glanced up without moving his head. "You are?"

"A good one. Worked a few years for one of the Big Four."

His next question was, "Why'd you leave?" What I heard was, "Why on earth do you work here?"

The rest of my section was empty, so I could chat. It took my mind off my headache. "You really want to know?"

"I asked."

"I hated 80-hour weeks. And I didn't want to impose them on other people either. Here I work hard five days a week, from 5:00 a.m. to 1:30 p.m., waiting tables and doing the books. Then I go home, have a life, and forget work until my next shift."

"Substantial pay cut."

"That's okay. I have no debt, more savings than 98.7 percent of my age group, and some fairly successful investments."

"Well, you're good at this too."

I chuckled, aggravating the pain in my head. "I bring you juice every morning. I get your check right. It's not rocket science."

He raised his furry, gray-and-white eyebrows in silence.

"I have mad skills serving whole meals too, if you ever want more."

"Good to know," he said.

"For example, tomorrow you could wash down a cinnamon roll with your juice. Or pancakes." I envisioned him eating pancakes very slowly.

"No, thank you. Watching my carbs."

"Nick's omelets are the talk of downtown. He says so himself."

"Don't like eggs."

"Ham, sausage, bacon?"

"Too much salt."

"Fresh fruit?"

He lifted his glass a half-inch. "This is fresh."

"Well then, unless you come for lunch or dinner, I guess that leaves juice. Or the coffee's pretty good."

"Don't drink it."

"We have grapefruit juice."

"Regrettably, it interacts with my medications."

"Tomato?"

"Love it too, but the salt again. And apple's too sweet. May I ask a question?"

"Sure."

"What is the proper level of gratuity for an establishment of this sort?"

"For an unpretentious downtown diner with great food and world-class service?"

There might have been a glint in his eye. "Something like that."

"Fifteen percent is kind of the low end of acceptable. Twenty's good. Twenty-five's excellent."

This was a longer conversation than I could remember having with Grandpa. Gruff sermons about correct behavior for girls and not raiding his raspberry patch weren't conversations.

He focused on the check again. "Twenty-five percent would be $1.30. That would feel cheap."

"Frank, I've never complained about your tips. You're always very kind. Thank you!" I put a hand on his shoulder, then froze. I almost never touched customers who had outgrown booster seats.

He froze too. I removed my hand, and we were back to normal.

"Thanks for coming in," I said. "See you tomorrow?"

"Most likely." He looked up and squinted. "I'm sorry. I've never quite been able to read your nametag."

"Millie. Short for Emily."

His eyebrows rose again. "I have a granddaughter by that name."

Of course he did. I scrambled for a response. "I hope she's younger than me."

"She's eighteen."

"That's younger," I said.

The front door admitted two guys and a girl, all teenagers. They were probably cutting school. "I'll get back to work."

"Good day . . . Millie."

"Good day, Frank."

"That's another thing," he said before I turned away. "You don't say, 'Have a good rest of the day.' That just sounds like wishing someone a good nap."

"Yeah, it does. See you tomorrow."

ON SUNDAY EVENING, MOM called, which was not the problem. The problem was that I answered, caller ID notwithstanding. An unforced error.

"I hate to think of you slaving away, waiting tables," she said after small talk. "I know how people treat waitresses."

"Did you ever wait tables?" I asked. I knew she hadn't. The next thing I planned to say was, "Don't judge what you haven't tried."

"No, but Grandma did."

"I didn't know that. Before she met Grandpa? Or was that how she met him?"

"Years later, when he was in the war. I was five or six, old enough to know it drove him nuts that she had to do that. I'm sending money."

"No, thanks. I'm fine." I had more money than she did.

"You're sure?"

"Decent wages, great tips, sound investments. I'm doing well."

"I'll send you $100."

"I'll send it back. Again."

"I want to help. You could be a little grateful."

"I said thanks."

"You said no, thanks."

That was plenty for one evening. "Mom, I have to go. Early shift, as usual."

"You deserve so much better, Millie. You had a career path."

"I know, Mom. Good night. Thanks for calling."

Her words echoed in my mind as I prepared for bed: "You deserve so much better."

They still echoed on my walk to work at zero-dark-thirty, as Nick called it. He sounded like a soldier because he'd been one, in the same war as Dad.

"You deserve so much better." What Mom's words meant was, "I'm so disappointed in you."

I'd told her a hundred times, and it was true: I was happy. I enjoyed my job, and I had job security, even if I didn't have a clear, upward career path. I went to plays and concerts, not always alone. I walked in the park and by the creek that burbled and sparkled through my little neighborhood. I volunteered at church. I sat in my favorite chair for entire evenings, reading books I loved. There hadn't been time or energy for any of that, when I worked 16-hour days in a cube. And so what if my best friends were from work? My friends were real people now. They weren't desperate to impress everyone.

I didn't care that others thought I'd lost my mind. But I was wired to care what Mom thought.

The blossoms and the cool morning breeze had worked some of their magic by the time I reached the diner, and it was a good thing. The whole morning was a circus. We were down a server, and the breakfast rush stretched into the lunch rush.

Frank came at the usual time, and his usual booth happened to be open. He was gone before I saw his ten-dollar tip.

Tuesday was back to normal, so I had time to ask, when I brought his juice and check, "What's up with yesterday's tip? Almost 200 percent?"

His voice was gruff. "Was it inappropriately large?"

"Kind of."

"Then I apologize."

While that hung in the air, I reminded myself that I was angry at Mom—and Grandpa—but Frank wasn't either of them, and I was a better person than this.

"Actually, I apologize. You were very generous. Unnecessarily so. Thank you."

"You're welcome."

An order was up, so I had to go. "Thanks for coming in, Frank."

I had another spare minute later, before he finished his juice, so I asked him my other question. "Why yesterday? You got less attention from me than usual."

He looked at me with upturned eyes. "If you must know, I heard those six patrons at that table behind you deciding to leave you a quarter each, glued to the table with pancake syrup—after they were profoundly rude to you in their words and their . . . liberties."

I wouldn't have said profoundly, but he wasn't wrong. "It's part of the job."

"Perhaps. But you deserve better."

I deserved better? He was Grandpa after all. Or Mom.

"Frank, you don't know me. How would you know what I deserve?"

His eyebrows twitched upward. "I know your work, and you're human. You deserve better on both counts."

I actually hung my head a little. In actual shame. "Thank you, Frank. Have a great day."

"You too," he said.

*   *   *

ON MY BIRTHDAY I had to answer Mom's call, and I had to act enthusiastic about the box she'd mailed late, which was still en route. I didn't care about the delay, and I was grateful for the gesture, but I didn't expect much. Last year's box had included some makeup I never used because the colors were too bold, the latest perky self-help book for women who wanted to have it all, and a cute but low-cut top she'd found for me, which I had worn exactly once, for two minutes, in front of my bedroom mirror.

"Ernst & Young is opening a big office here," she said in her helpful voice. "I heard they're having trouble finding enough accountants. You should apply. They're Big Five, right?"

"It's Big Four now. Arthur Andersen went away long ago."

"That's hardly the point," she said. "Not liking one accounting job doesn't mean you won't like another. You should aspire to something more than living alone and waiting tables."

There it was.

"That pretty much covers it, right, Mom? I'm twenty-seven and single. Grandpa would be so disappointed, even if he never really liked me. And I wait tables for a living, so you're more than disappointed. You're ashamed. I'll bet Dad wouldn't be ashamed of me if he were here."

Dad died when I was eleven. His Humvee hit an IED in Afghanistan, three weeks before the end of a six-month deployment that had lasted almost two years.

On his last leave, over Christmas, he asked me what I wanted to be when I grew up. I said I wasn't sure. Maybe a combat engineer like him. Maybe a teacher, because I loved my sixth grade teacher, Mrs. Neville. Maybe a waitress, because we were on a New Year's Eve lunch date, and the server was smart, pretty, and kind.

I decided to test him. "What if I want to drive a garbage truck?"

He grinned. "You're testing me again, right?"

I couldn't keep a straight face.

"Millie, you should be happy. If that means driving a garbage truck, just be really good at it. And shower thoroughly after work."

"Okay," I said. "But garbage is gross, so it probably won't be that. Are you happy?"

"I am. I'm good at my job, and I help people. I miss being home with you and Mom and your little brothers, but I'm protecting the people and things I love most, including you, and someday soon I'll come home to stay."

He came home that March. We buried him on a chilly, gray-brown day. After the school year ended, we moved three states away to be closer to Grandma and Grandpa.

Mom was still on the call, but my attacking her and Grandpa and invoking Dad's memory all in the same twenty seconds had bludgeoned her into silence.

Remembering Dad brought tears to my eyes. I wiped them away.

"I miss Dad too," she finally whispered. Then her voice got louder. "And you can stop saying Grandpa didn't love you. He did. He wanted you to be happy." I heard a deep breath. "And I'm not . . . I'm not ashamed of you, Millie. But all that education, all that work building a career."

"Education is for life, not just work," I said. "I read that some-where. I have a life now."

"If you insist on waiting tables, why does it have to be a diner? That's just about the bottom rung of the ladder. You deserve better."

"You should check our online reviews. People love us. Great food, great service, relaxed and friendly atmosphere, the whole deal. I'm proud of my work, and we're not the bottom rung."

"I've heard the speech," she said.

I ignored her, because just talking about it made me happier. "The best part is, people are themselves in diners. Customers, workers, management. No pretense, no illusion. At least a lot less than other places."

"I just want the best for you," she said. "Do you still want marriage and family?"

"When the time and the man converge, yes."

"How will that happen, waiting tables? How will you ever meet a good man in a diner? Or keep one interested, when he finds out where you work?"

"Would it help if I owned a diner?" I asked.

"You don't, do you?"

"No, but never say never. That would be a career path."

"Very funny," she said. "You should be meeting good men."

"I thought I'd start by being happy and having a life. Besides, Rosie Perez got Nicholas Cage in a diner. Julia Roberts got a guy in that pizza movie."

"I just want you to be happy."

My voice turned cold. "How many times do I have to say it? I'm happy. I'd be even happier, if my family didn't consider me a failure and a lunatic. You'd think at least my mother might believe in me, but she doesn't."

She said nothing for a full five seconds, so I decided we were done.

"I have to crash, Mom. Thanks for calling."

She retreated. "You're welcome. Happy birthday."

I SHOULDN'T HAVE REPLAYED our conversation in my head on the way to work the next morning, but I did, especially the parts where Mom said she wasn't ashamed of me, but I knew better, and where she refused to believe I was happy—which I really was, when I wasn't on the phone with her.

There was no remedy on my route. The blossoms were long gone, the leaves seemed faded and tired, and there was no cool breeze, despite the early hour. The oppressive, muggy heat matched my feelings rather than improving them.

I hid my dark cloud from the customers, but when things relaxed after the breakfast rush, my façade must have slipped.

Frank asked, "Is everything okay, Millie?"

I was an instant waitress-in-a-diner stereotype: hands on hips, curt. "Why do you ask?"

"You don't seem yourself today."

I snapped at him. "Frank, you're entitled to your juice, a place to sit while you drink it, and professional service, including an accurate check. Psychoanalyzing me is not in the package."

"I'm sorry," he said quietly. "I did not mean to offend. Or psychoanalyze."

I was trying to come down from my high horse. I should have waited to speak again until I'd succeeded. "What did you mean, exactly?"

He turned slowly toward me.

"To cheer you up a little. Encourage you. Offer some relief, however transitory."

My feet were on the ground now, my cheeks were hot, and my high horse was trudging away in shame. "Thank you," I murmured. "How were you going to do that?"

"I don't know. But I wanted to try."

His candor was disarming, but now he reminded me of Dad, not Grandpa, and I couldn't handle being disarmed and thinking of Dad just then. "Thanks for that. Here's your check. Have a good day."

"You too, Millie."

I couldn't tell him it wouldn't be good. He'd ask why, and I'd explain, including the fact that yesterday was my birthday. He'd wish me a happy belated birthday, and it would just be bad.

He left his usual two-dollar tip.

On Monday he came in with a man about my age, who was tallish, with short, curly blond hair I might have liked on myself but didn't like on a guy. Frank introduced him as Brad, a neighbor. Brad didn't say much, but he ordered an omelet and left a nice tip.

Frank didn't appear the next day—or for the rest of the week. I worried that he was ill or out of town. Or maybe he'd taken delayed offense at my little tantrum.

At lunchtime the next Monday, Brad came in alone, ordered a BLT on wheat toast and a cup of chicken soup, and did his best Frank impression. He stared straight ahead while he ate, not even looking at his smart phone.

As he finished his meal, I stopped at his table.

"Can I interest you in some pie?"

He looked up and nodded. I still hadn't seen him smile. "Sure. What do you have?"

When I brought his cherry pie, I asked about Frank.

"He hasn't felt like going out," Brad said.

"I hope he's not ill," I said.

"I think he'd prefer to be ill. His wife passed away last Monday evening."

My heart fell further than I knew it could fall over someone else's troubles. "I'm so sorry. Is he okay?" It was a stupid question.

Brad shrugged. "Not the first word I'd use. Wasn't a great surprise, but you know."

"What's his story? He's been coming here for months, but he never talks about himself. Or his wife."

"A while back she slipped into a coma. Wasn't a stroke. Something else. She came out of it, but not all the way out. She could eat and smile, and usually say hello and goodbye, but a lot of her was just gone.

"They put her in that place around the block, and he started spending every day there. He'd arrive by 7:00 a.m. and take a break later, while they bathed her and so on, which is when he'd come here. Then he'd go back and stay until late. He fed her, if she was too weak, but mostly he read to her for hours and hours. Jane Austen, the Bible, all her favorite books. She liked that, but he wondered how much she understood. Maybe she just liked his voice."

The more Brad said, the less Frank resembled Grandpa—unless I'd misjudged Grandpa too. I probably hadn't.

"Last Monday was their 57th anniversary," he said. "I took the morning off to help him celebrate by helping her celebrate, sort of. I don't think she understood, but he had a good day—until she passed away that evening. He said she squeezed his hand for a long time. Said she loved him, smiled when he said he loved her, then just sort of switched off."

He glanced up, shrugged, and looked down at his pie.

I couldn't move. "That's either really sad or really . . . wonderful."

Brad nodded. "I'm going with wonderful."

My eyes were about to drip, it was so wonderful.

"You're the one who objected to a big tip, right?" he asked.

"Guilty as charged," I said. "Why does he tip so well? Is he rich?"

"Not at all. Just generous. Besides, he likes you. You're reliable, friendly, intelligent. You remind him of his granddaughters. He doesn't get to see them very often."

"I don't know what to say."

"What's to say? He's lonely, he's old, and coming here helps." He looked up. "Thanks for that. He's a good man."

"You're welcome. He's welcome." I smiled wryly. "Everybody's welcome. Will he be back?"

"Probably, when he feels like facing life again. He lives in the next building, close to me. Speaking of which, can I get orange juice in a to-go cup, please?"

"Of course. I need to go in back for a minute. Then the juice is on the house."

I hurried to the office I shared with Nick, grabbed a sheet of official stationery and a matching envelope, and sat at my little desk. Maybe I did know what to say.

Dear Frank,

Brad told me you've been spending all day, every day with your wife, reading to her.

Something struck me.

No wonder your voice was hoarse, even in the mornings, with all that reading.

He said she passed away last week. I'm so sorry. When you're ready to go out again, we'll be happy to see you here.

Best wishes,

Millie

For a couple of weeks I watched for him, but he didn't come. On a Friday I traded shifts with a girl who had a date that evening. I worried that Frank might come in the morning, and I'd miss him, but I was starting to think he might never come back.

When I showed up for the lunch rush, Nick said, "Hey, that old guy asked for you this morning. I told him you traded shifts with Kaycee, so she could have her hot date tonight. Too much information, maybe? He looks even older now."

"His wife just died."

"Sorry to hear that. Anyway, he said you're very good at your job. Professional, kind, good at arithmetic. I said I'll talk to my accountant about getting you a raise. He seemed to know that's you."

"I don't need a raise, Nick. You gave me one three months—"

He was already gone.

I worked on the books in the back for a while, then returned to the floor as dinner loomed. We were never crowded for Friday dinner. We'd get a few young couples who didn't have much money, for whom going out at all was a treat. We had cheap specials for them. Younger patrons usually didn't tip well, but on Friday evenings the guys wanted to impress the girls.

When I saw Frank at a table—his usual booth was occupied—I nearly dropped four plates. He stuck out like a sore, wrinkled, stooped old thumb, but I was happy to see him. I greeted him more solicitously than usual, but he did nothing to encourage conversation. He wasn't impolite or grouchy, just monosyllabic.

I didn't press him to talk—until I saw him drop a crisp $50 bill next to the spotless plate where his meat loaf had been. He was halfway to a standing position when I closed the two yards between us and put my hand on his arm.

"Wait, Frank. I think you made a mistake."

He furrowed his brow and stared at me, saying nothing.

"I'm sure you didn't mean to leave that much."

He looked down at the table. "No mistake. Good evening, Millie."

I still held his arm. "I can't accept that."

"Is it inappropriate?"

"Maybe. I don't know." I took a deep breath. "I guess I need to know why."

Our eyes met again, but his grave expression didn't change. He spoke slowly, as usual. "It's Friday evening. You took your colleague's shift, I understand, because she has a date and you don't. The young males of our species must be hopelessly addled. All I can do is demonstrate that someone appreciates what you do and how well you do it." He cleared his throat with Grandpa's four staccato coughs, which was eerie. His Adam's apple bobbed, and his voice was noticeably gruffer. "And who you are."

Blood rushed to my cheeks, and tears pooled in my eyes. "Your wife was a lucky woman." His eyes darted to my hand on his arm, and I let go.

"I was lucky. I meant to thank you for the juice the other day. And your thoughtful note."

"You're welcome. Thanks for coming." My usual words sounded too routine, and now my voice was gruff. "It's good to see you. I'm so sorry about your wife."

THE NEXT MONDAY, HE came at the usual time, sat in the usual booth—and asked for a menu and ordered breakfast. "What about carbs and sodium and all that?"

He smiled faintly. "My wife is gone, my usefulness is waning, and it's too late for me to die prematurely. I've decided to eat what I like. Could you pack me a cinnamon roll, please, for a snack?"

This went on for weeks, with five-dollar tips. He put on weight and looked slightly less old.

On Christmas Eve, an hour before I planned to hit the road for Christmas with Mom and my brothers, he came in for a late lunch, after coming for breakfast that morning. He left me a twenty and a hundred. "This is no mistake," he said solemnly. "I'd be grateful if you'd accept it without protest. You've been good to me all these months."

A lead weight formed in my gut, and my voice trembled. "Is this goodbye?"

"No," he rumbled. "I'm flying off to spend a week with family, but I'll be back. This is the same gift my nine grandchildren are getting. Merry Christmas."

The immediate cause for tears was gone, but my eyes teared up anyway.

I tried for a mischievous smile. "For my college fund?"

"For whatever you wish."

"Thank you," I said. "Even without this generous gift, I'd miss you if, you know."

"I would miss you." He stood to leave.

"Frank, could you use a hug today?"

"I, well . . ."

While he decided, I hugged him. His frail arms shook as he hugged me back. We let go, I wished him a merry Christmas, and he shuffled out the door.

I clocked out and sat in his booth with bowl of beef barley soup. While it cooled, I pulled out my phone to text Mom. Then I switched to e-mail. It was less interactive.

Hi, Mom. Quick lunch, then driving. Good day for soup here (beef barley). I wish you knew some of our regulars. One old man reminds me of Grandpa, or sometimes Dad. He's eighty-something and newly widowed. Also generous and kind.

His neighbor, a guy about my age, comes in sometimes. He seems like a good man too. He wears a wedding ring, so it's not what you're hoping. But there are good men in diners. At least this one.

Hope you're well. I'm happy. See you in a few. M

My peripheral vision caught movement, and I turned to the window. A swirling winter breeze pushed a few brown leaves and bits of litter around the sidewalk.

It was definitely a good day for hot soup.

Invisible

I CAN BE INVISIBLE. No, really. I have proof. We'll get to that.

I can see myself in the mirror, and other people can see me if they want. You probably could if you wanted to. So I don't think my invisibility is supernatural. It's more like out of mind, out of sight.

It hasn't always been this way, and I don't just mean that people ignore me at school, though they mostly do. In the halls that's a good thing. Even as a seventh grader, I'm too tall for ninth graders to stuff me into a locker, but that doesn't mean they wouldn't try.

Mostly it's my sister, Joanie, and her best friend, Charlotte. They're both three years older than me, so they're sophomores. They go to high school.

Joanie's friends get to call her Jo. As for Charlotte, everyone calls her Shar—except me, because I like her real name.

I'm Stefan, but Stef is fine too. I'm an artist.

I especially like to draw in pencil. I'm good enough that my elementary school art teacher told my parents I had real talent and I needed a private art teacher. He showed them some of my work and explained what he thought was so "promising" about it.

They got me Mrs. Reynolds. I've had a one-hour lesson with her almost every week for the last two years. This summer we mostly worked on drawing people, which is where the Advanced

Drawing class at school started this fall. (It's usually for ninth graders, but they let me in early.)

I work pretty hard. I spend at least three hours drawing, most days. But maybe it's also a gift, like they say, because I know some things before people tell me. For example, most kids draw a human hand all stretched out, but hands usually don't look like that in real life. So you draw them in a natural pose instead, maybe resting on a table, with thumb and fingers relaxed. The thing is, nobody ever had to tell me that. I just knew.

My junior high art teacher is Mr. Giordano, or Mr. G. On my first day of seventh grade he told us to take the first half hour to draw one of our own hands, doing anything we wanted—except flipping the bird, he said, when one of the ninth graders asked. When we were done, he walked back and forth, behind each row of us, looking at our work. Then he asked if he could take my drawing for a minute.

"Okay, everyone. Good work. Now look at Stefan's drawing. Take a good look. Then I'll have you tell me why his drawing is better than we expect on the first day of class."

(I know I promised you proof that I'm invisible. We're getting there.)

Bedtime was 9:00 p.m. on school nights. About the fortieth time my parents caught me drawing in my room after midnight, they made a rule: No drawing in the bedroom. At all. Not even before bedtime, because obviously I couldn't be trusted. But it's not like they banished art from the house. They gave me a corner of the family room, sort of a nook, to be my studio. They even added some lighting, so it wouldn't be too dark. They told Joanie I could be there anytime I wanted, before bedtime, and if she and her friends wanted to be in the family room too, they had to leave my art alone, and they couldn't tell me to leave.

She didn't have that many friends over. I figured she didn't have many friends, because sometimes she was mean. Mostly it was just Charlotte. At first they left the room, if they wanted to talk without me hearing them—about boys, mostly, I thought, and maybe periods.

After a few weeks, they didn't leave the room. They just whispered. I heard most of it anyway, whether I wanted to or not. Usually not.

Pretty soon, though, they talked and acted as if I wasn't even there. And I don't mean they were just ignoring me. They'd forgotten I was there. I had become invisible.

It's true that I was usually concentrating on my work, so I didn't pay that much attention. But I heard things. Lately they'd been talking a lot about a problem I had never heard of before, which they really wanted to solve. I listened more carefully for a week or two, and I finally realized that having "virgin lips" was the problem of never having been kissed, when you really wanted to be. Or never having kissed someone, when you really wanted to, which seemed about the same.

That's my proof. They never would have talked about that—and they especially wouldn't have talked about certain boys they really wanted to help them with their problem—if I hadn't been invisible.

IN OCTOBER MOM SAID she was going to tell me what she and Dad wanted from me for Christmas. It was usually pretty hard to decide what to give them, so I was glad. She said I should draw portraits of each member of the family—Mom, Dad, Joanie, and me—for them to frame and hang on the wall, and I should sign them. I could do them any way I wanted, and she'd get the others to pose for me, if I asked. She thought the hardest one would be the self-portrait.

I didn't exactly have Mom and Dad pose for me, but I got their permission to draw them while they were sitting, reading, and watching TV. I took my first tries to my lessons with Mrs. Reynolds, and she helped me make them a lot better. She even coached me on how to include my signature so it would look good. By Thanksgiving my parents were done, and my self-portrait was mostly done—and no one but me and Mrs. Reynolds had seen any of them. Oh, and Mr. G, because they were also my semester project at school.

I didn't think Joanie would want to pose for me, so it wouldn't be good if Mom forced her to. I had to draw her when she didn't know it. My first few tries weren't good. I came pretty close on the Friday afternoon after Thanksgiving, when Charlotte came over, and they both sat on the sofa in the family room, while I drew in my corner studio. I had set up an easel just off my line of sight, with a photo of a boy standing in a wheat field, so she wouldn't realize I was drawing her, if she saw me looking that way.

They chattered about Charlotte's date that night with one of the boys she liked. His name was Andy, and I knew him from church. It was their second date, and she was hoping her lips would lose their virginity before the evening was over. I wondered without asking (duh!) if just any kiss was enough for that, or if it took a special kind of kiss.

Late Saturday morning, I was drawing in my corner again, when I heard the front door open. I heard muted squeals, but I kept working. Before I knew it, Joanie and Charlotte were in front of me. Charlotte was sprawled luxuriously—maybe even blissfully—on the sofa that sat at a right angle to the love seat.

"You have to tell me everything," Joanie said. "At least twice. This is so cool! No more virgin lips for you! I hope I'm next. Tell me everything."

My eyes went wide, and I almost made some sort of sound, which is a terrible idea if you're invisible. But it wasn't what you think. It was what I saw. Joanie was sitting with her chin in her right hand, and her elbow was on the arm of the love seat. Her eyes sparkled as she looked at Charlotte. It was the perfect pose for her portrait.

I turned to a blank page and began to draw.

When you draw three hours a day for years, sometimes you can work quickly and confidently, even when you're only in seventh grade. Ten minutes later, my first rough sketch was complete. Joanie was still in the same pose, and Charlotte still chattered away. Joanie interrupted now and then with questions about lips or hands or saliva.

Eww.

When she finally moved, it was okay. I'd sneaked a few photos with my phone for reference.

The truth—which, as her little brother, it was my job to keep to myself—was that Joanie was cute. She had an oval face with brown hair that curved around it and just brushed her shoulders. I couldn't do brown eyes perfectly in pencil, but her eyes were really pretty, especially when she smiled. When she listened to Charlotte talk about kissing, her whole face lit up. Her cheeks almost dimpled, but not quite.

I didn't get her eyes right until I took the drawing to my lesson, along with my photos. Mrs. Reynolds helped me see a few lines and some shading I could change to make everything work.

It was the best portrait of the four. It was a pity to waste such quality on my sister, but it was really a gift for Mom and Dad. I was proud of the whole series.

The next Saturday afternoon, Charlotte was back, but there was a cloud of gloom over her and Joanie when they flopped on the sofa together.

Joanie sounded very earnest. "I can't believe they grounded you for a month. You'll miss everything!"

"I know," Charlotte moaned. "All the Christmas everything. New Year's Eve too."

"Wait," said Joanie. "If you're grounded, how can you be here? Did you sneak out? That was probably a dumb idea."

"I'm not that dumb. The grounding specifically doesn't include your house."

"Why not?"

I wanted to know that too.

"Because you're a good girl, and this is a good family, and I obviously need all the good influences I can get in my life right now."

All that goodness gave me a warm, happy feeling on behalf of my whole family and our house, but Joanie eyed her suspiciously. "How obviously? Spill."

Charlotte shrugged. "I went out with him again last night, like I told you. The movie was good. The kissing was better. I was home on time." She sighed. "I like kissing Andy."

"What got you grounded? Somebody saw you and told your parents?"

"No. Andy came over this morning to bring me my ski cap. You know, the purple one? I left it in his car, so he'd have to bring it to me. Everyone else was out shopping, so I invited him in, and we sort of got carried away."

She eyed Joanie for a second. "I really like getting carried away."

Joanie sounded hesitant. "How carried away did you get?"

Now Charlotte blushed. "We just kissed."

"Just kissed?"

"For maybe an hour."

"Just kissed for a whole hour?"

"Well, it didn't seem like an hour. And there's kissing, and then there's kissing."

"What were you kissing? What was he kissing?"

Again, eww.

"Oh, no, we weren't doing that! Just on the mouth. And, um, in the mouth." I wanted to see her expression, but I didn't dare move my eyes.

"French kissing?" Joanie's voice was a dramatic whisper.

Charlotte breathed deeply, and I heard her exhale. "Yeah. We were pretty . . . focused. Didn't hear them come home. When Mom and Dad—and Emma and Ellie and Lizzy—saw us, he was sitting on that piece of our sectional that doesn't have arms or a back, and I was on his lap, and . . ."

"And?"

"I kind of had my legs wrapped around his waist."

I tried to imagine how that would work.

"That was my idea," Charlotte said. "I don't how long they watched us, before we knew they were there. Probably not very long. But the garage door opener's really quiet. It was this amazing, open-mouth kiss, and it lasted almost forever. Nobody made a sound—well, except us, probably—until we came up for air.

"And okay, so I'm grounded. I am so grounded. But it was totally worth it. I can live on just the memory for at least a month. And maybe Andy and I can sneak away and kiss some at church on Sundays. It's probably our only chance." She sighed. "Jo, he's really cute. And besides, we didn't take any clothes off, and nobody's hands wandered anywhere naughty."

There was silence for a moment. I held my breath. Finally Joanie spoke.

"Oh my gosh, Shar! Oh my gosh!"

There was a dry giggle from Charlotte. "Is that, 'oh my gosh, you little tramp,' or 'oh, my gosh, I'm so jealous'? Because with Mom and Dad it was pretty much the first one. I had a boy over when no one else was home, which is like a felony or something all by itself. And we were kissing. And my little sisters saw us.

"I admit it would have been better if we were standing up or something, and if it wasn't obviously that kind of kiss. And if I hadn't told them he'd been there for an hour. But I had to tell them that, because they could check the log on the stupid smart home system. But Mom is totally exaggerating this. We were not 'practically having sex with our clothes on.' I can think of ways it could have been worse with our clothes still on. So anyway, what do you think? Little tramp? Or jealous?"

"The second one," Joanie said. "Totally. But you should be more careful next time."

"I know, right? I regret not hearing them come home, but that's all I regret. Well, that and some of the Christmas parties and stuff. Oh, and the New Year's Eve dance. But Jo, I really like that boy, and it is so good when we kiss!"

"Okay," said Joanie with authority. "Here's the plan. We'll make a fancy lunch to celebrate. That'll take your mind off being grounded."

"With ice cream?"

"Totally with ice cream. Well, not totally. We'll make those Monte Cristo sandwiches you like. And some other stuff. Then we're going to hang out all afternoon and paint our nails and everything. And I want every possible detail."

"I'm in," said Charlotte. "I should run next door and tell the parents I'm here for lunch. I promised to check in personally about now."

I drew all through their lunch. I'd grab something later. Then they came to the family room for the girl stuff. I didn't pay much attention, until they started talking about Andy and Charlotte kissing again.

"Is Andy okay?" Joanie asked.

"He was really embarrassed. I mean, seriously, Mom was his Cub Scout leader and Dad's his Sunday School teacher, and he's hardly ever been in trouble for anything. He says he's never kissed anyone like that before. How could he not be embarrassed? But they didn't yell at him."

"What'd they say?"

"Well, I got . . . off him . . . and stood up. He grabbed his coat and stood up too. He held my hand, which was sweet. And very brave. He apologized, and Dad said, 'You should probably go,' and he did. I texted him later, to tell him I was grounded and see if he was okay. Here's what I wrote."

Joanie read aloud from Charlotte's phone. "'I'm so sorry we got caught. I know you're embarrassed. But that's the only part I'm sorry about. Are you okay?'"

"Now read what he said."

"'I'll be okay, Shar. I really like you. Your parents haven't talked to my parents yet. Maybe I should tell them first. But it was totally worth it. Sorry you're grounded. I probably will be later.'"

"Then some X's and O's," Joanie added, "which I think we have to take seriously, under the circumstances."

They started painting their toenails, while Charlotte narrated the whole hour of kissing in distracting detail. I tried not to look up from my work at all, but I looked a few times. And I didn't try not to listen.

One time, when I looked, Charlotte had moved to the floor, not six feet from me. She was wearing her short shorts—even in December—and a faded red t-shirt. One long leg was stretched out, and the other was bent at the knee, while she painted a nail orange. The one next to it was red, and the one next to that was purple.

If Joanie was cute, maybe even pretty, Charlotte was gorgeous, but I hadn't fully appreciated it before. She had curly blond hair, and her shirt and shorts traced some nice curves. Her eyes were green, and her cheeks dimpled cutely when she smiled. But it was her legs that made me need to draw her. I didn't quite understand that.

Her long, long, long, long legs. My view of them from my invisible corner was as good as if she were posing for me. Which she was. She just didn't know it.

She was breathtaking.

I had to breathe.

I'd never drawn someone in a pose like that before. I hadn't learned legs yet, and I had to sketch her legs about nine times before they started to look right. Overall, my sketch didn't come close to doing her justice, but it was a good start.

I knew this would be my best portrait ever, if I got it right. My teachers would call it candid and natural.

Too bad I could never show it to anyone else.

I drew all of her, including the cute little pout in her lips, when she concentrated on painting a nail. Her hands were hard to draw, like her legs.

I had trouble focusing when I imagined her arms and her long, long legs wrapped around Andy while they kissed. Weird things happened in my head and chest and stomach. My terror of getting caught pushed all that aside for a minute, while I sneaked a reference photo, but then it came back.

I WORKED ON MY masterpiece hour after hour, day after day. I took it to two of my art lessons, which really helped. I studied Charlotte a little more than before, when she was over during those weeks, and maybe not just for reference.

When it was done, I could look at my drawing and feel what I felt looking at her. She came to life on my paper.

I was an artist.

Then I made my mistake. Mr. G's assignment for our semester project was a series of four pieces, but he said we could have extra credit if we made it five. I didn't need extra credit, but I included my drawing of Charlotte with the other four anyway, when I handed them in.

Two days later, he called me to his table during a work session in class. He spread out my five drawings and leaned over them. He was already shorter than me, so I saw the top of his head and noticed for the first time that his black hair was thinning.

"Three of these are very good," he said, pointing his delicate, permanently stained fingers toward my self-portrait and my parents. While he described some details he liked, I wondered what he thought about the other two. Maybe I was wrong. Maybe they weren't even good.

He turned to my portrait of Joanie. "This one is even better. I remember your sister. In fact, I saw her the other day. And I guarantee you these portraits are a better gift for parents than anything I'll get for Christmas from my kids this year. It's good payback for funding all those art lessons."

My cheeks were warm. "Thanks."

"It's your first commission. Not your last, I'm sure. Well done."

He put the drawing of Charlotte directly in front of us and shook his head. "This piece is hands down the best work I've seen from you. Who is it?"

Now my cheeks were hot—because of his praise and his question. "Charlotte. My sister's friend."

"You've captured her beauty. There's life here. Passion too, kind of a poignant admiration. It's realistic. Heart-breaking, almost. It's not Impressionism, but it's the kind of everyday image they painted a lot. Hold that thought!"

He turned to his bookcase for a big, thick book and opened it next to Charlotte on his desk. "It's like Renoir's 'Young Woman Combing Her Hair.'" He pointed to a painting in the book. "See this one? It's a pose but it doesn't look posed. It's beauty, effortless and natural. She could be the girl next door."

"Charlotte is the girl next door," I said.

"Okay, I meant the Renoir, but that works. There's an even better example." He thumbed through the pages. "Here we are. Camille Pissarro. He was a guy, by the way, one of the early Impressionists, taught some of the most famous ones. This one is his 'Young Woman Bathing Her Feet in a Brook.' I saw it in Chicago once. Studied it for two hours. It's breathtaking."

He looked up at me. "Does she know you drew this?"

"No." I couldn't see my face, but scarlet turned out to be a color I could feel.

"She didn't pose for this? The pose is brilliant."

"No. She was just painting her toenails with Joanie in our family room."

"You should show her. Maybe give her a copy."

"First I'll have to apologize for drawing her without asking."

"I think she'll forgive you."

"I don't know."

"Well, it's up to you. But remember, our first semester exhibit is next Friday. I'm not a judge, but I think this could win the grand prize."

I was cheerful and light on my feet for days, after what Mr. G said about my art. Mom and Dad noticed, and I explained that he loved some of my drawings. They said they weren't surprised, and Mom's eyes twinkled.

I didn't worry about Charlotte then. I could do that later.

ON THE DAY OF the exhibit, after the bell, I stood for a while in front of my family series and admired the blue ribbon next to it. The last thing in the world I expected was Joanie's angry voice over my shoulder.

"What the hell? You jerk!"

We weren't allowed to swear at home, but that didn't stop her when we weren't home and Mom and Dad weren't around.

I jumped about six inches.

"You drew me without asking?"

"I'm sorry. I can explain."

"You better. I can break your arm."

I realized the bigger danger was the drawing she hadn't seen. That was around the corner. Charlotte really had won me the grand prize.

"Mom said that what she and Dad want for Christmas from me is portraits of all four of us. I don't think Dad knows. She probably decided for both of them and didn't even tell him."

She pursed her lips and glared. "Get to the point."

"I didn't think you'd ever agree to pose for me. I'm sorry, I guess, but I think I drew you really well. This is just about the best I've ever done. You're almost as pretty here as you are in real life." I wasn't lying, but I was laying it on a little thick. I'd never called her pretty to her face.

She stared at me. Her ears were red and her lips were still pressed together, and that was never good. Then she looked past me, at her portrait. She tilted her head a little this way, then that. Her mouth made about six different shapes, and some of the color moved from her ears to her cheeks.

She cuffed the side of my head and began to smile. "You know what? I'm sorry. This is really good. Mom and Dad will love these. You even did a nice job on yourself."

"Really?"

"Tell you what. Ask next time, but this time I won't kill you, on one condition."

"What's that?"

"I want a copy of mine. And could you digitize it for me too? I can already see it on my Instagram."

"Uh, sure. I can do that."

"You know what?" she said. "I want a copy of all of them. Even you. After Christmas. And I won't tell Mom and Dad how good these are. It'll be a nice surprise."

I was so relieved that my head went a little numb, which was weird.

"Let's go," she said. "Mom's waiting. She sent me in to get you."

Y Christmas morning my grand prize drawing of Charlotte was safely tucked away, and the four family portraits were framed, all 9-by-12, and wrapped together under the tree. Joanie had helped me choose the frames at Target, and she'd insisted on doing the wrapping. That was good, because she'd already told me my gift for Mom and Dad was a lot less lame than hers, and I knew that, if she helped with mine, she couldn't be so mad about that.

Mom had Dad unwrap them. He was speechless. He picked up each portrait in turn, holding it with both hands in front of him, looking at it, nodding slightly and smiling a bit, before passing it to Mom. He studied hers the longest.

When I looked at Mom, tears were dripping down her cheeks.

"These are so beautiful, Stefan. I never imagined . . ."

Dad reached for her hand, then looked at me and said softly, "Thank you. These are stunning."

After Christmas dinner there was pie, and that was perfect too—right up to the moment when Mom said, "Stef, you told us you won first prize with our portraits, and we can see why. But Mr. Giordano said you had an even better drawing, and it won the grand prize for the whole exhibit."

I nodded.

"Where is it? May we see it?"

Oh, no.

No, no, no.

I needed to swear, but I couldn't. I also needed to lie, and I couldn't do that either. I blushed terribly instead.

"Stef?"

"It's upstairs. I'll show you later." Maybe if I timed it right, I could show Mom and Dad, but not Joanie. Then she wouldn't kill me. I could swear them to secrecy.

Within twenty minutes I had the perfect chance. Charlotte came over for a video, and Mom excused Joanie from kitchen cleanup. They disappeared into the family room and closed the door.

Mom was in such a good mood that she excused me too, after a while. I ran upstairs and brought down my masterpiece. The table was already clean and dry, so I put it there.

"Son," said Dad, "this may be the best you've ever done. It's so real, so alive. Her face is perfect. And I know hands and legs are hard, but wow! This is art."

Mom was crying again, and she hugged me. "No wonder you won the grand—"

"Damn you, Stefani!" (Joanie called me Stefani when she was really upset, or when she wanted me to be. It worked both ways.) She slammed her empty steel popcorn bowl on the table. A few old maids popped out and scattered across the floor. The bowl followed them with a clang.

I hadn't heard the family room door open. If it was possible to shrivel with fear, I was doing it.

Mom and Dad started to object to her language, but she kept yelling. "You're a dead man! You are so freaking dead! You won't live long enough to be a dead man! You're a dead little boy!"

"Joanie! Calm down!" Mom hissed. "And watch your language. You know better."

Dad didn't sound as angry. "What's the problem, Joanie? He won the grand prize with this. It's practically a masterpiece." He leaned over and picked up the bowl from the floor.

Joanie's mouth fell open. She stared at Dad with her red, angry face, then at my drawing. I was ready to snatch it away, so she wouldn't rip it up.

She started to say something, then stopped, then started and stopped again. Then she shook her head and looked almost sad. But still furious.

"Honey," Mom said, "Dad asked you a question."

She exhaled loudly, and part of her face went pale. I'd never seen that before, and I'd seen her angry a lot. Her fists were at her sides, but I didn't fully believe they would stay there.

"She's my friend, and she's right in there." Joanie turned to me. "Did she know you were drawing this? It's not like Mom told you to draw her too. You can't use that excuse for this."

Then she really did go pale.

"When did you . . . That was when . . ." Her eyes were huge. "You were there the whole time, listening. You know what? You suck. You're not an artist. You're a voyeur. You violated both of us. I'm never going into that room again, when you're there."

Mom's tone was sharp. "Joanie, that is absolutely enough. Chill out. Now."

Dad's voice was calm. "Son, did Shar know you were drawing her?"

I hung my head, shaking it slowly.

"Does she know now?"

I shook my head again.

"She's about to," Joanie snarled, and strode purposefully toward the family room.

"Joanie, wait," Dad said quietly. Somehow that worked. She stopped and turned.

"What?" her lips quivered like she was about to cry. That's when I realized I hadn't just made her angry. I'd embarrassed her, maybe even humiliated her. And it was about to get worse.

"All in good time," he said. "Stef, do you know what a voyeur is?"

I shook my head.

"It's someone who watches people when he shouldn't, and maybe when they don't know he's watching and wouldn't want him to. It's a hard line to draw for an artist, I think."

I looked up and mumbled. "What should I do?"

"Shrivel. Up. And. Die," Joanie said. "You're a freaking perv!"

"Joanie, enough!" Dad said. "We're working through this. Be patient."

He turned back to me. "Maybe you should show her what you drew and apologize for not asking her. There's nothing wrong with the drawing. It's beautiful. She's beautiful. There's nothing embarrassing about her pose or what she's wearing or the way you drew her. You just need to tell her. And show her."

"What if she wants me to rip it up? Do I have to?"

"She'll rip you up," said Joanie. "I'll help her."

Mom silenced her with a glare, then turned to me. "Stef, that's one of those things you shouldn't worry about unless it actually happens. If it does, we'll talk first, before anything gets ripped up."

"Okay," I said. "When?"

"No time like the present," Mom said.

Oh, no. No, no, no, no, no.

"I'll get her," Joanie volunteered, and this time Dad didn't stop her.

On their way back to the dining room, I heard Joanie say—probably for my benefit too—"I'll help you kill him when you're ready."

Charlotte was usually cheerful, but she could be a little scary. Sometimes, not often, she was kind of a witch. This could go bad in several ways.

But she was smiling, which was the one thing I wasn't prepared for at all. "You drew a picture of me, Stef?" I had turned it over before she arrived. "Can I see it? The ones with your family are really good."

"Yes, and yes, and thank you, and . . ." I looked up at her. "I'm sorry."

"For what?"

"I didn't ask if I could draw you."

"Oh, that." She waved dismissively. "Can I see it?"

I turned it back over. My hand shook so badly that she must have noticed.

Even if she was being nice about it so far, I still thought she might hit me or something when she saw it.

She didn't hit me. She didn't even look angry. Her smile got bigger.

"I don't know what to say, Stef." She took her time studying my drawing. "This is amazing. I knew you were good, but . . . look at my hair and my face. And my hands and feet. Even my toes. This is amazing!"

"It won the grand prize in the junior high exhibit last week," Mom said proudly.

Charlotte looked up at me. Her eyes were so bright.

"Really? We won the grand prize? Can I get a copy of this? Please?"

Joanie stared in disbelief. "You want a copy?"

"Sure. Why not? It's incredible. And look." Her voice was suddenly deeper, and she grinned. "I have pretty nice legs." She stared at Joanie for a moment. "Jo, why are you pissed?"

Mom and Dad wouldn't correct her language, I suspected, and I was right. Not for just "pissed."

"Okay, first of all, he drew you without asking, and you didn't know he was doing it."

"I can fix that," she said.

"What?"

She took one step toward me and kissed me on the cheek. My face burst into flame. "Stef, you can draw me anytime you want. And if you want me to pose sometime, just ask. Did you get a cool ribbon or a trophy?"

I started to tell her about the ribbon and the $50 check, but I got drowned out. In fairness, I wasn't talking very loud.

Joanie was loud. "Dammit, Shar, think about where we were when he drew this."

Mom huffed, shook her head, and raised her arms in frustration. Joanie was officially in trouble, if she wasn't already, once Charlotte went home.

"We were in your family room, painting our nails. He was in the corner being an artist, as usual. I mean, I don't remember him there, but obviously he was."

"No kidding. Remember what we talked about? While he was there listening? Which I always totally forget, by the way. It's like he's invisible."

I couldn't tell if Mom was amused or suspicious. "What were you talking about?"

Joanie blushed, but Charlotte didn't—which seemed pretty strange, given what I'd heard that day.

Charlotte turned to Mom. "I was telling Jo about my date with Andy. You know, Andy Beeler from church? I told her how he brought me my ski cap the next day, after I left it in his car—on purpose, of course—and my parents caught us kissing in the living room and grounded me for a month. Eleven days and counting down, by the way."

Dad's eyes twinkled—but so did Mom's. Joanie was wide-eyed, maybe because Charlotte told the story so calmly.

"If you're grounded," Dad asked, "how is it you're always over here?"

Charlotte giggled. "Mom and Dad say Joanie's a good influence on me, and so is your whole family, and I need all the good influences I can get right now."

Joanie shook her head and face-palmed.

Charlotte turned to me. "I really would love a copy."

"A peace offering for your parents, Shar?" Dad might have been teasing her.

She giggled again. "Maybe. Or maybe I'll give it to Andy and tell him he gets to keep it for a while, but he has to return it when we break up. Which we will, right? Because we're in high school? Maybe I'll hang it in my bedroom. That's after I show it to Andy. He won't be seeing it there."

Mom and Dad laughed. Joanie groaned and did a two-handed face-palm this time. Dad said, "Stef, why don't you make her a copy right now in my office?"

"Um, I thought I would draw a copy."

Her face lit up. "My own drawing? Really? I could pay you."

I shook my head, and I should have said no thanks, but I just said, "No."

"Up to you," she said. "Now come here." She reached toward me.

This was weird. I took one hesitant step. Apparently that was enough. She put her hand on my shoulder, which gave me chills. Chills and sudden visions of long, long, long, perfect legs.

"Stef, I already have a boyfriend. That's why I'm grounded. Well, more or less. So you can't be my boyfriend. Not that you would want to be. You're a little young. Or I'm a little old. And kind of a ditz sometimes, I guess. But you are now officially my favorite artist."

I was speechless. Also paralyzed.

"Well," said Dad, sounding amused. "What do think of that, Stef?"

I had no thoughts at all, of any kind. Then my brain started to reboot, sort of. "I could make you a photocopy. For now, I mean. Could I give you the new drawing in a couple of weeks?"

She beamed. "Perfect! Tell me when it's ready, and I'll come get it." She kissed me on the cheek again. Which made me a little dizzy. And which was also, you know.

Perfect.

Joanie was still fuming.

"Come on, Jo," Charlotte said. "Lighten up. Little brother here is an artist." She turned back to me. "Artist Stefan, you will never be invisible to me again. I promise."

She put her arm around Joanie, who looked rigid. "I love how he drew me! You have to forgive him. Or let him off the hook or whatever. For my sake. Because we're friends."

Charlotte was good at cheering up Joanie. Joanie stared stiffly, then produced a faint smile. If she looked at me, it was only for an instant. "Okay. But we have to be a lot more careful where we talk about some things. And who else is there."

Charlotte shrugged, and I could have sworn she winked at me. "Okay, maybe. But it's not like he didn't know boys and girls kiss, until he heard us talking about it."

Mom spoke up. "Still, Joanie's right. There may be some things he doesn't need to hear. And some things you two shouldn't have very much to say about for quite a while yet."

I got brave for a minute. Or maybe stupid. I can never tell in advance. "I don't actually listen that much. I mostly ignore you and focus on my work."

That turned out to be a smart thing to say, because then Joanie couldn't be sure what I'd heard and what I hadn't.

"Girls," Mom said. "Time flies. You should finish your video, if you're going to. Shar, we'd like to remain a good influence on our favorite juvenile delinquent. Let's try to get you home on time."

"Okay," said Charlotte, sounding bouncy. "Stef, want to come with us? You can draw while we watch. As usual. Or you can watch with us. And I'm not kidding. You will never be invisible to me again. Oh, and you can show me what you're drawing whenever you want. Especially if it's me."

Joanie rolled her eyes back into her head, but she didn't say anything.

"What a merry Christmas this turned out to be!" Charlotte exulted, as I followed her and Joanie down the hall. "I love how he drew my face. And Jo, for a seventh grader, little brother really knows legs."

Joanie cursed under her breath, and it was a really bad one, but Mom and Dad didn't hear it. And I wouldn't tell. It was still Christmas, after all.

I Made Muffins

WHAT WOULD YOU SAY if you were standing at the front door of a nice guy you just met, and it was 6 a.m. and still dark, and you were delivering fresh baked goods he wasn't expecting, but you hadn't rung his doorbell yet because you hadn't figured out what to say, and he opened the door and found you there?

I said, "Here. I made muffins," and held out a paper bag with two large muffins. They were fresh from the oven.

He took it, smiling faintly. His eyebrows were all the way up to where his hairline might once have been. Now he had no hairline. But he could have looked quite a lot worse. If he'd had an oversized mustache, and little tufts of fur protruding from his ears and nose, he'd have looked like Mr. Nixon, my middle school principal.

That's what I had thought at the Christmas Eve party, 34 hours earlier. Now I could hardly think at all.

"Good morning," he said in his even baritone. "Thank you. You made muffins?"

The winter air was cold, but my face was hot. "Muffins. Morning. Uh, airport? See you. Merry Christmas."

Except that Christmas was yesterday, I thought too late.

Now only one eyebrow was raised. "Would you like to come in for a minute?"

"No. Uh, time. Airport. Sorry. Thanks."

"You're hurrying to the airport?"

I nodded vigorously.

"Then I won't keep you. May I walk you to your car? We can speak in complete sentences on the way."

That didn't help me stop blushing at all. "Okay."

"So it's 6 a.m., and you're heading to the airport, and you've already made muffins. From scratch?"

"Right. Yes. Still on Eastern Time. Couldn't sleep."

"You made them for me?" Again with the eyebrows.

I took a deep breath and told a version of the truth.

"I made a double batch for Annalisa's family with the last of the raspberries, and I remembered that you liked them. I was going to have them bring you some, but I saw you out here shoveling snow, and I thought I'd deliver them myself, while they're hot. The family's still sleeping the sleep of the just. Or very soundly, at least."

I took another deep breath, then finished my scatterbrained speech. "See? Complete sentences. Well, some of them. Were. Some of them were. Complete."

He smiled again, not faintly at all. "Thanks for thinking of me. This is a welcome surprise."

"Yes, I'm welcome. I mean, you're welcome." My shoulders slumped. "Sorry."

This was a disaster.

He was almost laughing. I could hear it in his voice. "No need to be sorry. And you can be welcome too."

We reached my rental car. He pulled a card from his wallet, wrote something on it, and handed it to me. "If you'll text me, so I have your number, I'll text you back and tell you how much I enjoyed them."

"Oh, you don't have to do that."

"Up to you. If you don't want the feedback, don't send me a message. But have a safe trip. Thanks again for the muffins. And merry Christmas. Well, Boxing Day."

The truth was, I wanted him to have my phone number. I'd wanted him to ask for it on Christmas Eve, at the party Annalisa and her husband threw for the lonely singles in their congregation—the ones who didn't have family in town, and weren't away visiting family, and were able and willing to go out after dark.

"That's about twenty out of seventy," she'd said. "Most of them are a lot older than we are. And it's an anti-loneliness party, not our own non-alcoholic Yuletide singles bar."

Feeling like an outsider, I had spent most of the evening helping in the kitchen, cleaning up and preparing plates of leftovers for the singles who'd stayed home. When Annalisa brought a relatively young guest back to meet me, because he'd praised my raspberry dark chocolate muffins, my face and neck had done their own raspberry-shaded thing. Then we'd talked some—more coherently than this morning. He'd asked where I was from, then said he'd never traveled back East, but wanted to. He was a history teacher, mostly US history, and he was writing a book for teenagers about the Civil War.

He was soft-spoken, and he'd helped me wash dishes while we talked. And yes, I had checked. His ring finger was as empty as mine.

"Thanks for the help. And the conversation," I'd said, when we were finished.

"My pleasure," he'd said, as loud whoops erupted from some party game. "Good company back here. Quieter too." He'd smiled wryly. "And younger."

He was nice, I'd thought, not weird or creepy. And okay to look at.

He was nice at 6:00 a.m. too. And still okay to look at. But maybe I was a little creepy.

I took his card.

Unfamiliar freeways, rental car return, airport security, a gate change, and boarding kept my mind busy for a couple of hours. Finally I was sitting in an aisle seat on my 737, watching the flight attendants jam someone's carry-on further into an overhead bin, so the door would stay closed and we could push back on time.

A little family sat across from me. Part of a family, at least. Their row was about a foot forward of mine, so I could watch them, and they wouldn't notice.

A mom was in the middle, youngish, prettyish, and altogether too together for having just dragged her little girls through the airport. I'd spent five days wrestling, cuddling, and trying to reason with Annalisa's adorable daughters, ages three and five, and loving every minute of it. But there was no way I could have had Bonnie, my friend's younger girl, sitting quietly but awake in the window seat, and Lindy, her five-year-old, chatting happily on the aisle.

Annalisa and I had been college roommates for our junior and senior years. I had dated as much as she'd studied, and studied very nearly as little as she'd dated. Three years later, she was married and expecting, and I . . . wasn't.

I was okay with it at the time, and content with my accelerating career in PR, but now I wanted what she had—now that I thought it would never happen. Dating had gone so abominably after college, and not dating had gone so much better, that I had convinced myself that giving up was for the best. I was resigned to a dotage of confirmed and infamous spinsterhood. At least I could try for infamous.

Hailey, the five-year-old across the aisle, told her brown-haired mother—whom I also envied—to look at the board book she was reading. Then she told her again, more insistently. Finally winning the attention she demanded, she stabbed at a page with implacable authority.

"This button is for kissing. See? You push this button for kissing."

"What about this one?" asked her mom.

"That one you never push. Not ever. Not for any reason. It's not allowed."

I had no idea what any of it meant—except that, like my best friend, this woman I had never met had two beautiful daughters—and judging by her ring finger, a husband—and I had no one. I blinked back tears.

I decided it was time for a post-mortem on the muffin conversation debacle. I already felt rotten enough that thinking through it couldn't make me feel much worse. But it was still painful. I'd been a complete dork—which is to say, I'd been myself. Not my vivacious, social self from college; that version of me had been AWOL for at least a year. Not even my reasonably personable, professional self from the office; that part seemed to have gone somewhere without me for the holidays.

He'd been, what? Patient? Mildly amused? Maybe a bit stiff about complete sentences? Which I totally deserved.

He'd been a bit cool but not cold. Was he indifferent to me or merely caught by surprise, unaccustomed to flushed and flustered visitors bearing unsolicited baked goods on weekday mornings, when dawn had not even begun to paint the wintry eastern sky?

Could I have been more awkward? Was I creepy? And why did I have to babble like that?

Next year, if Annalisa invited me again, which she probably would, I should arrange for prior commitments elsewhere. Unless she happened to mention that a certain neighbor had moved away or married, or was on safari in another hemisphere.

Under the circumstances, it seemed pointless to like him, but I liked him anyway. I had liked him when I went to his Sunday School class with my friend, two days before Christmas. He'd been intelligent, witty, insightful, and encouraging, one of the better (and more human) teachers I'd seen at church in a while. I'd liked him on Christmas Eve in the kitchen, when he helped with the dinner dishes without being asked, and without showering me with tired pickup lines or too-slick-by-half advances. He was the one interesting single guy I'd met lately.

So I made muffins for him and stopped on my way out of town to dork everything up.

Off and on for the next few hours, I watched the little family across the aisle and yearned morosely for a life I'd never have. I wasn't even functional anymore, in a meeting-a-guy sense. The first, simplest step toward a family of my own was now beyond me.

"Mommy, will you read to me?" asked the little girl in the window seat. I could barely see her, but her sweet, tired, earnest voice broke my heart.

"Of course I will, Rachel," said one of the two luckiest women in the world.

Tears pooled again. I fumbled in my purse for a tissue and found his card instead.

We'd begun our descent, and the flight attendant was collecting trash. I knew what I had to do, and there was no sense in delaying. I closed my eyes and dropped the card into the trash bag, along with my empty plastic cup and my napkin. Then I leaned back against the headrest, awash in something that felt a lot like relief.

Later, on the ground, as the rows in front of me emptied, I stood up into the aisle. Looking down at my seat to make sure I wasn't leaving anything behind, I saw that something had fallen to the floor.

His card. Which I thought I had thrown away.

I reached down to pick it up, then stopped myself. Then I reached down again and stopped again. The woman in the adjacent seat picked it up and handed it to me.

"Thank you," I said too calmly.

He'd circled his cell number, but he'd also left a note. "Thanks! I owe you one, next time you're in town."

I stared at the words, trying to figure out what they meant. He'd given me his phone number and more or less asked for mine. After I'd been a total spaz. He wanted to see me next time I was in town. Unless he was just being polite.

My thoughts played ping pong with my heart as I walked through the terminal, then stood for ten minutes, waiting for the baggage carousel to start. Every minute or so, my eyes darted to the mom and little girls I'd watched on the plane. They were maybe ten feet away.

I pulled out my phone. My hands shook, but I managed to send a message. "Vince, this is Marnie. Remember me? The addled purveyor of early-morning baked goods and awkward conversation? Just arrived in Charlotte. I'll be delighted to hear how much you liked the muffins. Happy New Year!"

A horn sounded three times, a light began to flash, and the baggage carousel squeaked to life. Two little girls cheered, and their mom looked at them with a smile that grew quickly from tired to radiant.

I wanted to smile like that.

Their bags were among the first out, and I watched them leave. My bags were nearly the last to tumble down onto the carousel. I wrestled them into submission and headed for the economy parking shuttle alone.

Kissing Santa

B EA SCOWLED INTO ONE of her bedroom mirrors. Medium brown wasn't her color—if it was anybody's color. It helped to remember that the thrift store dress was a costume. She would wear it only once. And reindeer were, after all, brown, as she knew from the Christmas cartoons she watched as a child, plus every kitschy Christmas reindeer thing anywhere.

At least the weird little antlers were cute, like an outdoorsy tiara. She adjusted their angle, then turned to her best friend, Cee, who was studying herself in the other full-length mirror. "I'm only doing this because I need the extra credit," Bea grumbled. "I can't flunk Current Events. How gross do I look, really? You can tell me the truth."

"Mirror, mirror on the wall," Cee chanted. "Who's the hottest reindeer at the mall?" It was a fair question. Cee was hot too.

"Meet Santa and His Reindeer" was happening at the mall, and it was Saturday, so it would be overrun with parents and little kids. The woman in charge, the Current Events teacher's wife, was using that to make things difficult.

Necklines should not be even the tiniest bit daring, she'd said, and very little leg, if any, should show above the knee. But there were other ways to flatter a figure, and Bea and Cee had figures worth flattering. So they went for—what was the word?—snug. Mrs. Rollins hadn't forbidden that.

Bea's dress, er, costume was not quite bodysuit snug, but she'd get some looks at the mall. The looks she wanted most were from a certain boy in the class. He would be there too.

Cee's reindeer costume was darker brown and a little less snug. You take what you can get at the thrift store. But Cee's question for the mirror was still a toss-up, Bea thought. The answer depended on whether the mirror preferred long brunette hair like Bea's or long blonde hair like Cee's.

Cee made her voice lower. "The hottest reindeer at the mall will be . . . Beatrice. Cecily will be a close second."

Bea gave Cee a patient look. She opened her mouth to repeat that medium brown was not her color, but she changed her mind. "Or maybe the other way around," she said.

Cee beamed. "Brown isn't my best color either, but we're reindeer. What can we do? Besides, you still look amazing. And we both know you want more than extra credit for Christmas. You want to lock lips with Santa."

"It sounds almost naughty when you say it that way," Bea said more cheerfully. "I like it."

"I don't blame you," Cee said, as they headed for the coat closet near the front door. "Mark Nielson is the hottest of all possible Santas, and maybe the first one in forever with a six-pack. Mr. Rollins is kind of hot too, for a teacher."

"He has a wife, you know."

Cee slipped into her coat. "No kidding. It's not like I'm into him."

"I have a question," Bea said. "When Mark and Rudy were flirting with us in class yesterday, do you think they flirt with lots of girls like that? Or do they maybe like us?"

"Hoping for the second one," Cee said. "Here's your coat."

"Me too," said Bea. "Dibs on Santa." She knew Cee preferred Rudolph anyway.

"Dibs on Rudolph," Cee said, and they stepped outside.

Rudy Girardi—or today, Rudolph the Red-Nosed Reindeer—was in Santa's league, hotness-wise. In real life they were best friends, just like Bea and Cee. Rudy was brunette-hot and tall. Mark was blond-hot and a little taller.

"Let's invite them for ice cream after the thing, just you and me," Cee said. "We should ask them before it starts, before someone else snatches them away. You aren't the only reindeer having warm fuzzies for St. Nick."

"Gross! Do you have to say it like that?"

"Okay, you're not the only reindeer who's enamored about Santa."

Bea backed her car carefully onto the street. "What's enamored?"

"Use your context," Cee said.

"On that topic," Bea said, "I can't believe Vicki."

"Skanky Miss I Will Be a Reindeer if I Can Be the One Named Vixen?"

"I'm not sure I knew that word either, before this week."

"If we were pulling a sleigh," Cee said, "she'd probably want to be in the back row, right in front of Santa, when he's driving. So he could appreciate the view."

"I should be the other one in the back row," Bea said. "To give Santa a choice."

Cee smiled broadly. "Both those views are choice," she said. "For the east end of westbound reindeer."

"I know, right? Lucky Santa."

While Bea drove, Cee looked in the little mirror on the sunshade and straightened her antler tiara. "The idea is for Bea and Cee to be lucky, so there's ice cream, followed by Santa kisses for Bea and some reindeer nuzzling for Cee."

"So you be in the front," Bea said, "right behind Rudolph. He leads, right?"

"We won't be in rows like that, but if we did, I'm totally there."

The parking spot they found was surprisingly good for the Saturday before Christmas. They both left their coats in the car. Bea didn't actually shiver until she was just inside the doors.

The mall was crowded, and they got plenty of looks as they made their way to the center plaza. It was no wonder. Most of the other women they saw were wearing winter coats or at least bulky sweaters.

The plaza was decked out with trees and lights and every other Christmas thing Bea could imagine. Canned Christmas carols played on tinny speakers. When the song switched from "Deck the Halls" to "Rudolph the Red-Nosed Reindeer," Bea and Cee linked arms and sang the rest of the way. That got some looks too.

A maze of crowd control ropes was already mostly filled with moms, dads, and little children. Big signs said, "Meet Santa Claus here, 11:00 a.m. to 1:00 p.m. Children 8 years and younger, please."

They reported to a backstage area behind some curtains, for a costume check and instructions. Chiseled, strawberry blond Mr. Rollins was adjusting Santa's wide, shiny black belt. His Asian wife, who was shorter but scarcely less hot than Bea or Cee, inspected the reindeer one by one. She pursed her lips while she considered Bea's outfit, but finally she nodded.

"Nice antlers, you two," she said to Bea and Cee. "Where'd you find them?"

"Amazon Prime," said Cee, and Mrs. Rollins turned to the next reindeer.

"Look," said Cee. "Now's our chance. You ask them."

Santa's belt was okay now, apparently, and Mr. Rollins had moved on, leaving Santa and Rudolph by themselves, talking quietly.

Before Bea knew it, she was talking to Santa. "I know you're Santa and he's Rudolph, and we're just ordinary reindeer, but would you two like to go out for ice cream after we're done here?"

Santa raised his eyebrows dramatically and looked at Rudolph. Rudolph smiled a crooked, adorable smile. He was definitely smiling at Cee, which was perfect.

"Ho, ho, ho," rumbled Santa. "Such lovely reindeer. What are your names?"

Bea opened her mouth to say "Bea," which was stupid, because the boys already knew their real names from school, but Cee spoke first. "She's Dancer. I'm Cupid."

"Ho, ho, ho." Santa looked Bea up and down. "Santa and Rudolph would love to go for ice cream with Dancer and Cupid. Ho, ho, ho!"

"Awesome," said Cee. "Meet you here when we're done?"

"Ho, ho, ho!" said Santa.

"He means yes," said Rudolph. "You should get your candy canes. It's almost time. Rollins put a case over there."

On the way they nearly bumped into Vicki, whose sandy hair had pretty red and green highlights that weren't there yesterday in class.

"Oh, hi," said Bea.

"Hi," echoed Cee.

Vicki looked Bea up and down more quickly than Santa had. "Hi. I thought I was Vixen."

Vicki's dress was nearly the same shade as Bea's. It wasn't quite as snug, but it looked better. The neckline was kind of daring, just a little, and there was a cute slit up one side of the skirt. How did she ever pass inspection?

"You're a good Vixen," said Bea. "I'm Dancer." She raised her arms above her head and twirled. "Cee is Cupid," she said when she came around. She started another twirl but bumped into someone and stumbled. Two strong, red-sleeved arms with white fur cuffs caught her and held her up.

She forgot about twirling and just enjoyed Santa, er, Mark, for a moment.

"Ho, ho, ho," he said. "Starting out front in two minutes." He left her standing on her own two feet.

Vicki glared at Bea. "Yeah, like he said. Ho, ho, ho."

Bea took a fraction of a second to see if anyone else was watching, then stuck out her tongue.

"Charming," said Vicki, and stalked away.

For the next two hours, Santa's job was, of course, to be Santa. Bea wanted to be one of the two reindeer assigned to stay with him, to usher parents and children to and from Santa's red velvet lap, but Mrs. Rollins looked right past her and picked two other reindeer, including Vixen.

Rudolph was nearby. His job was to get parents and children in a happy mood as they neared the head of the line—a role for which, Mr. Rollins said, the most famous reindeer in history was uniquely qualified.

Bea, Cee, and the other four reindeer worked the full length of the line, which grew by the minute. The rope lines looked as crowded as airport security on the day before Thanksgiving, but whoever set them up left room for reindeer to move along the line, handing out tiny candy canes wrapped in cellophane and chatting up impatient children and their tired parents.

At least the moms seemed tired, Bea thought. Some of them were almost unfriendly. It was weird, because most of the dads she talked to were cheerful. But it didn't really matter. This whole thing was for the kids anyway. And it was a good job for a reindeer: bringing Christmas joy to little kids.

Twice Bea offered to sub for Vixen so she could take a break, but she refused. Bea thought of bringing her some hot chocolate or wassail and spilling it on her dress, so she'd have to leave her post next to Santa to clean up, but she went back to work instead.

Mrs. Rollins closed the line at 12:45 p.m. Bea could see it was still more than fifteen minutes long, but a little overtime was okay. "This was fun," she whispered to Cee when they met at the end of the line.

Just then, a little girl in the last family asked, "Are you reindeer? You're pretty."

"You're right, honey," said their dad, who was losing his hair but had a nice smile. "Reindeer."

The mom frowned. She was short and a little bit . . . bulky. "Yes, they are reindeer." She picked up a curly-haired toddler. "Mason, see the reindeer?"

Mason looked suspiciously at Dancer, then Cupid, and started to howl.

His mom blushed. "Sorry, girls. He missed his nap."

"Yeah, sorry," said the dad, with a nice warmth in his voice.

"I feel sick," said an older boy. He went wide-eyed, bowed his head slightly, and vomited on the floor. Bea stepped out of the way just in time, then stared in horror.

The boy looked up at his mom, but she was already on the floor, cleaning up the viscous mess with baby wipes. A thin stream of slime oozed down his chin and dripped onto his shirt.

He looked up at Bea and Cee instead. "I feel better now."

"Good. Merry Christmas," squeaked Bea. She turned away, pulling Cee with her. "I am so going to hurl."

"No, you're not," said Cee. "Let's go restock our candy canes or something."

"We're pretty much done," Bea protested. "We don't need any more."

"Beats hurling in front of Santa, not to mention spoiling the gentle homewrecking effect your snug deerskin is having on some of the dads."

"The . . . my . . . what?" Bea squeaked. "The dads? Real reindeer skins are pretty snug, aren't they? When they're on actual reindeer?" Her stomach lurched. "I still might hurl."

They went backstage together, but the case of candy canes was empty. Bea stared at the empty box anyway, if only to keep her mind off her stomach.

Cee put an arm around Bea's waist and spoke gently. "You okay now?"

Bea took a deep breath, then another. "I think so. Let's go back out."

The other reindeer had what was left of the line covered, so they just stood near Santa, on the opposite side from Vixen, and smiled. When the last family came to the front of the line, the mom said, "Just her," and indicated her daughter. "The baby is scared, and this one"—she put her hand on the older boy's shoulder—"just threw up."

"I feel better now," said the boy. "I could just stand and talk to Santa. I don't have to sit on his lap."

While Vixen guided the little girl to Santa, Rudolph sat on the floor in front of Mason, whose chin was quivering. "Are you scared of Santa?" Rudolph asked.

Mason shook his head.

"Good," said Rudolph. "Because he's really nice. Wait, are you scared of reindeer?"

Mason nodded.

"What's your name?"

"Mason." His chin quivered more.

"Have you heard of Rudolph?"

Mason nodded again.

"You know Rudolph is the nice reindeer, right?"

Mason nodded.

"Do you know which reindeer I am? I'll give you a clue." Rudolph reached up to his nose and tapped it, and it glowed bright red.

Mason's eyes grew wide.

"I'm Rudolph. Fun nose, right?"

Mason nodded vigorously.

"If I stay with you, would you like to sit on Santa's lap?"

The little boy hesitated, then nodded once more.

Rudolph looked up at the mom, who smiled and nodded her approval.

Bea glanced at the dad just then. He was smiling at her, not Rudolph. Her cheeks warmed, and she gave him a shy smile.

"Your sister's just finishing with Santa," said Rudolph. "It's our turn, Mason."

When it was the older boy's turn, he stopped in front of Santa and said, "I can stand here. I barfed, and Mom says I might be gross."

Santa's face turned from jolly to serious, and he made a show of inspecting the boy, even had him turn around. "Ho, ho, ho! I don't see anything gross. And I know gross. For example, reindeer poop is gross. Watch your step around here, okay?"

Bea stifled a giggle.

Santa slid to one side of his little bench. "Come sit by me. Yeah, just like that. Ho, ho, ho! What should Santa bring you for Christmas?"

Cee's breath was warm in Bea's ear. "These guys aren't just hot. They're *nice*. They're amazing!"

Cee was right. Hot and nice. Hot and *really* nice. Maybe they had little brothers and sisters to practice being nice to at Christmas.

At the end, Mr. and Mrs. Rollins thanked everyone, and Mr. Rollins said, "Good job, everybody. See you in class."

THE ICE CREAM PLACE in the mall was packed, but they found a tiny table for two and crowded four chairs around it. They were still in costume, except that Rudolph had put his nose in his coat pocket, and Santa had unpinned his thick, white beard.

"You reindeer ladies stay here, and we'll go order," said Rudy. "We're buying. What do you want?"

"Cookies and cream," said Cee. "One scoop on a waffle cone."

"And you, lovely Dancer?" asked Mark.

She gave him a troubled look. "I don't know."

"Come with us, then. Cee can hold the table. Okay, Cee?"

At the counter, Rudy ordered Cee's ice cream first.

"And for you?" the pretty brunette in the apron asked, as she handed him Cee's cone.

"That one looks good." He pointed. "What is it?"

"Spumoni."

"What's that?"

She shrugged. "I don't know. It's new. I think it's Italian. It's pretty good."

"Cool. Do you know who I am?"

"A reindeer, maybe?"

He reached into his pocket, pulled out his LED nose, attached it, and turned it on. "Not just any reindeer. I am Rudolfo, the Italian-a Reindeer-a Stallion. I'll-a have-a the-a spumoni. Two-a scoops in a sugar cone." He slipped the nose back into his pocket.

The girl giggled. "My pleasure, Rudolfo."

"*Grazie. Molto bene.*"

She took Mark's order next and showered him with flirty small talk. Bea had lagged behind, staring into the case and trying to decide. She settled on chocolate fudge brownie and looked up just as the girl aimed a dazzling smile at Mark and gave him his cone.

"Thanks," he said. "Looks good." Bea assumed he meant the ice cream.

"My pleasure," said the girl, and it wasn't the voice she'd used for Rudy. There were words Bea didn't know, lots of them, but she knew *sultry*.

When Mark turned to Bea and reached out his hand, which she took, the ice cream girl's smile vanished.

"Bea, I mean Dancer, are you ready to order?" Mark asked.

When Bea was back at their table, enjoying her ice cream and her view of Mark, a little redheaded girl appeared at Mark's side.

"Excuse me," she said, and all eyes turned to her.

She looked up at Mark. "You're not the real Santa. I know because the real Santa is fat and the real Santa has a beard."

Bea saw his eyes twinkle. "You're right. I'm not the real one. And you know what else?" He nodded toward the others. "These two lovely creatures and that butt-ugly one are not real reindeer."

"I know that. I'm not stupid. I'm seven and a half. And I'm telling my mom you said 'butt.'"

Mark smiled warmly. "You're a smart little elf, aren't you?"

"I'm not an elf! I'm a girl!"

A woman arrived at their table just then, looking embarrassed. She briefly made eye contact with Mark. "Sorry," she said, then pulled the girl away.

"Merry Christmas to all!" Mark's voice boomed. "Ho, ho, ho!"

The woman turned back for an instant. "Thank you."

As they moved away, Bea overheard the girl say, "He's not the real Santa, Mommy. Santa is fat. And he said 'butt.'"

Rudy quietly mimicked the little girl's voice. "Santa is fat. He says naughty words. And what's a ho, Mommy?"

Bea nearly choked on her ice cream.

A few minutes later, Cee interrupted their chatter. "Rudy, are you okay?"

His face was red, and his voice was strained. "Not sure. I—" He looked down at the ice cream cone in his hand. "What's in spumoni?"

Nobody knew.

"Look it up, okay?" He face was bathed in sweat.

"How do you spell it?" asked Cee.

"Ask Siri," he said.

A moment later, she said, "Cherry, pistachio, and either chocolate or vanilla."

"Uh-oh," Rudy said.

"Is that bad? Are you okay?"

"You're wearing my coat," he wheezed. He'd offered it five minutes earlier, halfway through the ice cream. It was another benefit of the girls leaving their own coats in the car.

"I'm sorry. Are you cold?"

"Not cold. There's a thing in the pocket. I need it. Long, plastic."

Cee pulled out something that looked like a fat pen, but with labels all over it. "What is it?"

"Epi pen."

She looked it over. "What's it for?"

"Has a needle. Stick it in my leg, and I don't die."

"Die? Of what?"

"Ana— . . . Anaphylaxis. Allergic to . . . cashews and pistachios. Please?" He held out his hand, and she gave it to him. In an instant, he removed a cover, turned the epi pen over in his hand, and stabbed it firmly into his thigh through his pants. He held it there for several seconds before pulling it away. Bea stared in shock.

A small bloodstain grew on his pant leg, and Bea closed her eyes before she got nauseous again. That's when she heard Rudy's rapid, shallow breathing and started to be scared for real.

"How does it work?" Cee asked.

Bea opened her eyes but was careful not to look at Rudy's leg.

Rudy set the epi pen on the table and leaned against the back of his chair, which creaked loudly. "Epi is epinephrine. Can't explain how it works. Just does."

"Good thing you had it with you," Cee said.

"Always have it with me." He stopped for a breath. "Have a spare at home. Carry that now. Replace this one. Kind of expensive. Beats dying."

"Are you feeling better?" Bea asked. "You look a little better."

"Starting to."

"Is there anything else we should do?" Cee asked.

"I'm supposed to go to the hospital after I use it."

"The hospital!" Cee sounded as if she might cry.

"Just in case," he said. "But you should all finish your ice cream first. It's not a life-or-death emergency. Not anymore."

"I'm done with mine," Cee said. "Thank you, though."

"Me too," said Bea, who felt a little queasy after all. She couldn't eat the last two bites.

"Moment," said Mark. The last inch of his cone disappeared into his mouth, and before Bea thought he should have been able to, he swallowed and said, "Let's go."

"We'll all go," said Cee.

"We came together," said Mark.

"So did we," said Cee. "Two cars or one?"

"Two," said Rudolph, "in case they want me to stay."

Cee looked down at Rudy's leg. "I think you're still bleeding."

Mark pulled two napkins from a dispenser and handed them to Cee. "Bea and I will get the cars and pull them up to the door. You two stay here a little longer. Cee, press those against his leg." His eyes twinkled. "Where it's bleeding."

Cee hesitated.

"Trust him," said Rudy. "He knows first aid. Wow, I feel weak. I can walk though. In a minute. Might need to lean on you, Cee."

Cee held the napkins to Rudy's leg, and Bea and Mark went for the cars.

To Bea's delight, Mark rode to the hospital in her car, and Cee drove Rudolph's. Bea tried to follow them, but Cee drove like it was still an emergency.

"Not a very nice Saturday before Christmas for Rudy," Bea said as she pulled into a parking space and turned off the ignition. The lot at the hospital wasn't nearly as full as the lot at the mall.

Mark snorted. "Are you kidding? Did you see that pretty girl with her hand on his thigh?"

Bea started to giggle.

"Now they're in there together," he continued, "where he may get a bed and a private room."

"Naughty Santa!" Bea exclaimed. Then she laughed until she felt more like a Jell-o pudding than a reindeer.

He just sat in his seat and smiled at her, until she mostly settled down.

"I like your laugh," he said. "I like that you laugh at my jokes."

"I have to. You're a very funny Santa."

"You're Santa's favorite reindeer. Let's go in."

They used the emergency entrance, where they got some looks. Rudy and Cee were nowhere to be seen. "Like I said," Mark muttered. "They got a room."

A nurse pointed them to Room 4. They found Rudy on a bed, half-sitting. Cee was pressing gauze to his thigh.

"Hi, guys," said Rudy. "Could you check the vending machines for some cashews, please?"

Cee looked puzzled. "Cashews? Aren't you—"

"He's allergic to those too," Mark said. "He likes how things are going." He gestured toward Cee's hand on Rudy's leg. "This is the most affection he's had in months."

The door swung open and a female doctor swept in. She was shorter than Bea, with darker hair, and pretty old. She was at least forty, judging by her face, and her white coat wasn't really flattering. She stopped short. "Three visitors? Santa and two reindeer?"

"Three reindeer," Mark said. "The one wheezing and bleeding on the bed is Rudolph."

"Were you doing a party?" She looked at Bea from head to toe. "Tell me this isn't for an adult film."

"It was for kids," Bea said. "At the mall."

"God help us," said the doctor. "Okay, I'll let you all stay, but keep out of the way. She put a hand on Cee's arm. "Young lady, I think you can stop that now."

The doctor sat at a computer screen. "Rudolph—nice coincidence—I'm looking at your chart. Okay, not bad. First time using the epi pen?"

"Third, I think."

"Well, you got it right. You have a spare at home and a current prescription to replace the one you used?"

"Yep."

"Are you feeling better?"

"Yeah, a lot."

"Good." She turned off the screen, stood, and moved to put her stethoscope on his back. "Breathe deeply. And again." She pressed the inside of his wrist with her fingers, then stepped back. "Okay, I'm pretty sure you'll live. I want the nurse to check your vitals every fifteen minutes for another half-hour. Then you can go, if you still feel better. I see you're eighteen, but did you call your parents?"

"Yeah. They're a couple hours away, but they know."

"Did you drive here?"

"Cee drove my car." He nodded toward her.

"Smart. You should be okay to drive, if you're okay to leave. But no more spumoni. It's bad for celebrity reindeer," she said without smiling even a little.

"That's for sure," said Rudy.

For a moment the doctor looked at Cee, who hadn't left Rudy's side. They were holding hands now. "Merry Christmas, everyone." She turned to Bea. "I hope you get your Christmas kiss from Santa."

Bea thought the doctor smiled a little as she said that, so Bea smiled back. Then she looked up at Mark, who had the sort of happy, inviting, kissable look that made even a brown thrift store dress worthwhile.

"I like her," said Bea. The next thing wasn't easy to say, but she couldn't *not* say it. "I think a lot of reindeer dream of kissing Santa at Christmas. This reindeer most of all. I guess it's obvious, if the doctor can see it."

He grinned. "Your whole face just got bright like Rudolph's nose. But you're way prettier."

That was when Santa kissed Dancer, the reindeer, and she kissed him back. Except she felt more like a girl than a reindeer, so she was pretty sure it was really Bea and Mark who were kissing, despite the costumes. It was amazing.

Mark looked over her shoulder, and she followed his gaze. Rudy and Cee were in their own little world, like they hadn't seen a thing.

"My mom used to kiss it better," Rudy murmured.

"Kiss what better?" Cee asked.

"Whatever was hurting."

Cee leaned over and kissed him on the lips. "Your lips looked like they hurt. How are they now?"

"I feel half-cured. No, one-third cured."

Cee kissed him again, for longer, which made Bea want another kiss of her own. She looked up into Mark's eyes again and matched his smile.

"You know I'm not the real Santa, right?" he asked.

"I don't know anything like that at all," she said. "Next you'll tell me I'm not a real reindeer."

"Are you a real dancer?" he asked.

"I'll prove it to you sometime."

"May I walk you to the sleigh, Dancer?" He looked back at the others. "We're out of here, guys. Don't do anything Santa wouldn't do."

Bea's laugh was more like a snort.

Outside the emergency entrance, Mark stopped. "Remember a little while ago, when Santa kissed Dancer?"

"A reindeer never forgets."

"I thought that was elephants. Which you are totally not. This one is Mark kissing Bea, if you don't mind. Sort of merry Christmas for real and maybe we could do this again soon."

She didn't wait for his lips to come to hers. She went to his.

Even though it wasn't Christmas yet, it was officially a merry Christmas—so merry that "soon" turned out to be when they got to her car, and again when she dropped him at his house.

At home she danced from her driveway to the door, then floated up the stairs to her room.

She checked her phone for the first time since the mall. There was a message from Cee from before, telling her which room they were in at the hospital. Then a new message: "I got reindeer nuzzles," followed by a reindeer emoji, a heart, and another reindeer.

A message arrived from Mark. "If you want," she read, "I want to wish you Merry Christmas again. Maybe on Christmas Eve. Personally. Then Happy New Year later. New Year's Eve party with me Dancer?"

"It's a date Santa," she replied.

"I'll do better than the red suit," he wrote.

"I can do a lot better than my deerskin," she wrote back.

"Hard to imagine," he wrote.

She sent him a blushing smiley. Her whole face felt like a blushing smiley. Good thing red was a Christmas color.

The Old Man and the Chicken

T HE TINY OLD BARN had a sloping metal roof and walls made of scrap two-by-fours, laid flat, staggered like long bricks, nailed together, and painted barn-red on the outside against the weather. It had stood for 63 years and might stand as many more.

The only window was covered with chicken wire, because half the barn had long been used as a chicken coop. In winter, to conserve heat, the opening was covered inside and out with clear, thick plastic. It always came off in the spring, until one year the old man hadn't bothered to remove it. He was too tired, and he knew he'd still be too tired in the fall, when it was time to put it back on.

The chickens would be fine in the summer heat anyway, he reasoned. He could leave both doors open during the day. The side door led to an outdoor run that was twenty feet square and fenced tightly enough to keep the skunks out. In front the inner door was a screen of sorts, a hinged wooden frame with more chicken wire. The solid plywood outer door was weathered but intact.

A metal handle turned, hinges creaked, and the old man stood in the doorway. He carried a tall, four-legged stool and a bulging plastic grocery bag that was starting to tear near the bottom.

"Just me, chicken. Where are you?"

He closed the door behind him and flipped an ancient switch. A large incandescent bulb softened some of the shadows cast by light from the window.

"There you are."

From a corner near the roost, a scruffy Rhode Island Red hen stared at him with one eye, then the other, and went back to scratching in the dirty straw.

A row of nests stood along one wall, two feet above the floor. He checked each one. "No egg today, I see. But not to worry. You're only one hen, after all, and it's winter, and you're about as old as me, in chicken years." He coughed deeply, but only once. "I'm too lazy to cook an egg more than once a week anyway.

"I'll sit over here for a few minutes, out of the way. That's why I brought this stool. Took me three times as long to get out here, dragging all this stuff."

He hung the plastic bag on a nail he'd driven into the wall years ago, for an unremembered purpose. Then he struggled awkwardly to find a place on the uneven dirt floor where all four legs of the stool could sit firmly.

"There," he gasped, winded, and sat down to rest a while. The stool was in the open doorway between the two halves of the barn. He slumped his shoulders and hung his head, but he was careful not to fall asleep. If he did, he'd surely fall off the stool—and even if he didn't hurt himself, he'd use half a day's energy trying to pick himself up again. Besides, he hadn't changed the straw on the barn floor in a while.

Finally he took a deep breath, exhaled, and slowly stood.

"Okay, chicken, as you've already gathered, this is not my usual visit with feed and water. But don't worry. It's not the end for you. I don't slaughter chickens anymore. Even if I did, there'd be no point in trying to eat you. You're too much like me. Not enough meat, and what there is would be shoe leather."

He leaned against the wall to rest from the exertion of standing up.

"I quit raising chickens to eat when Mother died. That was nine years, eleven months, and twenty-nine days ago. I counted again today, in the half hour between *Dragnet* and *Bonanza* on that rerun channel.

"You were one of that summer's pullets. We kept two dozen of you for eggs. Remember that? You probably don't."

He took a few breaths, gently wheezing.

"Can you believe Mother and I were married 49 years? Didn't quite make 50. Always thought I'd be the first to go. Anyway, that leaves the two kids and me. Joshua still lives in England with his wife and three of my grandkids. He says they might visit for a couple of weeks next summer. I hope they do. Think either of us will be around by then?

"They already called today—Josh and his family, I mean. It's a few hours later there. Six, maybe? Don't remember exactly. It just changed a few weeks ago, when we got off Daylight Stupid Time. Still haven't fixed all my clocks. Anyway, did I mention it's Christmas Eve?"

He paused to let his lungs catch up.

"Mary's still in Virginia. You've met her, I think. If she could ever have stayed more than a day or two and gotten to know you, she'd have named you. She used to name all the chickens. Then she'd cry when we butchered them. She'd cry again at dinner, when Josh asked which one we were eating. We didn't track that, but that didn't stop him. I told her a thousand times, never name an animal you plan to eat. But she had too big a heart to listen. Still does.

"She's big in another way right now. Humans reproduce a little differently. Don't know if you knew that. Anyway, number three—that's grandchild number six for Mother and me—is due in February. They'll do their Christmas with the twins tomorrow, and she'll call me in the afternoon. She'll be too tired to talk very long, and the twins are barely two years old, so they won't talk much. Kevin—that's her husband—will be on the phone with his mom or sisters, so I probably won't talk to him at all. Good man, though. I think he's good to her.

"They bought me a little artificial Christmas tree a couple of years ago, and they'll ask about it if they remember, but it's not worth putting up for just me. It's in the garage somewhere."

He eased himself away from the musty wall and stood almost straight.

"Let's do this." He coaxed a red extension cord from the plastic bag.

The hen drank from a two-gallon cylindrical aluminum waterer that was taller than she was. She dipped her beak into the water in the pan around the bottom, then craned her neck to swallow.

"Water hasn't frozen hard yet, has it? Warm winter so far, but that ends tonight. There's a cold front coming about 6 p.m., if you believe the annoying guy on Channel 4. Maybe an hour later, if you believe that pretty girl on Channel 7. I'd rather believe her, you know?"

He talked in bursts, between breaths, which came more quickly as he uncoiled the extension cord and snaked it up into the rafters just above his head.

"Josh thinks I should sell the place, go live with him in England for a while, maybe a year—and Mary thinks I should stay with her for a while after that—and then decide where I want to live. I told them I'd think about it, and I've been thinking about it. I wouldn't be so lonely, probably. No offense. You're fine for a chicken. And if I left, somebody would want you."

He stared at the chicken for a while, then shook his head.

"All these years, and I still don't know whether chickens can count. But you might have noticed that there were three of you last winter, and now there's only you. I didn't eat the other two, I promise.

"Point is, for the first winter in your life, you don't have any other hens to huddle with, so you'll need some extra heat. We used to have a cow in the other half of the barn, and she kept it plenty warm, but that was before your time.

"If you had children in a nice, warm coop in England, would you go? Or would you want to stay here? Does a chicken ever want to see the world, beyond what's across the road?" He chortled at his own joke.

"I wanted to see the world, including England. Never saw much of it, and now I don't even want to. Just thinking about that kind of travel makes me tired. And I don't want to be a burden on anyone when I get there."

He fumbled around in the shopping bag and pulled out a small black box with an electrical cord attached.

He nodded toward the wall. "See the fuse box next to the outlet up here? It's a ten-amp fuse, but it's old too, and we don't want to blow it. So I spent some time back in October figuring out how to do this. Mary got on the Internet and found these two little heaters. They draw 200 watts each, so we should be okay, even with this 300-watt bulb going.

"These are made for heat at your desk when your office is cold, not that you know what a desk is. Or an office. They're low-powered, so they don't blow breakers on the circuits all the computers plug into.

"She e-mailed me pictures of a few models. I wanted to see if the strain relief on the cord looked strong enough that we'd be okay hanging them in here by their cords. We both studied the pictures, and we agreed on this model, even though they cost a few dollars more. She ordered them for me. Had them shipped here.

"They're very light. I think they'll hang okay. I'll wrap their cords around one of these rafters. I practiced in the garage the other day with an old two-by-four.

"Okay, time to rest," he said, making his way back to the stool. He still held the heater.

The feeder was next to the waterer. The hen scratched for grain beneath it.

He rested in silence. The hen hopped up onto the roost, a set of two-by-fours, wide side up and arranged in parallel, and she rested too. Finally he broke the silence.

"I'll still have to bring hot water, to melt the ice in the waterer and keep it from freezing for a while, so you can drink. At least I think I will. But these will help. I tested them on my dining room table for a couple of hours. First I turned off the furnace and let the house cool.

"By the way, they make a heater for this waterer, but I never bought one. Heard those things sometimes set a coop on fire." He chuckled again. "Not the right way to roast a chicken. No offense.

"Two of these little things were too much for me at dinner, but I was testing them in a 60-degree house. Actually, it got down to 58, and I'm allowing for the fact that the thermostat in the hall shows between two and three degrees higher than the actual temperature.

"I figured I needed a better test, so I opened the windows. Got the dining room down to about 50 degrees. These weren't quite enough by themselves, but they helped. It was noticeable."

The hen didn't appear to be listening.

"I'm talking in your sleep, maybe," said the old man. He contorted his slack, unshaven face into a grin, but it didn't last. "You know, I'd like to see my kids a lot. Their kids too. And they'd do their best to make me feel welcome. But it wouldn't be long before I felt like a burden. I'm a burden here too, but less of one. This is my home.

"Okay, time to work again." He stood up with great care, steadied himself with a hand on the door frame, and looked up at one of the rafters. "I figure I'll put them both on this rafter. It's the closest to being centered over this half of the barn. I'll put them a few feet apart, one closer to your roost, and one right about here, closer to the water and the feeder. And the nests. Those must be cold places to sit.

"This one's first, so I don't disturb you over there until I have to."

For ten minutes he said nothing. He needed all his strength and concentration for the work. He brushed most of the dust from atop a six-inch span of the rafter, wincing in annoyance when some of it fell into his thinning hair. But it was better falling there than in his face. If he sneezed too hard, he might need to change his pants. Not even that was easy anymore.

He painstakingly wrapped the heater's cord around the rafter.

"Time to rest again," he rasped.

He shuffled unsteadily to the stool, sat, and tried to stay awake. For a few minutes, his were the only sounds. He blew his nose twice into a handkerchief he pulled from his pocket, and he cleared his throat every half-minute or so.

He yawned and shook his head.

"I'd better talk, or I'll fall asleep. I imagine your Christmas plans are a lot like mine tomorrow: business as usual. But I have a surprise for you. Nothing scary. I think you'll like it.

"Had some Christmas dinner invitations, but I don't have the endurance for visits anymore. I was never good at it anyway, without Mother. Besides, after all this work today, I'll be pretty wiped out tomorrow. A couple of the families who invited me said they'll bring leftovers. Those will probably last me a week."

He exhaled loudly. "Good people, all those neighbors. Known them for years. Don't know anyone but family in England, or Virginia for that matter."

He cleared his throat, then cleared it again.

"Mother sure could make a Christmas feast. I'll bet Mary can too. I hope that husband helps a lot this year.

"I've never seen Katrina cook much—she's Josh's wife—but maybe she does. Or he does. He used to be a good cook. One way or another, they don't seem to be starving.

"Come to think of it, I don't cook much either, and I'm not starving. People bring me more food than I can eat during the holidays, especially fruit. Oranges, even, and they're expensive this year. Bad frost in Florida or something like that. I give most of them to the other people who visit me. Don't have much else to give them, and it's too hard to peel an orange with these hands.

"Almost brought you the rest of a pretty good meatloaf the other day, but I ate it myself. Not sure you like that sort of thing anyway. Or if it's good for you. I probably used to know that."

He fell silent again, and his head began to droop. He bolted upright, then stood more quickly than before.

"Almost fell asleep there. Can't have that, for the previously mentioned reasons. Did I mention them? Doesn't matter. Let's get that second heater installed, shall we? May have to disturb you. This one goes right over your head."

The hen still dozed on the roost.

Practice made him more efficient, but exhaustion made him weaker. As he held up the second heater in one hand and tried to push the cord over the rafter with the other, he missed. The cord fell, hitting the chicken across the back. She squawked and half-flew, half-fell to the floor at his feet, then raced away.

"Criminy! Sorry about that. Didn't mean to startle you. These old hands, you know? Sorry to scare you. Hope that didn't hurt."

The chicken's squawks gradually calmed down, but she paced and clucked for a while in the other half of the barn.

After a few more minutes, he announced breathlessly, "Both attached, both plugged in. Ready?"

She didn't answer.

He looked around but didn't see her. He eased himself past the stool and into the other half of the barn.

"Where'd you go, chicken? I said I was sorry about the cord."

He checked the rafters. He didn't think a chicken could get up there, but you never knew. Then he had a thought. He shuffled over to what used to be the cow's manger, but had since been used to store bales of clean straw—except that the last bale was now mostly used. He'd have to talk to one of the farmers about getting a few more bales.

He looked down into the wooden box and laughed aloud. "There you are, sitting like you belong there. That's the last clean straw we have. Got your own little Christmas Eve manger scene, don't you?"

He shook his head. "That's pretty good. I'll flip the switches, and we'll see if your new Rube Goldberg heating system actually works. You can come over here and watch, if you want to. Not that my telling you that makes any difference."

When he reached the nearest heater, he paused. "Cross your fingers that the old fuse works better than the old hands. Well, cross whatever you've got. There's a spare fuse in the garage, but I'd probably have to call somebody to help me replace it.

"Turning on heater number one. You'll hear the fan."

He steadied the heater with one hand, while he flipped the switch with the other. It hung about eight inches below the rafter, right in front of his nose.

"I'll bet money that I bump into these things a few times before spring. Remind me to duck, okay?"

He waited and watched, then reached for the second heater. "Heater number two coming online. Cross whatever you crossed before. We'll have about six amps on the circuit. Hasn't had that much of a load in years, probably."

He pressed the switch, held up his hand to feel the heat, then retreated to his stool.

"I'll sit with you a little longer, make sure this keeps working. Not too long."

The hen perched on the side of the manger, eyeing him.

"Usually don't stay this long, do I? Getting tired of me?" He shifted uncomfortably. "I'm getting tired of me. At least I get to stay home, mostly. Don't have to do that long commute to the plant anymore. It wasn't so bad, I guess. And it was necessary. Can't be a plant engineer by remote control, and Mother and I wanted a little bit of land. It was worth the commute. And the kids certainly learned to work."

He smiled faintly. "We wanted this little bit of land, with the creek and the mountain view. Didn't know about the neighbors then, but we'd have wanted them too."

He stared at a wall, then slowly arose. He walked up to the two heaters, inspected them once more, followed the extension cord back to the outlet on the wall, and reached out to make sure it was firmly plugged in.

"You know, they say not to plug a heater into an extension cord, but this is a good cord, and these low wattages will be fine. Shouldn't be any risk of fire. And you'll be a little warmer out here all alone. I'll be back later."

He opened the inner and outer doors, stepped carefully over the threshold, and closed them firmly behind him.

A T SUNDOWN HE APPEARED again, carrying a small plastic leftover container full of grain and a silver bucket with two or three inches of steaming water.

"Hey, chicken. Me again."

This time, the hen waited a foot back from the feeder.

He poured the water carefully into the waterer, then put the feed in the feeder. The chicken attacked the feed as soon as he stepped back.

"Okay, little lady, enjoy your dinner." He peered into each nest, looking again for the egg he didn't expect to see. "The heaters seem to be helping, but we'll see how they do when the cold front hits. Both channels pushed its arrival back a couple of hours in their forecasts just now."

He put his hand on the door latch. "Coldest night of the winter tonight. Think warm thoughts, if you think at all. We'll see what Santa brings you when he comes. I'm leaving the light on tonight, for extra heat. Shouldn't bother you too much. Mostly lights the other side. Oh, and it shouldn't keep Santa away. See you in the morning. Merry Christmas!"

The hen may or may not have been listening. She alternately pecked at the grain in the feeder and scratched in the dirty straw on the floor below.

The old man disappeared, shutting the outer door firmly against the impending weather.

*

J UST AFTER SUNRISE THE next morning, he opened the door again.

"Merry Christmas, chicken!"

The hen was on the roost. She didn't move when he entered.

"Hey, it's not too bad in here. Out there it's four degrees, and I don't mean Celsius. Looks like your water froze, but just barely. This will take care of that."

He poured in the warm water, as he had a thousand times before.

"You alive over there?" He looked more carefully. "Yeah, you look like it. No need to wake up yet, if you don't want to. It's Christmas morning at home, just you and me. No children to keep us from sleeping in. There's a luxury."

He put the morning's feed in the feeder, then turned to see the hen blinking at him.

"You're awake. I have a gift for you."

He reached into his coat pocket and pulled out something wrapped in a paper towel.

"Brought you a treat for breakfast. I know how you like cantaloupe rinds, so when Paul and Eileen—they live next door—when they offered to pick up some groceries, I had them bring a cantaloupe. But this is more than the rind. I left half an inch of fruit on it. See? Never did that before, and it was harder than it sounds. So here are two thick slices for your Christmas breakfast."

He unwrapped them, then bent slightly and dropped them carefully onto the straw. "You should get to them before they freeze, because they might." He stuffed the paper towels back into his pocket.

"Ouch!" He shook his hand, then held it up. Two large band-aids on his left index finger were stained red.

The hen watched him.

"Nothing to worry about, but this is why I was late. Sliced my finger when I sliced the cantaloupe. Don't think I need stitches—but if I do, I'm not bothering anyone today. Hurts some. Hurts like the dickens, when I catch it on my pocket like that. Just a little Christmas wound for an old man trying to be an elf. Anyway, there's more cantaloupe where that came from, for dinner tonight and probably a few days after that. I'll just be a little more careful when I cut it."

He watched the hen for a minute.

"Yeah, I should still leave the light on."

He looked around, as he always did before leaving.

"Knew I forgot something. Left my stool here. Thanks for not messing it up for me."

He looked at the hen again, this time in much the same way as she looked at him: head cocked to the side, favoring one eye, motionless.

"Okay with you if I sit for a while? Think I'll move the stool so I can lean on this post."

He fussed at that, trying to find a suitable place. "Can't have a wobbly stool," he muttered.

It took longer than before, but he was patient. Finally he sat. "Pretty stiff from all that work yesterday, but it was worth it. Temperature's not too bad in here."

The hen hopped down and attacked the nearest strip of cantaloupe.

He mumbled, as if talking to himself more than to her.

"Watched a Tabernacle Choir Christmas concert on PBS while I waited for my finger to stop bleeding. It was pretty good. The neighbors' daughter was a dancer in one of those, years ago, when she was at the U. Probably watch some football this afternoon and try to be awake when folks bring leftovers. There's some good cooks on this road."

He fell silent. His head and eyelids drooped.

"Be nice to have the kids here for Christmas," he whispered. "But they can't this year. And the house is such a mess that they probably wouldn't want to. If they came, they'd spend the whole time cleaning. It needs it. I don't have energy for a lot of housework, just like I don't have energy to go see them."

He took a deep breath. "Phone calls are easier. Cheaper than they used to be. Their phone plans have free long distance. International, even. It's incredible. If flying were as easy as calling . . ."

He stared at the wall for a while. The hen moved to the waterer for a drink, then picked at the cantaloupe rind again.

"Good news for you and yours today. No, not glad tidings of great joy. Well, maybe those too, but what I mean is, hardly anyone's eating chicken today. Your people are grossly underrepresented in Christmas dinners. Live nativity scenes too. Don't usually see chickens in those. But you had to be there, right? Some of you probably looked at the baby Jesus the same way you look at me. Wonder if Mary let you perch on the side of the manger."

He chuckled. "Facing the Baby, I hope. They had to launder those swaddling clothes by hand."

He watched the hen until she happened to look toward him.

"Did you hear sleigh bells and reindeer last night?" he asked.

His question hung in the air, unanswered. She drank at the waterer again, then returned to the cantaloupe. He gave the back of his head a good scratch, then blew out a breath.

"The kids used to be happy to do chores on Christmas, even when they were hopped up on too much candy." He shifted on the stool. "I was about to say I never enjoyed those Christmases enough, but that's just a cliché. Truth is, I loved them. Then the kids grew up and went away. Children do that, you know. They come back for visits—the human ones do—but not as often as you want.

"I remember sitting in my easy chair after Christmas dinner, with little Mary on my lap. She didn't want her new toys. She wanted me to read her new books to her. So I did. We must have done that for an hour. When she fell asleep in my arms, I just held the little angel for another hour or more. Mother said I should get up and put her to bed, but I didn't want to.

"Now she reads to her own kids and holds them, I guess. In theory, I could move in with her and read to my grandkids. But this is home, you know?"

He heaved a loud sigh and closed his eyes. When he opened them again, he inspected the bandage on his finger. His gold wedding band caught his eye, and he stared.

"Mother's last Christmas was a lot like the one I told you about, except that I was reading to her, not to Mary. I sat next to her bed, right there in the house, forty yards from here. Read to her until she fell asleep. Then the pain would wake her, and she'd squeeze my hand until it receded a little, and I'd read her to sleep again.

"Did that a lot of days. Nights too, for a while there. On Christmas she wanted me to read from Luke. Second chapter, you know? Didn't have to read it, though. Memorized it when I was a boy."

His eyes closed.

"'And it came to pass in those days, that there went out a decree from Cæsar Augustus, that all the world should be taxed. (And this taxing was first made when Cyrenius was governor of Syria.) And all went to be taxed, every one into his own city.'"

He opened his eyes. The hen was still working on the cantaloupe rind.

"That was more of a census than a tax, you know."

He cleared his throat, then cleared it again.

"'And Joseph also went up from Galilee, out of the city of Nazareth, into Judæa, unto the city of David, which is called Bethlehem (because he was of the house and lineage of David): To be taxed with Mary his espoused wife, being great with child.'

"The Romans would have been fine with him reporting in Nazareth, where they lived, or so I've heard. It was Jewish tradition that sent him back to . . . his home."

He watched the hen hop up onto the roost, then stretched out his left hand and stared at his ring again, blinking back tears.

"His home." The old voice was like gravel. "Anyone you miss at Christmas?"

He sat awhile, staring and blinking, breaking the silence with an occasional sniff. Finally he looked up.

"Enjoy the cantaloupe. There's plenty more where that came from. Guess I already said that. I'd better get back inside."

He stood slowly, then turned to pick up the stool, but didn't. He looked back at the hen.

"Think I'll leave this for a while. You have your own roost. Leave mine alone again, okay? May as well keep using it."

His voice fell nearly to a whisper, too soft to be steady. "Here we are, home for Christmas. Where we belong, I suppose. Home 'til we both shake off this mortal coil. The good people of England and Virginia will have to come to us, when they can."

Old man and old hen stared at each other.

"Almost forgot," he said more firmly. "Last night I came up with one more thing I can do for you. Remember I said you should never give a name to something you plan to eat? I should give you a name, in case you still worry about that sometimes. Let's think of good one this week.

"In the meantime, Merry Christmas. See you tonight. At least I can travel this far."

Hinges squealed and creaked, and old man disappeared into the winter chill.

Christmasing with Preet

T HERE WERE 104 ROOMS—THE sign called them "smart apartments"—in Verdant Meadows, the largest assisted living facility in town. So Alli made 104 identical holiday decorations to pin to the small, eye-level bulletin boards on the residents' doors.

She worked for hours with her colored pencils, until she had drawn a poinsettia she could bear to have people see. She scanned it, arranged four identical images on a page, and added two words beneath each image in a legible but noticeably festive typeface: "Happy Holidays!"

She'd planned for the message to be "Merry Christmas," but the manager of Verdant Meadows mentioned that about one in four residents didn't celebrate Christmas. So she changed it. She didn't want to offend a single person, let alone 26 strangers, with her signature good deed at Christmas. That would ruin the feeling.

She used her mother's photo printer with a glossy photo paper, inspected each page for printing glitches, then meticulously cut the pages into quarter-sheets with a paper cutter. That way the cuts would be neat and the size uniform, and the decorations would stack beautifully until she and the other girls passed them out. She printed and cut one extra sheet, so she'd have two spares, plus one to keep for herself and one to enclose in her thank-you letter to the manager for giving his permission.

She'd been smiling ever since she finished her drawing. As her preparations neared completion, her smile grew. So did the warm Christmas feeling inside her. She wasn't just using her artistic gift at Christmas, which was already a happy thing. She was also using her gift for organization to give her artistic creation to a hundred people or more—and to help the other girls get a warm Christmas feeling too, by making it possible for them to help.

It was also nice that she could probably use this in the Volunteer Service section of her scholarship and college applications, and maybe some other things. But the feeling mattered more.

Just the thought of spending time with old people made her squeamish, so she planned for the hour before dinner on the Saturday before Christmas. Most residents and staff would be in the ballroom, enjoying a Christmas concert by musicians from the local community college. It was the big event of the season, the manager had said, except for Christmas dinner on actual Christmas. A lot of the residents' families would attend with their loved ones.

It was a perfect plan. She and the other girls could avoid actually meeting anyone as they made their rounds.

She'd invited and reminded seven girls from church, and most of them would come. People tended to show up when she invited them. One or two girls could take each of the four wings, and they'd be in and out in less than half an hour.

She arrived early, ten minutes before the concert would start, if it was on time. Ten minutes after the concert began, she and the other girls would divide and conquer. Meanwhile she sat on a bench outside the main entrance and watched families arrive, plus a couple of musicians with instruments in black cases, who hurried as if they were late.

The decorations and push pins were in four Ziploc bags in case of weather, but the sky was clear with no breeze. There was snow on the ground but not the roads or sidewalks. The sun had just set, but her hands, feet, ears, and face were nearly as warm as her heart.

She heard music when the front doors opened to admit an especially cheerful batch of visitors. Her smart phone said 5:02 p.m. At 5:03 p.m. she saw a familiar figure approaching from the parking lot.

"Preet," she whispered to herself, and had an embarrassing flashback. The first time she'd met Preet at church, a few years ago, she'd asked, "Is that a foreign name? Are you from someplace foreign?"

"It's Hindu," Preet had said.

"Are you from . . . where's Hindu? Do you speak Hinduese or something?"

By now she knew, of course, that they speak Hindu in India. Preet was from Montana. She didn't look Indian, but Alli had never seen anyone from anywhere who looked like Preet.

She was too tall, too thin, and too pale, almost albino, though the mild winter chill had painted some faint color on her face. Her hair was strawberry blonde, cut to shoulder length, with curls at the bottom. Her gray winter coat was too grown up for any girl under 30, at least. It hung open now, revealing Preet's typical ensemble: black jeans and a gray tee shirt, with gray sneakers to match. She wasn't beautiful, but she was certainly exotic, which sounded nicer than strange, and her clothing was a perfect gray/black frame for her coloring.

Preet already wore the facemask the manager insisted they wear indoors. It was black too. It made her gray eyes seem big and expressive, sort of like Alli's colorful holiday Disney mask made her own brown eyes sparkle when she looked in the mirror.

Alli said hi, Preet said hi, and Alli invited her to share the bench while they waited for the others. Preet sat, then just shrugged when Alli thanked her for coming. Preet was that way at church and school too. She showed up, but whatever the group was, and whatever they were doing, she kept to the fringes of it and didn't say much.

At 5:10 p.m., Alli's planned starting time, there was no group, just Alli and Preet. The warm Christmas feeling in Alli's heart was slipping away. She sent a text message to the other six. "We'll wait ten more minutes," she wrote. She tried to suppress her disappointment and, if she admitted the truth, her anger at the other girls for being late and not telling her.

Four of the six didn't reply. One said sorry, she was sick. The other said sorry, she still wasn't back from her grandma's house in another city.

By 5:20 the warm feeling was pretty much gone, but the good deed still had to be done. "I guess we can't wait anymore," Alli said. "It's just you and me."

In the lobby she handed Preet two of the four stacks. "I'll take A and B wings, and you take C and D, okay?"

"Okay," said Preet. It was her first word since saying hi.

"We don't have time to knock or stop and talk, and most of them will be at the concert anyway. Just pin it to the little bulletin boards as fast as you can. Leave room for other stuff above it."

"Okay."

Each side of each corridor had thirteen numbered doors, with even numbers on one side and odd on the other, but skipping #13, probably for the same reason they skipped the 13th floor in some of the tall buildings Alli had been in.

Alli did the odd side of A Wing from the near end to the far end, then did the even side on her way back. She did the same in B wing. Preet's longer legs must have made her faster, because she appeared when Alli still had four doors left.

"I'm done," Preet said. "You were right. I didn't see anyone at all." Preet made it sound like a sad thing.

Alli couldn't remember hearing so many words come out of Preet's mouth at once. Maybe she was excited about Christmas. Her face still had a cheery glow that reached beyond her mask—but it didn't reach Alli's disappointed heart.

"Thanks for helping me, Preet. You're the only one who came."

"Except you."

"True," said Alli.

"Here, I'll help you finish." Preet reached out her hand, and Alli gave her two of the remaining decorations.

As Preet reached to put the last decoration on the last door, it opened. She started and made a little noise.

"May I help you?" said a slow, deep, gruff male voice. Alli couldn't see the voice's owner.

"Oh, hi," said Preet. "Merry Christmas. We're putting this little decoration on everyone's door. Is it okay if I put it on yours?"

"Let me see it."

Alli imagined the man nodding.

"Go ahead. Thank you," he said. "I'll close my door now. Good evening."

As the door latch clicked, Preet looked at Alli with raised eyebrows, then turned back to the door and pinned the decoration.

They stopped out front to take off their masks, put on their gloves, and button up their coats. The sun was long gone, and a breeze had come up.

"Thanks for coming when no one else did," Alli said. "I guess I said that already."

"I'm glad I could help," Preet said. "This is a nice thing. And you did most of the work. Did you draw the flowers? They're beautiful."

Alli felt oddly self-conscious. "Yes."

"I always like your art," Preet said. "I wish I could draw."

"Thanks. Do you want to go out for ice cream or something? If you have time?"

Preet surveyed the winter scene around them. "Now? Ice cream?"

"Hot chocolate?" Alli asked.

"That sounds nice," Preet said, "but I have to go somewhere."

Preet's response disappointed Alli more than it should have, considering her offer was just a required gesture to thank the one girl who came to help. Something must have shown on her face, because then something showed on Preet's.

"Do you want to come with me?" Preet asked. "I'm going to—"

"Yes," Alli said, then blushed at her sudden eagerness.

Preet smiled faintly. "I'm going to visit an old lady on my street. She's usually kind of cranky. You can come with me, if you want."

"What are you doing there?"

"We talk, and I read to her. Could be half an hour. You don't have to come."

"You came to my thing. I want to come to yours."

"Okay. You can park your car at my house, and we'll drive to her place together."

Preet's tiny car seemed like it should be too small for its tall driver, but it wasn't. They drove at least a mile past Preet's house, Alli guessed, to a neighborhood where the houses were a lot bigger and nicer than Preet's, even though it was the same street. They parked in the driveway of a house that was all steep angles and beautiful stonework. It was dark, except for the porch light.

"Who is this woman?" Alli asked.

"She's the midwife who delivered me."

"Seriously?"

"She and my mom became friends. She delivered my little brother too. She used to come to our house for dinner sometimes, and some holidays, but she doesn't get out much anymore."

Alli was having second thoughts. "How old is she?"

"You should ask her that," Preet said.

"I don't think so. What would she say?"

"Probably something like 'still well south of a century.' I think she's almost eighty. She's blind now, and she lost most of the feeling in her hands, so she can't read Braille, and she doesn't walk very well. I think she has depression too. I don't really see how she could help it. But we won't say anything about that to her."

Alli resisted the temptation to stare. Why was Preet never this talkative before?

Preet knocked loudly at the door. There was no response. She bent to pick up three small gifts from the step, the sort of things neighbors gave their neighbors at Christmas.

"Here, hold these," Preet said.

There were two small plates of cookies, one covered in festive cellophane and one in everyday plastic wrap. The third item was roughly the size, shape, and weight of a brick. It was a loaf of the much-loved pumpkin bread from a local bakery, frozen solid. The ink on the tag had run. That must have been before it froze.

"Are we taking them? Isn't that stealing?"

"We're not taking them." Preet knocked again, then startled Alli by calling loudly through the door. "Mrs. Gunther, it's Preet. I brought a friend with me, but she's nice."

Preet turned to Alli. "I think the speaker's broken again."

A bolt clicked. "It's electronic," Preet explained, and opened the door. "She uses voice commands. Come on in." Preet switched on a light in the entryway.

A sour, citrusy odor assaulted their nostrils. They looked at each other and cringed.

"Preet?" called a gruff voice from somewhere further in.

"Hi, Mrs. Gunther. I brought my friend Alli. We just did a Christmas thing together."

"I don't celebrate Christmas."

Preet turned to Alli and spoke gruffly, under her breath. "She doesn't celebrate Christmas."

Alli suppressed a giggle, and Preet's face broke into a smile Alli didn't remember seeing before.

"I heard that," said the woman. "Hang your coats by the door, take off your shoes if they're wet or snowy, and turn on a couple of lights so you don't trip over something. I'm in my chair."

Her chair was a large, leather recliner which dominated—Alli didn't know what to call it. Did people with big houses have sitting rooms? Mrs. Gunther herself was a white-haired, medium-large mass of wrinkles and splotches, huddled under a red-and-blue plaid blanket.

Preet introduced Alli as a girl from church, and Mrs. Gunther extended a hand that seemed nothing but skin and bones. "Tell me what you look like, Alli."

Alli squeezed the old hand gently and let go. "I, uh, I'm about six inches shorter than Preet, almost as thin. My hair's light brown. It's pretty curly. My eyes are darker brown. That's about it, I guess."

"Thank you," said Mrs. Gunther. "Now ask me why I don't celebrate Christmas."

Alli looked at Preet, who shrugged.

"Why don't you celebrate Christmas, Mrs. Gunther?" Alli asked. "Are you Jewish?"

"I'm no more Jewish than you are."

"Then why not?"

"It's too commercial. The Christmas holiday should be a holy day, but now it's turned into a whole season for spending more than you can afford on gifts for people who mostly don't need or appreciate them anyway. That's why I don't celebrate Christmas. It's too commercial.

"And Preet," she continued, "I didn't answer you the first time because I thought you were just one of the neighbors or one of the people from some church. They keep bringing me stuff, and if I don't let them in, they leave it at the door."

"I'm glad you let us in," Preet said.

"I suppose there was more stuff at the door, and I suppose you brought it in."

"Two small plates of cookies and a loaf of bakery pumpkin bread. The pumpkin bread is frozen solid."

"I can't eat the cookies," Mrs. Gunther said. "Too much refined sugar. Some of the neighbors should know that. You take them. One plate for each of you. If you don't want them, just throw them away."

"Thank you," said Preet.

"Thank you," echoed Alli.

"I suppose you noticed the lovely stench," said Mrs. Gunther.

"What is it?" asked Preet.

"Some of them brought me fruit the other day. I think it must have been two weeks ago last Friday. They caught me off guard and I let them in, and they left it on my counter. I ate an apple or two, but some oranges fell and rolled away, I think. They must be rotting somewhere, and I'm too helpless to find them."

Preet looked at Alli. "You stay here and read to Mrs. Gunther," she said. "I'll take care of the fruit."

"You shouldn't have to do stinky chores for an old woman," said Mrs. Gunther.

"I don't mind," said Preet. "What are you reading today?"

"Still working on Dante's *Inferno*. Do you think your friend reads well enough to handle that?"

"I'm a pretty good reader," Alli said. "I'll do my best."

"Thanks," said Preet, and disappeared.

Mrs. Gunther handed Alli a thick, hardback book. "The place is marked."

Alli opened to the marked page and was dismayed to see that it was poetry. She read silently through the first few lines, to see if she could read it at all, then began.

> UPON the margin of a lofty bank
> Which great rocks broken in a circle made,
> We came upon a still more cruel throng;
> And there, by reason of the horrible
> Excess of stench the deep abyss throws out,
> We drew ourselves aside behind the cover
> Of a great tomb . . .

As she read, Alli heard chairs, then something heavier, scrape across the floor in another room. She thought of asking Preet if she needed help, but she wanted to keep reading, so Mrs. Gunther wouldn't complain when she stopped.

She did stop reading when Preet appeared in the doorway. "I found the problem," Preet said. "Two oranges rolled under that little table by the window in the dining room. They were sitting on the heat vent."

"No wonder they're rotten," said Mrs. Gunther. "They stunk up the whole house."

"They were kind of gross," Preet said lightly. "Don't you have someone who comes in to help you every day?"

"Her mother's visiting from Boston. I gave her two days off."

"That's nice of you," said Preet.

"She'll be back in the morning," Mrs. Gunther said. "The stench has only been the last couple of days."

"I can't just leave rotten oranges in the kitchen garbage," Preet said. "I'll take it all out and replace the bag."

"Thank you, dear. I'm sorry you have to do this."

"I don't mind. I'm just glad I found them. Oh, I found some air freshener too."

Mrs. Gunther nodded. "Alli, please continue."

Alli resumed reading, trying not to visualize any of it in her head.

> A death by violence, and painful wounds,
> Are to our neighbour given; and in his substance
> Ruin, and arson, and injurious levies;
> Whence homicides, and he who smites unjustly,
> Marauders, and freebooters, the first round
> Tormenteth all in companies diverse.[1]

It was challenging enough that Alli didn't notice the minutes passing until Mrs. Gunther interrupted.

"Young lady, if you don't mind, would you please set down the book for a minute and go see what's taking Preet so long?"

Alli obeyed. The next room had a piano in it. The one after that was a dining room, and beyond it a large, well-lit kitchen. There was no sign of Preet.

"Preet?"

"Down here!" Her voice was muffled.

Alli stepped all the way into the kitchen, then stopped short. Preet's head and shoulders were in the cupboard under the large sink. There was a small white garbage bag, obviously full, on the floor at either hip. The smell was a lot worse in here, and it wasn't just rotting oranges.

"What are you doing?"

Preet emerged from the cupboard and slipped something that looked foul into one of the garbage bags. "Cinch that closed, would you please?" She stood and began to wash her grimy hands at the sink.

Alli made a face, when Preet couldn't see it, but she took two reluctant steps forward, reached down, and cinched the bag closed. It was clean enough on the outside, but the stench of the contents made her queasy.

"How's Dante going?" Preet asked.

"Difficult. Grim. I think it's about hell. She sent me in here to see what's taking so long."

"Tell her I spilled some garbage, and it took a minute to clean it up."

"More like she spilled some garbage, and it took you ten minutes to clean it up."

"I spilled a little too, but tell her what you want. I'll take these outside and come spell you with Dante. I don't like it either.

Check her water, please, and bring it for a refill if it's mostly empty. She never wants it more than half full, or it's too heavy."

Back in the sitting room, Alli explained, "Preet spilled some garbage and had to clean it up. She's taking it all out. She'll be right back."

When Preet appeared in the doorway again, she held an orange in each hand. "Mrs. Gunther, two of these oranges are good. Shall I slice them for you? Are you hungry?"

"You don't need to bother."

"Are you sure? They're beautiful. It would be sad to waste them."

"Do what you will," said Mrs. Gunther.

Preet disappeared.

The old lady said, "You watch. She'll slice them neatly and serve them on a plate, arranged just so. Your friend is kind but not very obedient."

"Oh, she's not—" Alli stopped. "She pretty much does things her own way."

Mrs. Gunther grunted.

"She said you delivered her. Do you know why they named her Preet?"

"I did, but that was many years ago."

"Seventeen, I think," said Alli.

Mrs. Gunther's blind eyes gave Alli a look, which was creepy. "It's a Hindu name, but she's not Hindu. I seem to recall that her parents were honoring a friend or neighbor or some such person."

"What does it mean?"

"You should ask her."

There was a beeping sound from the kitchen. Mrs. Gunther grunted. "What's that silly girl doing? You don't slice oranges with a microwave."

"Want me to go find out?" Alli asked.

"No. Read me some more Dante, please. She'll be back soon enough."

Alli cringed but resumed reading.

After a few more minutes, Preet appeared with a platter of sliced oranges and pumpkin bread, along with napkins and three small plates. She filled one of the small plates.

"Mrs. Gunther, there are four orange slices to the right. I removed the peels and the little weird bit in the center. To the left is a thick slice of pumpkin bread, cut in half. It was frozen, but it thawed okay. Now it's warm. Here's a napkin too, and there's more of everything."

"You go to too much trouble, Preet."

"You need to eat, Mrs. Gunther."

Preet and the blind old woman somehow shared a look which Alli couldn't decipher. She reminded herself that Mrs. Gunther hadn't always been blind. And maybe she wasn't completely blind.

"Thank you," said Mrs. Gunther. "Let's have your friend keep reading, please. She does tolerably well."

The compliment pleased Alli, even if the poetry didn't. As she read, she managed a few glances at Mrs. Gunther, who ate carefully but hungrily. Preet ate too, then took over the reading so Alli could eat.

When Preet stopped reading to separate two pages that were stuck together, Mrs. Gunther sounded almost shy. "Alli, could you please serve me another slice of pumpkin bread? And a few more orange slices, if there are any left?"

When only a single bite of pumpkin bread remained on her plate, she reached out and found Preet's arm. "Preet, dear, that's enough Dante. I can't concentrate anymore."

Alli did her best to hide her relief from Preet. Poetry about hell had given her the opposite of a warm Christmas feeling.

"Would you like me to take your plate?" Preet asked Mrs. Gunther.

"Yes, please."

"Here, let me get a couple of crumbs too." Preet deftly picked a few large crumbs from the front of Mrs. Gunther's sweatshirt, then took everyone's plates and napkins to the kitchen.

Mrs. Gunther didn't say a word to Alli while Preet was gone. Alli tried to think of something to say but couldn't. She hadn't felt this helpless in a conversation for a long time. At least the dark, heavy effect of reading Dante was starting to fade.

When they heard Preet's footsteps, the old woman finally spoke. "Alli?"

"Yes?"

"You read reasonably well for a high school student."

"Thanks," said Alli.

Mrs. Gunther nodded slowly, and Preet was back.

"Mrs. Gunther, we finished the oranges, and I sliced the rest of the pumpkin bread and put it in the fridge. It's at the front of the second shelf from the top, to the right. I'll come back tomorrow, and if it's still there, I'll help you eat the rest of it. I lit a candle earlier in the kitchen to help with the odor, but I just put it out, so you don't have to worry about that."

"I don't have any candles," said Mrs. Gunther.

"It was with some of the Christmas stuff on your counter. A Christmas candle."

Alli thought Mrs. Gunther nodded, but it turned out she was nodding off. The girls shared a glance, and Preet looked at the old woman, smiling gently.

"Good night, Mrs. Gunther," Preet whispered. Then her look turned mischievous. "Merry Christmas, Mrs. Gunther."

The old woman's blanket had slid down to her lap. Alli gently pulled it up to cover her arms and shoulders.

"Good night," Alli whispered. "Merry Christmas."

They showed themselves out.

"I can't believe you did all that yucky cleanup," Alli said as they walked down Mrs. Gunther's sidewalk. "Her maid or nurse or whatever will be back in the morning. And why did you slice the oranges when she told you not to? She said you would."

They stopped at Preet's car. Preet looked almost sad. "Most days, all she eats is her Meals on Wheels that comes at noon."

"Oh."

"Those are probably enough, I think, but today's and yesterday's were still in the fridge. They come with a little card that lists the date and everything in the container. I couldn't see that she'd touched any of it."

"She didn't eat for two days?"

"At least," Preet said. "Eating is hard for her. If no one's there to help her, she usually just doesn't. She gets up to refill her water, when she's thirsty enough."

Alli didn't know what to say. No, she knew one thing. "What does your name mean?"

Even by the streetlight she saw the tall girl's cheeks color. "Is that important?"

"She said I should ask."

Preet nodded but didn't reply.

Suddenly Alli had plenty of words. "It should mean Christmas. What you just did is a thousand times better than my Christmas project."

"You made 104 people's Christmas a little nicer, plus their visitors," Preet said, "and what you drew for them is beautiful. It was a good project."

Alli felt a flicker of Christmas warmth, but it didn't last. "Thanks. Do you know why it was 104?"

"Because that's how many rooms there are at Verdant Meadows?"

"Because I picked the care facility with the most rooms in it."

"So you helped more people."

"I picked it because I thought a three-digit number would look better on my application for that big service scholarship. Maybe in my college application essays too. And the more people I got to help me, the better it would look, but then it was only us two."

"It was still a good thing."

"Yeah," Alli said drily. "So good that I did my best to avoid actually seeing anyone while we padded my resume by looking like we were helping old people."

"It was good, Alli. You shared your talent."

Alli sighed. "Thanks."

They drove back to Preet's home in silence. Alli spent the time comparing herself to Preet. She couldn't imagine what Preet was thinking.

When they arrived, before Alli got into her own car, she turned to Preet. "Thanks again for coming to my little project." She huffed softly. "No one else did."

"You're welcome. It was fun. Thanks for helping me with Mrs. Gunther. That's less fun, I guess. Dante in particular."

Alli smiled in spite of herself. "Spilled garbage and rotten fruit in particular. If you want some company sometime, when you visit her, I wouldn't mind going with you again."

Preet nodded. "Okay. Merry Christmas, Alli. You deserve it."

"Merry Christmas, Preet."

Preet waited until Alli was in her car with the engine started, then gave a little wave and turned up the sidewalk toward the door.

Alli rolled down her window. "Preet?"

Preet turned.

"You never told me what your name means."

Alli thought she saw Preet's cheeks color again in the porch light.

"Look it up." Preet waved and slipped into her house.

"Well, I asked," Alli murmured to herself as she pressed the brake pedal and slipped her car into reverse. She thought of Preet wishing the old man at Verdant Meadows a merry Christmas, Preet emerging from under Mrs. Gunther's kitchen sink, Preet picking a few crumbs off the old woman's sweatshirt—and Preet thanking Alli for helping her.

"I helped some," she told herself, and felt a little better inside.

Her foot was still on the brake. She shifted back into Park and reached for her phone. "Meaning name Preet," she typed into the browser's search box.

She tapped on the first two results. "Happy or joyful," said one. "Beloved. Peace, harmony, love," said the other.

She set her phone on the passenger seat and reached for the gear shift lever again. "Like I said," she mused aloud, "Preet means Christmas."

---

1. Canto XI, Henry Wadsworth Longfellow translation.

Keep My Secrets?

I FROZE WHEN MOM knocked. "Feel like driving to the airport?" she asked through my bedroom door.

"Why would I want to?" It seemed like a reasonable question.

She turned the knob but only cracked the door. "Because no matter how old you are, Mike, or how far away you go to school, I'm still your mother. May I open the door?"

I was home for the holidays, currently wrapping Dad's Christmas gifts for Mom—which I was bad at, but he was worse. The real secret, if she could have seen it, was in my head. I was thinking about expanding the little business my parents didn't know I ran at school, if I could do it without my grades slipping or someone ratting me out to the university. Demand exceeded my supply, even at the high end.

I buried the last unwrapped gift. "It's safe."

The door swung open. "Dad's at work, Mallory's helping me, I'm up to my armpits in cookie dough, and Jill's flight lands in 30 minutes. Meanwhile, Kathy's by the side of the road, waiting for a tow truck." Her voice turned tired. "That's why you want to, smart aleck. But mostly the mother thing."

I smiled. "Okay already. You had me at tow truck."

Her eyebrows arched. "Not at Jill?"

I shrugged. Jill was Kathy's daughter, Kathy was Mom's best friend, we were neighbors, and Jill and I had been friends since we were toddlers. We had one of those comfortable friendships you could pick up where you left off, after a month or a year. The thought of seeing her for the first time since last Christmas made me a little nervous, and our first minute might be awkward, but then it would be like old times.

"Thanks," Mom said, and closed the door.

I was downstairs in ten minutes. It would have been three, but . . . Jill. A guy has to have some pride.

I stole a sugar cookie. "Can I take the 4Runner?"

"You may. Keys are in the cupboard. Stop for lunch, if she's hungry. Use the card."

"Matchmaking again, Mom?"

"Feeding my neighbor's offspring. And my own. You turning down free food now?"

"Just asking. Anything for you and Mal?"

"No, thanks." Her smile was mischievous and smug. "You clean up nice."

"THIS IS LIKE RELIVING our first date," Jill said from across our tiny table at a trendy, socially-aware sandwich shop I thought she'd like. "Only the food's better. And you're not wearing that silly velour shirt you thought all us girls would want to touch."

I could laugh at the distant past. Her relaxed, girl-next-door smile helped. She looked older, but her green eyes hadn't changed, and her hair was still what she called "honey blonde."

"Hey, it was my first date," I said. "What did I know? You thought you weren't pretty enough, so you masked that tiny birthmark on your cheek. Never saw you do that before."

"I was masking the not-so-tiny prelude to a zit," she said, "and I thought, why not try for normal? Besides, it was my first date too. What did I know?" She smiled distantly. "I did want to touch your shirt. For it, not you."

"And I've always thought you were pretty, with or without the birthmark. Like now."

She looked concerned. "Are you coming on to me?"

"No, much as our mothers would like that. Did you want me to?"

"No, thanks."

I grinned. "So it really is like our first date."

She smiled too. "Our only date. I'm singing in Church on Sunday. You'll be there, right?"

"Usually not, but I can't stay home on Christmas. Don't want that topic over Christmas dinner. But now I can look forward to it."

"What happened? You were the most committed church-going boy I knew."

"Topic for another day," I said.

"You mean that, or you just don't want to talk about it?"

"Does it matter?"

"It does to me," she said. "And it's not just you. I'm stuck too. At least you're at a state school. I somehow picked a church school, where chronically missing church is not an option."

"You went for the music scholarship," I said. "Seems like *you* want to talk about things."

"I kind of do, but not today. Short night, long week." She cocked her head. "Do you want to talk about things?"

"Just you and me? Yeah, I'd like that."

She swallowed the last bite of her sandwich and wiped her mouth and fingers. "Here's an idea. I have Christmas shopping to finish tomorrow. And start, technically."

"Me too."

"Let's go shopping together," she said. "Lunch will be on me. Our parents will think it's something else, but we'll just be two old, platonic friends, platonically shopping and lunching together. Pick you up at 10:00?"

At BREAKFAST THE NEXT morning, Dad, Mom, and my sister Mallory all got the family twinkle, when I said Jill and I were going shopping for a few hours. I ignored them. Ten minutes later, Jill sent a text.

"Mike, not good. Sore throat, headache. Maybe sick, or too little sleep for too many consecutive nights. If I want to sing tomorrow, I have to rest today. Also avoid cold air and not talk. So sorry!"

"I'm sorry too," I replied. "Is your shopping something I can do while I'm out?"

"Are you sure?"

"Small price to hear you sing tomorrow."

"Some of it's pretty feminine. But I'm singing twice, so it might be worth it. You're sweet!"

"Then I'm your elf. List, please."

"Thanks! Let's still get together before we leave, okay? Been thinking how much I miss that."

Her shopping went smoothly enough. The most feminine adventure was lotions for her mom at Victoria's Secret, but I handled that okay. Got some extra too.

A T 8:00 A.M. ON Christmas I texted her. "Merry Christmas! Please say you're in good voice and feeling well."

She called me back. "Merry Christmas! Yesterday helped a lot. I'm rehearsing in a minute."

"What are you singing?"

"'The First Noel' and a new song by my roommate Heather. She wrote the words too. They're in the program. This morning is the world premiere. Hope you like it. Both, actually."

"I will. Break a leg."

S HE SANG "THE FIRST Noel" early in the program. Her rich mezzosoprano was clear and powerful, without sounding too operatic or too Broadway for church. She didn't use or need a microphone, and I didn't hear one false note. The big crescendo in the last chorus all but blew me away.

I texted her: "Gorgeous! Powerful!"

She sent a smiley.

While the program plodded on, I read and reread the words of the new song. It seemed pretty ordinary until I heard it.

Kathy's piano accompaniment was sparse but beautiful. Jill's voice was different from before—still strong enough to fill the chapel, but meeker and simpler somehow. I wondered how good she had to be to make it sound so natural and so flawless too.

By then her roommate's words were familiar.

When I think about the manger,
Cradle of the infant King,
I'd approach it, though a stranger,
Bringing lullabies to sing.

When I think about the mother,
Blesséd Mary, in that place,
I would bring her cooling water,
She who bore God's Gift of grace.

When I think of gentle Joseph,
Guarding Mary, guarding Him,
I would bid him rest an hour,
While I watched by candle dim.

When I think about the shepherds,
Summoned by an angel throng,
I would join them, kneel in wonder,
Learn to sing a Shepherd song.

When I think about my Savior,
Born and died a lowly Lamb,
I would praise Him, follow, serve Him,
Offer everything I am.

The last two lines repeated, almost:

I will praise Him, follow, serve Him,
Give Him everything I am.

Even the children near me were still, as her voice and then the piano faded to silence. I sneaked a sideward glance. Dad looked pensive; Mom and Mallory had tears in their eyes.

I, for once, didn't mind being in church.

After the service Mom and Mallory gushed to Jill about her singing. Then Mom and Kathy decided our families would get together at our house for dessert after Christmas dinner.

* * *

"CHERRY PIE IS THE best," Jill said. We were all in our big living room. She and I were on the love seat, but not snuggling or anything. She set her plate on the coffee table and leaned back.

"You ate like three bites," I said.

"I'll finish after I sing. Then I'll need seconds."

"We're making you sing for your dessert?"

"I love to sing."

"Works for me," I said.

Kathy played our piano, and Jill sang the same two songs by Mom's request. Even when she sang only loud enough to fill the living room, her voice was strong and steady, then tender and soft but not weak. It pulled at my heart.

She listened graciously, while Mom and Mallory gushed again, and she told them about her roommate, when they asked.

Mom shifted gears without warning. "Jill, Mike, it's unseasonably warm outside. You should take a walk."

Kathy nodded her approval.

Jill and I traded knowing glances. "Pie or walk?" I asked.

"Both," she said. "I'll finish this, then we can walk. Then more pie."

"**H**OW MUCH OF WHAT you sang do you really believe?" I asked, as we rounded the first corner. It was too warm to see our breath.

"I don't know what I believe anymore," she said. "I don't disbelieve everything. Why do you ask?"

"When you sing, I want to believe. You're very convincing. Then the song ends."

She smiled shyly. "I'm a singer. I sing what they put in front of me, and I sing it as well as I can. But like I said, I don't disbelieve everything."

"That new song's amazing," I said.

"Heather's amazing. She mostly composes for orchestra. She's headed somewhere big for a master's program in composition next year. Juilliard, Curtis, Manhattan maybe. Big."

"Her roommate's amazing too," I said. "You could sing my fast food receipts, and it would be beautiful. Do you have a fan club? I want to run for president."

I could see her color by the streetlamp. "You're overdoing it a little, maybe?"

"Maybe about the fan club," I said. "Not about your voice."

She took my arm. "Today's Sunday. Tuesday we visit crazy Aunt Tonya, and I fly back on Wednesday for some weekend gigs. Can we do our long lunch tomorrow?"

S HE TOOK ME TO a French café for a fancy four-course meal. I couldn't pronounce anything, but she was happy to help. Three years of high school French, another in college, and last summer in Paris had her sounding pretty French to me.

We made small talk about shopping and gifts. The first course was cooked vegetables served cold with a vinaigrette, which I liked more than I thought I would.

She speared her last zucchini slice with her fork, and the small talk was over. "Any girl would be lucky to nab you for a boyfriend," she said.

"Are you coming on to me?"

There was something soft about her smile. "No. I'm already lucky you're my friend. I can't spare you in that role."

"Even after a year of not seeing each other?" I asked.

"We've always been friends." She hesitated. "Did you want me to come on to you?"

I answered carefully. "If our schools were closer, and we wouldn't be a total cliché, and you didn't already know me too well, you wouldn't be my last choice."

"That's a lot of *if*s. Would I be next to last?"

"Way better than that."

Since Sunday I'd been having a few small second thoughts, wondering if the impossible could ever be possible.

"What are you not telling me?" she asked.

I didn't answer immediately, but she waited. She always knew when to do that.

Finally I said, "Two things, I guess."

When I didn't continue, she asked, "What two things?"

"The first thing I want in a girlfriend is a friend as good as you. Haven't met one yet."

"You will," she said.

Our entrées arrived. Mine was something delicious they'd done with chicken. Hers was beef, and when I sampled it, I loved it too. We ended up sharing both.

She set her knife and fork on her empty plate. "May I confess something?"

"To me? Always."

"I measure guys against you." A wry smile flashed across her face and disappeared. "Haven't found the right one yet."

"You will," I said. "Besides, I'm not that good. That's my second thing. I'm not a very good person at all. Speaking of confessions."

"What are you talking about? You did a girl's Christmas shopping for her, in some very girly places. You donate plasma every month. I've known you forever. You've always been one of the good guys."

"Keep my secrets?" I asked quietly.

"Of course."

"I lied about donating plasma."

"O–kay," she said slowly. "But you didn't lie to me. I heard that from your mom. Lying to her isn't good, if you did."

"Yeah."

"Why is not donating plasma important?"

"I lied so they wouldn't be suspicious that I always have a little extra money. More than they realize, and they would hate the source."

She stared at me. "You cannot possibly be a drug dealer."

"No."

"Or a male prostitute."

"No."

"Or a human trafficker."

"No."

"Then what would they hate?"

"I sell papers."

She cocked her head and studied me. "You mean like school papers? Term papers?"

"Yeah."

"You write for one of those sleazy online services?"

"Those are a rip-off," I said. "Too easy to get caught. I ghost-write original papers to order. I even customize them to the person's voice. I charge top dollar. There are some desperately lazy rich guys out there."

She grimaced. "Wow."

"They'll kick me out of school if they find out. I'll be lucky to get into any school after that."

"But the money's worth the risk?"

"Has been."

"How'd you get into that? I mean, I know you can write."

"I started helping people write their own papers, but that's too much work for some of them. Some guys. No women."

"Why not?"

"Too complicated. It's easy not to care what guys think about me, but I'm afraid I'll start to care what some girl thinks."

I already cared what one girl thought of me. That girl was staring at her plate.

She looked up. "That's not good."

"It's called academic fraud, I think."

"They'd get kicked out too?"

"Probably, especially if they did it more than once."

"Do they?"

"It's mostly repeat business, and there's plenty. I write at least three short papers a week, or one long. Just for English and GE classes."

"How much?"

"Short papers, $500. They take maybe half a day. Long ones, $1500, and a couple of days, give or take."

"Holy crap," she murmured.

"Like I said, lazy rich guys."

She stared at her plate again. "Well, it's not like you're a serial killer or a drug dealer."

"More like a male prostitute," I said.

"Not even that, Mike."

"But you're not pleased."

She met my eyes. "No."

Dessert arrived, some fruit that was out of season but perfect.

After a few bites, I stopped and took a deep breath. "What I didn't say before is, if I were good enough for you or even close, I'd hit on you. You're . . ." I shrugged. "You're you."

"Believe it or not, that's debatable." She smiled sadly. "I'm not so good either."

"So you're not sure you believe what they say you have to believe to go to that school. And maybe you wouldn't go to church if you didn't have to. My thing, any school would kick me out. Your thing, hardly any other school would care."

She frowned, and her chin trembled.

"Sorry to disappoint you," I said. "I won't blame you if we can't be friends anymore."

Her eyes looked troubled. "Can we go now?" She hadn't finished her fruit.

"I can get an Uber, if you'd rather."

She shook her head. "You're with me."

She paid the check, and neither of us spoke.

When she pulled us into the empty lot of a neighborhood park and turned off the engine, we still didn't speak. We just stared straight ahead.

She finally turned to me. "Mike, I'm a fraud too." I hadn't heard her voice so unsteady since she broke her arm when we were six.

"You can't fake singing like an angel."

"That part's real." Her voice broke. "And thanks."

It was my turn to wait. My heart began to ache for her instead of myself.

"Promise you'll keep my secret, Mike?"

"You don't even have to ask."

She nodded. "I know. I might hit on you, except for one thing nobody knows. Except you, in a minute."

I tried not to imagine.

"I'm not all that interested in guys," she said. "I'm not . . . physically attracted . . . to men."

"Are you—"

"Am I attracted to women? Oh, yes."

Somehow my inner turmoil receded. "You'd be all over me, but you play for the other team?"

She winced. "That's a little crass. I'm not in the game yet. But I'm thinking about tryouts." She turned red. "Or the information meeting before tryouts. Something like that."

"They have those?"

"It's your metaphor."

"Right. So . . . goodbye church school, goodbye church?"

"Potentially," she said. "But I don't want to lose my voice teacher or my scholarship. Voice scholarships are hard to get."

"Are you sure you're . . ." I swallowed my half-asked question.

"Yeah. Sorry. Are you shocked?"

"Didn't see this coming."

She gave me a wry smile. "Want to try and talk me out of it?"

"Does it work that way?"

"No. I tried for a long time. Long before our first date. Long after too." She shook her head. "There are some good guys at school. Freshman year, I let some of them kiss me. I tried to be physically attracted. Thought maybe I could at least be bi. This year, I quit trying. I am who I am. I think. Haven't told anyone until you."

"I can't even imagine how tough that is," I said.

"It helps to tell you. Thank you."

Her face crumpled. I reached for her hand, and she clung to mine. I expected sobs, but she just stared straight ahead, looking morose. Now and then a tear rolled down her cheek.

I thought through all the years I'd known her, looking for hints of what she'd just revealed. I found nothing. Then I began to imagine what it was like for her, especially at a church school. And how hard would it be at home? If she came out, would she ever come home again?

She took a deep, ragged breath, and her voice was gruff. "Do you still want to be my friend?" She sniffed twice. "You don't have to. I'll understand."

"Of course I do. Do you still want me for a friend, knowing what you know?"

She looked at me with the same sad expression and nodded. "I love you. As, you know, as a friend. Always have."

"I love you too," I said. "As a friend. Always have."

"Thank you. We should go. It's getting cold." She started the engine. "When we get there, could I have a long hug, please?"

"Long as I get one too."

"That's how it works," she said.

O N MY FRONT PORCH and still in my arms, she said, "You know how you asked if I believed what I sang?"

"Yeah."

"I want to. I just don't see how someone like me fits into all that."

"I don't know either," I confessed. "Wish I did."

"Yeah." She took a deep breath. "I want to be a good person."

"You already are."

"I'm not honest about who I am. But I don't know if I can stop pretending yet, and start jeopardizing . . . everything."

I had nothing to say. No right to have anything to say.

"There's a lot of good in you," she said.

I could change the subject too. "Take you to the airport Wednesday?"

"Our moms will rejoice."

"On the same false pretenses," I said.

"If they think we're more than friends with shopping, lunch, and airport transportation privileges, that's on them," she said. "I've never said we were more."

"Me neither," I said. "But they hope."

"Someday we have to tell them." Her eyes widened. "Not this week."

O VER DINNER MOM AND Mallory traded little smiles, until Mom finally said, "We saw you on the porch with Jill, looking cozy. Anything to tell?"

"Just friends, Mom."

Not *just* friends, I thought. *Friends.*

"Looks to me like you love her," Mallory said. "And she loves you."

I nodded. "As friends."

"Does she have a boyfriend at school?" Mom asked.

"Don't think so," I said.

"Do you have a girl you're not telling us about?"

"Not at the moment," I said.

Mallory took over. "So what's stopping you? She's amazing. And I'm your sister, so you can't be a complete loser."

"We're friends."

"You say so," she said, then changed the subject.

The subject in my head didn't change. I flashed back to Jill saying she'd understand, if I didn't want to be her friend anymore.

I wouldn't understand. And she'd sounded so vulnerable.

"There's a lot of good in you," she'd said.

"That's not good," she'd said before that.

I knew she was right.

O N Tuesday I worked on what to tell my clients, if I decided to quit. They probably wouldn't want just a normal, honest level of tutoring. But they couldn't rat me out without ratting themselves out—and their brothers and their houses. They were all from two fraternities.

I'd probably want to sell the gently-used Lexus SUV I'd bought in August, which my parents didn't know I owned. The payments would be a problem. But I loved my ride. Great electronics.

Heated, air-conditioned seats. It looked great on the road and in a parking lot.

Maybe one more semester. I could finish the school year, not leave my clients hanging, and get ahead some. I'd have an even longer runway if I added a few extra clients.

If I had a clear exit strategy and was executing it, maybe Jill wouldn't be too disappointed.

"B EFORE I FORGET AGAIN," I said Wednesday, as we zoomed toward the airport in the Toyota, "I got you something for Christmas. Sorry it's late. Hope it's small enough to pack." I pulled a gift bag from behind her seat.

"From Victoria's Secret," she said in mock wonder. "My friend Mikey is growing up."

I smiled. "Hope you like it. I have the receipt, if you want to exchange."

"Is this . . . ? Oh, vanilla's perfect! Body spray *and* lotion? This is what I'd exchange for. Thank you! But I don't have anything for you."

"You bought me lunch, remember? Plus I got to hear you sing."

"True, but we're early, so let's make one stop before the airport."

"I don't need anything," I said.

"I won't buy anything. It's just a stop."

"It" was a big music store near the freeway. Colorful window signs announced the Holiday Piano Extravaganza.

"If we're not buying anything, why are we at a store?" I asked.

"You'll see." She pulled a leather folder from her carry-on. "In we go."

Jill told the sales lady, "We're looking for the right piano, a small grand. Bigger than a baby."

"Excellent," she said. "They're all to your right, as you see. Take your time. Looks like you brought music."

"If it's okay, I might sing too."

"We love that here."

Jill plinked on a few pianos, then insisted I sit beside her on the bench of a polished black Steinway.

"You're singing for me?" I asked.

"Playing and singing. You can turn my pages for the first one. When I nod."

"There's more than one? Cool!"

"The first is because of you. The second is because I want to sing it again."

The first sounded like a Broadway song. The title was "Old Friends." The jazzy piano accompaniment was fun, and if there was anything her voice couldn't do beautifully, it wasn't this.

She played the last riff, turned to me, and smiled. "Like it, my old friend?"

I'd been smiling since she sat us down. "I like it a lot. Thank you."

The new Christmas song was next. She turned to me for the last two lines, and I saw tears in her eyes.

> I will praise Him, follow, serve Him,
> Give Him everything I am.

She let the final notes ring. I thought she was about to tell me something, but her gaze shifted, and the sales lady appeared beside me.

"It's a beautiful instrument," Jill said. "The sale ends Monday, right?"

"Right," she said. "May I ask about the song you just sang? I've never heard it before. I'm sure I'd remember it."

"It's new," Jill said. "Unpublished."

"It's beautiful," the lady said. "Is it yours?"

Jill smiled sweetly. "No. I have very talented roommate."

The lady glanced at me.

Jill chuckled. "He's not that talented. He's a bit of a writer, but he's not my roommate."

"We have a publishing imprint now," the lady said. "Would your roommate be interested?"

Jill pulled a business card from her folder. "Heather's card. You should ask her. Tell her Jill said to call. But I'm sorry. We'll have to come back. We're due elsewhere."

In the car, as I reached to put the key in the ignition, Jill stopped me with a hand on my arm.

"I felt bad pretending I might buy it," she said. "Especially when I need to stop pretending . . . other things."

"She got something out of it," I said. "Heather too, maybe."

"Maybe. Mike, I want to be a good person." There was a catch in her voice. "I'm going to work on that."

"But?"

She looked at me for a long time. "You know the last line of Heather's song?"

"I know it well."

"I doubt God wants everything I am."

A tear tumbled toward her chin. I stopped it with a finger.

"I'm not God," I said. "So I don't know."

She faced straight ahead. "We should go."

She was quiet until we merged onto the freeway. "I'm going to work on that," she repeated. "Being a good person."

"How?"

"Maybe take a while and figure out what I believe. Then figure out who I am, if I can, and see where it leads."

"Where do you start?"

"I think by trying to believe again. Christmas is good momentum for that. When I sing Heather's song, among others, I want to believe more than I do." She sniffed. "It's like she wrote it for me. Not just for me to sing. She probably didn't." She sniffed again. "She doesn't know I might be hopeless."

I reproved her with a look, and she approximated a smile.

Too soon we reached the airport exit.

"Jill, if you ever want to talk . . ."

"I will," she said. "Same goes for you."

"Even knowing what you know?"

"I thought about that. I know you're my friend. I never thought you were perfect. I'll still write my own English papers."

"Here's what you don't know," I said. "I've been thinking too. I'm quitting. I have to."

"School or fake papers?"

"Papers. I'll just tutor. Maybe call myself a writing coach. Less money, but some. Then I can feel honest again and stop worrying about getting expelled."

"Just quitting? Cold turkey?"

Traffic stopped, approaching the terminal, so I could look away from it for a moment. I looked into my oldest friend's eyes and decided.

"Cold turkey. I had an exit strategy with one more semester, but yeah. I'll call my clients this week and tell them I can't anymore."

"I'm so glad. What brought this on?"

"The truth? I want you to be proud of me. To know who I am *and* be proud of me. Guess it would be nice to be proud of myself too."

She nodded slowly and reached for my hand. "I'll be proud of you. Thanks for keeping my secrets. And hanging out. And the rides."

I smiled for the first time since the store. "Being your holiday beard is a good gig."

Traffic started to move.

"Friend is more than beard," she said. "Can I tell you something?"

"Seriously? Never ask me that again."

"I know. It just gives me an extra moment to gather my courage. It's actually a question. Someday, when I find someone, if I find someone, do you think you'd want to meet her?"

"Sure."

"It's just that you might be the only one I know here who wants to."

"I hope not. But yeah, count me in."

"Thank you. If I have children someday with the help of a sperm bank somewhere, and we happen to end up as neighbors, would you ever let my children be friends with yours?"

"Yeah, I would. You want children?"

"Not wanting a man doesn't mean I don't want babies." She smiled wryly. "I'm . . . queer that way. What do you think?"

"Third-generation friends? That would be cool."

"Thank you," she murmured. "Will I see you at spring break?"

"I hope we're both at the same time."

"Hadn't thought of that," she said.

"If not, we'll figure it out," I said, as we pulled up to the curb. I hopped out and offloaded her suitcase.

She took my hands and smiled sadly. "We'll figure it out. Good motto for both of us. Happy New Year, Mike, and I'm hugging you again. Then I'm going to miss you. I may sit and cry, when I get to my gate."

"Happy New Year, Jill. I mean it."

We finally let each other go. She walked into the terminal, and I drove away.

My Christmas break was a few more days, but it felt like it was over.

It felt like it was good.

Acknowledgments

Besides Christmas, the stories in this collection have at least two things in common.

First, each was much improved by the thoughtful attention of my critique group, Good AF Writers ("AF" for American Fork), a chapter of the League of Utah Writers.

Second, these stories began as annual Christmas gifts for my mother-in-law, Kay Gardner Hancock. Every Christmas, she receives that year's offering with enthusiasm and gives welcome encouragement in return. Then I draft next year's story while the Christmas spirit lingers.

My friend and neighbor, Chris Wettstein, an artist of considerable talent, helped with the realism of the artist's work in "Invisible."

I thank these and more. Especially this next one.

My musical wife, Heidi, took the verse I wrote for the new Christmas carol in "Keep My Secrets" and turned it into an actual carol for solo voice with piano accompaniment—an extraordinary Christmas gift.

Finally, none of this would mean as much without you, the reader. Thanks for reading!

**"New and full of surprises."
—2025 Utah Book Awards**

a 2025 Utah Book Awards Notable Read
winner of a 2024 Silver Quill Award

The Dad Who Stayed (a novella) is a child's view of family, friends, church, school, and a progressive 1970s university town. Then twelve unrelated short stories explore friendship, family, and romance in the lives of characters from seventh grade to old age.

"Every emotional payoff, whether flash-of-lightning funny or tearfully joyful, is earned through a rich depth of honesty that is the polar opposite of sentimentalism."
—Darrin McGraw, co-author of *Animal Future*

High school sophomore Jenny Miller goes to dances but doesn't dance. Sitting is safer, in case she has a seizure. When she meets a boy who likes to sit and talk with her, an unexpected but welcome adventure begins. He even persuades her to dance with him.

It's not quite the blissful romance of her dreams. He's an athlete, and he's too popular to be interested in a girl like her—according to other girls, and she fears it might be true. Then jealousy turns to bullying.

Meanwhile, these two believing Latter-day Saints are breaking a few of the many dating rules they learned at church, where some are eager to judge and to assume the worst.

Amid rumors, judgments, and bullying that turns breathtakingly cruel, can they face another day? Is fitting in at school or church worth the price? Is love? And which of the many things they hear at church does God actually expect them to obey?

A long novel for teen and adult readers who enjoy long novels.

About the Author

David Rodeback had eleven Christmases in Boulder, Colorado, then nine in rural Southeast Idaho. Santa has since found him in Pennsylvania, Idaho again, upstate New York, and lately in Utah.

He served a two-year mission in western Pennsylvania and New York for the Church of Jesus Christ of Latter-day Saints, then completed degrees at Brigham Young University and Cornell University. He is Chief Marketing Technology Officer at a Utah manufacturing company.

He has worked as a speech writer, editor, translator, and writing instructor; has won a Telly Award as a writer for commercial video; has managed and advised political campaigns; has spent more than 30 years in lay leadership in his church (but prefers to teach); has blogged off and on for two decades on topics from politics to faith; and has seen exactly 66 words of his writing carved in stone. Since beginning to write fiction almost a decade ago, he has won a handful of prizes for short fiction.

He and his wife have four children and two grandchildren.

Let's Connect!

David is easy to find on Facebook (authorDavidRodeback), and at Medium, Simily, Goodreads, and Amazon, or you can connect more directly here:

Author website: DavidRodeback.com
Blog: BendableLight.com
E-mail: author@davidrodeback.com

Want to bring David to your classroom, writing group, or other venue, in person or virtually? Use the e-mail address above.

Sign up for David's quarterly e-mail **newsletter** with the QR code. (It points to DavidRodeback.com.)